# THE DAY SHELLEY WOODHOUSE WOKE UP

LAURA PEARSON

Boldwood

First published in Great Britain in 2024 by Boldwood Books Ltd.

Copyright © Laura Pearson, 2024

Cover Design by Lizzie Gardiner

Cover Imagery: Shutterstock

Every effort has been made to obtain the necessary permissions with reference to copyright material, both illustrative and quoted. We apologise for any omissions in this respect and will be pleased to make the appropriate acknowledgements in any future edition.

A CIP catalogue record for this book is available from the British Library.

Paperback ISBN 978-1-78513-639-9

Large Print ISBN 978-1-78513-640-5

Hardback ISBN 978-1-78513-638-2

Ebook ISBN 978-1-78513-641-2

Kindle ISBN 978-1-78513-642-9

Audio CD ISBN 978-1-78513-633-7

MP3 CD ISBN 978-1-78513-634-4

Digital audio download ISBN 978-1-78513-637-5

Boldwood Books Ltd
23 Bowerdean Street
London SW6 3TN
www.boldwoodbooks.com

*To Sue and George – with endless thanks*

# 1

## NOW

There's light, soft whirrs and squeaking sounds. The drag of a curtain pulled across. I'm flat on my back, in bed. Not my bed. Not my home. And then back to darkness.

A series of beeps, light pressure on my arm, the scratch of Velcro. I don't know where I am. I look up, to a ceiling of square tiles with stained patches. My bed's metal frame, the sheets white and crisp.

The smell of vegetables boiled for too long, a steady click-clack of shoes on tiled flooring. A touch on my arm, skin on skin.

Hospital. But why? I rake through my memories. The pub, the flat, David. My mind catches on David's name like a jumper snagged on a metal fence. But it's too hard to think about it. I fade out.

My eyes are open, and there's a middle-aged woman standing in front of me.

'Shelley?' she asks. 'Do you know where you are?'

'Hospital,' I try to say, but no sound comes out.

'Don't worry about that, Shelley. It might take a while for you to speak again. You've had a tube down your throat. You're in the hospital. You were involved in an accident.'

I open my mouth, try to speak again. Try to ask for water.

'Try not to worry about anything. I'm Angela, and I'll be looking after you during the days while you're in Intensive Care. It's one nurse per patient in here, so you get special treatment.'

Intensive Care? I've never been inside an Intensive Care unit before. They are for the people who are really ill, the ones who might not get better. Am I one of those people?

I look around to find a window but all I see are other beds, other people being kept alive. Tubes and wires snaking over skin and sheets.

'I'll leave you to wake up slowly,' she says, and bustles away.

I take in the surroundings. Six beds, too far apart for us to speak to each other. I'm on the far end, away from the nurses' station. A couple of the patients have someone sat beside them, holding their hand. None of them look to be in good shape.

I can feel sleep creeping up on me, and for a moment I try to fight it, but it's too strong.

* * *

Later, Angela passes by, and when she glances at me, I speak.

'What day is it?' It comes out as a croak, but I'm so relieved to have my voice back that I don't care.

'It's Tuesday, love.'

It doesn't really tell me anything. The last thing I can remember is Saturday, but have I lost days or weeks?

'How are you feeling?' she asks.

There is pain, but it's dull. When I tell her that, she asks where it hurts, but it's so hard to specify. It hurts everywhere. I feel at a disadvantage in this conversation. She's standing, looking down at me, and I'm lying down. Plus, there's all this stuff she knows about me. What my body looks like, how long I've been here, what happened to me. And I don't know anything. Or do I? I see David again, only this time he isn't pottering in the kitchen, he's standing over me, his face puce. *No*, I think. *No. Not yet.*

'I don't know why I'm here,' I say.

Angela's brow furrows. 'Try not to worry about anything. You are safe here.'

I feel like I might cry suddenly. I'm scared. That's the truth of it. Angela pours water from a jug into a plastic cup and hands it to me. I try to sit up, but she puts a hand on my shoulder to stop me, reaches for the remote control and adjusts the bed.

'The physio will be round soon, and she'll help you with your mobility.' She looks down at her feet, at her sensible shoes, then back up at me. 'Do you know the date?'

I want to say that I don't know how long I was out for. 'It's September 2017,' I say instead. 'I don't know the date. Twelfth, maybe? Was I in a coma?'

'Yes,' she says, nodding as if for extra confirmation. 'Now, do you know who the prime minister is?'

'Theresa May,' I say. Does she think I'm stupid? Brain damaged?

'How old are you?'

'Thirty.'

She shuffles on her feet a bit before asking the next question. 'Shelley, do you know what happened to you?'

I think I'm going to say I'm not sure, but that isn't what comes out. 'It was David,' I say. 'My husband. He tried to kill me.'

'I'm so sorry to hear that.'

I don't know what to say. But it doesn't matter because Angela is called away by one of her colleagues. She tells me she'll be back. When she's gone, I feel unsettled. To my left, the bed is quite a distance away and it's hard to make out whether the shape in it is a man or a woman, whether they're conscious or comatose. Opposite, same story. A thought comes, out of nowhere. Has anyone died in here, since I came? It's quite possible, surely. This is where you come when things are as serious as they get. What if I have lain here, unconscious, while someone took their last breaths beside me? Does it matter? It shouldn't, I suppose. I don't know these people. They don't know me. But it feels a bit chilling, all the same. I try to push the thought out of my mind. I will concentrate on what I know.

And so, I repeat the things I know, in my mind. My name, which is Shelley Woodhouse. That I am thirty years old. I am the landlady at a pub called the Pheasant. And that, a few days ago, my husband David tried to kill me.

Angela's back and I don't remember falling asleep, but I must have done.

'Do you need anything?' she asks.

There are so many things I need. To know what happened, why I'm here, when I'll go home. Whether it's safe for me there.

'I feel like my memories are scrambled,' I say. 'Confused, out of order. I feel like they're out of my control.'

'I think that's pretty normal, Shelley. Don't be too hard on yourself. Why don't you start with something you're sure of, from your childhood perhaps, and go from there?'

## 2

THEN

Six years old and gap-toothed. I'm in the playground, trying to cross to where the other girls are playing, while simultaneously scratching my scabbed knee and avoiding the football game that's taking place. Annabelle Harris turns, puts her hands on her hips and watches me approach. There are five of them. Emma Clacton and Sophie Giles holding either end of the skipping rope, Tessa Lynes jumping in time to 'Granny's in the kitchen' and Lucy Jeffers waiting her turn. Annabelle overseeing things. As I get close, I see that Annabelle is frowning, her eyes squinting as if the sun is too bright. But it is October, and dull. I stop and line up the two sides of my jacket, sticking my tongue out as I pull up the zip.

'You can't play with us,' Annabelle says. A pre-emptive strike.

'Why not?' I don't understand. Yesterday, we were best friends, our heads bent in close, giggling.

'Because you don't have a dad.'

Later, I would reflect that there's one moment in every person's childhood where they realise that what they thought was commonplace is, in fact, not. In the moment, though, I can't think of a single thing to say and just stand there, my mouth opening and closing like a fish. I think about other people's houses, about their families. Sometimes a mum and dad, yes, sometimes brothers and sisters, sometimes pets, but surely not always a dad? I've never noticed. At home, it is me and my mum, Tina, and her mum, Granny Rose. My mum told me once that Granny Rose moved in the very day that my dad moved out, when I was still a tiny baby. I kept hold of that piece of information throughout my bedtime story and then wrote it down in my secret notebook along with the other things I knew about my dad, namely that he was a liar and he didn't deserve to have a family.

'Oh,' I say eventually. And then I turn and walk away, pretending not to hear Annabelle and the other girls giggling and whispering as the skipping rope thwacks against the tarmac in a steady rhythm.

Later that day, I sit on the stool in front of my mother's dressing table, with her beside me. She is getting ready to go to work. I'm dressed in blue and green striped pyjamas, while she is in a tight, black skirt and a clingy top with big flowers and a low neck. She is doing her makeup, carefully applying mascara. I take a blusher brush and swipe it over my cheeks, pretending. Inside, I practise what I want to say. *Annabelle said I couldn't play because I don't have a dad.* But I don't know how my mum will react. I don't want to make her upset or angry just before she leaves for the night.

Granny Rose appears in the bedroom doorway, tapping her watch. This is how it is every night that Mum works. I try to stay as close to her as I can for as long as possible, but Granny Rose is strict about bedtime.

'Have you done your teeth?' Granny Rose asks.

I haven't. I jump off the stool and dart into the bathroom. If I'm quick, there might be time for Mum to read me a story. But no, when I emerge, Mum is already on her way down the stairs, calling out to us that she'll see us in the morning. Disappointment settles in my stomach like a stone.

'Do you want to choose a book, love?' Granny Rose asks.

I kneel in front of my small bookcase and run my finger along the spines. I pull out a book about dinosaurs having a party, and once I'm in bed I scooch up close to the wall so there's room for Granny Rose. We're halfway through the story when I have a thought. Maybe I can say what I wanted to say to Granny Rose. It won't upset her the way it might upset Mum. So as soon as she closes the book and leans in to kiss me goodnight, I speak, and the words come out in a rush.

'Annabelle said I couldn't play because I don't have a dad.'

Granny Rose pauses in mid-air, her lips slightly puckered. She pulls back, considers. 'Which one is Annabelle again? The one with the bunches?'

I nod.

'Well, I could tell you a thing or two about her family.'

My eyes widen.

'But I won't. Listen, children can be awfully cruel. In my experience, they decide who they're going to be mean to and then come up with a reason for it.'

I think this is something I'll need to pick apart later. But for now I have questions. 'But why don't I, when everyone else does?'

Granny Rose sighs. 'Because some men don't stick around and do the right thing, I suppose. And your dad was one of them.'

'Where do you think he is?'

'I don't know, love. I never think about him. He chose not to be part of this family, and it gave me the opportunity to step in and live with you both, and I'll never be sorry for that.'

I nod solemnly. I want to ask another question, to prolong this time snuggled up next to Granny Rose, who smells of floral hand cream and home, but I can't think of one.

'You know,' she says, 'you're a good girl. Such a good girl.'

I am. I make a point of it. Dad left and I don't want to risk anyone else deciding to go, do I?

'You're a good Granny Rose,' I say, and she laughs.

'Night night, love,' she says, getting off the bed slowly, one hand on her back. She slides the book back into its spot on the bookcase and leaves the room, turning off the light on her way out. In the pitch darkness, I feel around the bed until I find Big Ted and Small Ted. I lay Big Ted next to me and place Small Ted in the crook of my neck, and I think about Mum, who won't get back from work until the middle of the night but will still get up to have a coffee and a cigarette in her dressing gown while I have my Coco Pops tomorrow morning before school. I've been to the pub a handful of times, have drunk orange squash and eaten bags of crisps sitting on the high bar stools on the occasional Sunday afternoon, so I can picture Mum there, making drinks and taking money to put in the till. Having three different conversations at once, throwing her head back in laughter, and generally being impossibly glamorous.

I want to work in a pub when I'm older, but when I said that to Mum, she just looked a bit sad and said I should aim higher than that. I didn't understand. In the pub, Mum is like a queen, everyone wanting to talk to her, everyone knowing her name. I want that. I ache for that.

Sleep is tugging at me as I ponder what aiming higher means. I know that Annabelle's mum and dad both work in offices and she goes to a childminder after school every day while I go home with my mum and play Snakes and Ladders. Is that really better?

# 3

## NOW

A petite woman comes to my bedside and introduces herself as Fern. She's one of those women whose age is hard to determine. She's got sharp eyes that flit around the room and shiny, dark hair that's tied up in a neat bun. She says she's a physiotherapist. Like Angela, she tells me she's been looking after me while I was unconscious. Which begs the question – how long have I been unconscious?

'What does that mean?' I ask.

'Well, it's important to keep your body moving, so we just come in a couple of times each day and do some gentle stretches of your limbs, your fingers, that kind of thing.'

It's so strange to think of someone stretching out my limbs while I was unconscious that I don't ask another question.

'It's good to see you awake,' she says, and her voice is kind, and I believe she means it.

'You were lucky to catch me. There's a lot of sleeping going on.'

'Good. Rest is essential for recovery.'

Who are these people who choose this life? Working with

patients who are at the gateway between life and death, trying to ensure they go one way and not the other. How do they do it?

'Do you know when the police will come?' I ask.

She looks slightly taken aback. 'The police?'

'To take a statement. About my husband. He's the reason why I'm here.'

'Oh,' she says. 'Gosh, I'm sorry. I don't know. I think maybe you'd need to talk to your nurse. But rest assured, you're safe here, Shelley.'

Angela said that too. About me being safe. How do they know?

I look at Fern, take her in. She's not the kind of woman who would end up in an abusive relationship. At least, I imagine that's what she's thinking. She is neat and contained and I bet she has a boyfriend or a husband who does his fair share of unloading the dishwasher and hanging out the washing. But nobody thinks it will happen to them. That's the tragedy of it. One of the tragedies.

There's a part of me that wants to take hold of her hand – which is small, with flawlessly French manicured nails – and tell her to be careful. To be alert. But how would she see me? Just another sad woman who was taken in by a cruel man. And I suppose that's what I am, at the end of it all.

Fern gets me to stretch out my fingers and then curl my hands into fists, then the same with my toes. She lifts one leg up at a time and bends it at the knee. She's stronger than she looks. All the time, she talks about what we're doing and why. It's so that my muscles won't seize up when I'm ready to try walking. It's not as simple as just standing up and setting off, she says. When you've been lying down for a long time, you have to take things slowly. Step by step. Which raises the question I steel myself to ask next. 'How long have I been here?'

'A few days,' Fern says. 'Three or four.'

'When will I be ready to go home?' I ask.

And I know she's not the right person to ask but the thought has only just occurred to me. When will I be able to get back to running the pub? And who's doing it now? Is it closed? Dee will have taken over, I'm sure. But she won't want to manage on her own for long.

Fern looks a bit uncomfortable. 'That's not for me to say. You'll have to talk to one of the doctors.'

I turn my face away from her so that she won't see my frustrated tears, and I don't know whether that's why, but she brings the session to a close.

'I'll be back later,' she says. 'It's good to get you moving at least twice a day. Anything you can do in between visits is great, too. All of that will help with your recovery.'

*Recovery.* It's a word I associate with alcoholics and drug addicts. But I suppose it applies to me too, now. It all feels overwhelming, and then I feel sleep coming over me gently like a blanket being laid by a friend.

*  *  *

The doctor is a tall, thin woman with cropped hair. She looks like a pencil with a rubber on the end. She introduces herself as Dr Jenkins.

'Do you remember meeting me before?' she asks.

I shake my head. She's distinctive. I'd remember her.

She lists my injuries, most of which aren't serious. Cuts and bruises. It's the brain that's the problem.

'We can do scans, but we never know for sure how someone is going to recover after a brain injury,' she says.

It feels wrong. How can they just not know?

'So it's just a case of wait and see?' I ask.

'Pretty much. You have what's called a subdural haematoma, which is a bleed on the brain. It's very small, and we think you might get away without having surgery, but we're keeping a close eye on it.'

A bleed. On the brain. It feels like a punch. But I should have known by the fact that I'm in Intensive Care. You don't end up here from cuts and bruises.

'Do you have any questions for me?' she asks. 'I know it's a lot to take in, but I'll come to see you every day and you can ask me anything you think of.'

I feel like I have questions, but I can't quite grasp them. I'm sliding towards sleep again. 'Thank you,' I say. 'No questions.'

And I don't remember her walking away.

When I wake up, David is on my mind. I haven't let myself think about him, not properly, but I close my eyes and let it in, knowing I'll have to eventually. We're in our bedroom and he's standing over me, shouting and swearing, and I'm trying to get him to understand, to look at me and talk to me rationally, but he's too wound up. There's no talking to him when he gets like this. I know, by now, that it will end in some form of violence. That he will hit me, or kick me, and I've had enough of taking it, so I turn my back on him and storm out of the room. I haven't done that before, and he doesn't like it. He likes having all the power, being in control. He likes to see me cowering. So he comes after me, still hurling abuse, and it's funny but it's like I go into a trance and I notice these tiny things I haven't ever seen before, like a little pull on the landing carpet and a mark on the wall where someone's hand has been. But I can feel him behind me, his breath on my neck, the bulk of him getting ready to strike me, and I am determined not to curl inwards, not to show him I'm scared.

'You're a fucking liar, Shelley!'

I could tell him no, I could defend myself, but it's never got me anywhere in the past. If I can just get away from him, get down the stairs to the pub, he won't follow me down there and he certainly won't do anything while other people are watching. So I hurry, one foot in front of the other, ignoring the stream of vicious words he's spewing. And I almost make it, I really do. I'm at the top of the stairs when I feel him shove me, and I remember thinking, *I didn't think he would go that far. I didn't think he would do something that could kill me.* But he has.

I lie there, tears streaming down my cheeks. It was too much, to let it all in like that. I need to go more slowly, like Angela said. I need to let the memories in bit by bit. Starting with what I'm sure of, what I know.

# 4

## THEN

'I don't like broccoli,' I say.

Mum laughs, but it's brittle. 'Of course you do, don't be silly.'

When I keep pushing it around my plate, her face gets stormy. 'This isn't like you,' she says.

She means that I usually eat what she puts in front of me and do what she says. But I can't do that tonight. I can sense that Mum's nervous but I don't really understand why. Is it because of this man, this Mick, she's brought round to meet me and Granny Rose? I'm not keen. He's not very tall and he has too much hair. On his arms, his hands, everywhere. It's gross. I can tell, too, that he isn't kind. I won't say that to Mum, because I know exactly what will happen if I do. Mum will sigh and say that you shouldn't judge people on first impressions, or on what they look like, and that you need to take the time to get to know someone. She will ask me to 'just this once, give me a break'. But there's something about his eyes, which are brown and normal-sized but not spaced correctly. Slightly too close together. I push the chicken around my plate, not really hungry. I cannot tell Mum that I don't like Mick because his eyes are too close together, so I say nothing, try to focus on the fact that I know there's ice cream for pudding.

Mum met Mick in the pub. It's the only place she goes, really, so it's not surprising. I can picture it, Mum looking glamorous, standing there behind the bar. Powerful, somehow, and beautiful. Mick going in for a quick drink after work and chatting to her while he drank down that first pint, then asking for a second and giving her a smile. Is she so easily won over that it could have been any man who smiled and showed her a bit of attention? But no, that isn't fair. It's been years since she was with my dad and she hasn't had a boyfriend in all that time. If she is happy, then she deserves that. It's just, there's this feeling I can't shake. Like Mick is going to pick everything up and move it around, and nothing will ever be quite the same again.

It is Mum's night off and she doesn't have many of those. When she does, we always do something together, the three of us, me and Mum and Granny Rose. Sometimes we watch a film; sometimes we have a Snakes and Ladders tournament. I wonder what we'll do tonight. When Mick will leave. Mum clears the plates. She doesn't say anything about my uneaten broccoli but she gives me a look. Then she brings out a tub of ice cream and a stack of bowls and spoons, and stands at the head of the table serving us.

We've got that chocolate sauce that sets solid on your ice cream and I am chipping away at it with my spoon when Mum speaks.

'Thanks for offering to put Shelley to bed, Mum. We'll get off as soon as I've cleared the table, if that's all right.'

The disappointment pierces my chest, pins me to the back of the wooden dining room chair. Granny Rose puts me to bed practically every night. And much as I love lying next to her and having stories, and the fact that Granny Rose can always be persuaded to read one more, I long for Mum to be there. I understand that Mum has to work, of course she does, but this is something different. This is her choosing not to spend her evening off with us, choosing to spend it with this man instead, and it makes me hate him. I drop my spoon into my bowl and it clatters, making them all turn to look at me, but I am gone, away from the table and up to my room where I can cry without them seeing. Without *him* seeing.

I know that one of them will knock on my door. Will it be Mum, or Granny Rose? I take a deep, gulping breath and go to open the door and am half relieved and half disappointed when I see Mum standing on the other side. She looks cross.

'What's going on, Shelley?' she asks, pushing into my bedroom without asking first. 'Why are you being so rude?'

I don't think I'm being rude, so I don't know how to answer that. All I know is that I already don't get enough of Mum, and now I'm going to get even less. Will Mum understand that, if I try to explain?

'Mick's eyes are too close together,' I say, knowing even as I speak that it's the wrong thing. That it will make Mum even more cross and won't help me to be understood.

'That's ridiculous,' Mum says. She has her hands on her hips and I notice that she's wearing lipstick and her hair is down. She's a cross between the mum who I get to see here, at home, and the mum who goes to work at the pub. I want to tell her that she looks pretty, but how can I when we're in the middle of an argument? 'Look, you've been acting like a spoilt brat all night. Mick brought you that teddy and you barely said thank you.'

'I don't want it,' I say.

It's true; I don't. I have seen those same bears on the market and they are three pounds each or two for five pounds and it crosses my mind to ask, cruelly, whether there's another girlfriend somewhere with another kid who has one just the same.

'I don't understand you,' Mum says. 'It's not as if I'm asking him to move in. He's just a nice man who wants to spend time with me. Why don't you want me to have that?'

*But you have me*, I want to scream. *Me and Granny Rose. Why do you need him?* I say nothing, though. Throw myself down on the bed dramatically and wait, my face in the duvet, until I hear Mum sigh loudly and leave the room. When the door closes, I flip over and enjoy being able to breathe freely again. I go over something Mum said. *It's not as if I'm asking him to move in.* I didn't even know that was an option, but now I do, it's all I can think about. Is that the future? Mick in Mum's bed and sitting at the breakfast table like a pretend dad? That can't happen. I'll do anything to make sure it doesn't.

# 5

## NOW

At lunchtime, a young man with frizzy hair who can't quite meet my eye tells me that I was unconscious when they took orders so I've got cottage pie and that's that, but I'll be able to choose my dinner. He puts the tray onto my table with a clatter and leaves. I lift the lid and see exactly what I expected. A clump of pale mashed potato with greasy mince oozing out at the sides, and carrots and peas that look like they've been cooking for days. I use the remote control to change my position slightly so I'm more upright, and I take a few half-hearted mouthfuls before giving up.

I look down at myself, notice for the first time that I'm wearing pyjamas rather than a hospital gown. But they're not pyjamas I recognise. Not my pyjamas. They are soft cotton, pink and green stripes. Someone must have bought these and brought these in for me. David? I feel a bit anxious at the thought of him being here while I was in a coma, but if not David, then who? For a minute or two, I feel totally alone, and I remember losing sight of my mum in the supermarket when I was five or six. Everyone was so big, so busy. How could I let them know that I was there and that I needed help?

To stop myself from thinking for a while, I start testing the limits of my movement the way Fern showed me. I've clearly got a catheter in, but no other tubes. I move my head, then my shoulders, then my arms, going down my body to test for pain and limitation. It hurts to stretch either of my arms. What do I look like? I could ask for a mirror, but I'm not sure I want to. If I'm horrific, scarred for life, I'll need a bit of time to come to terms with that.

I must have fallen asleep, because when I open my eyes again, Angela's here, wheeling the blood pressure monitor. She looks at the meal I've discarded and grimaces, as if to say that she understands. That she would do the same. But I'm not ready for camaraderie. I look away.

'Who brought me these pyjamas?' I ask.

She looks at the pyjamas in question, and it's like she's playing for time.

'Has my husband been here? David?'

'No,' she says, quickly. 'No, he hasn't.'

'Why wasn't anyone here when I woke up? Has no one been in to see me? And if they haven't, where did these pyjamas come from?'

Angela pulls the curtain around my bed, puts a hand up to tell me to stop. To calm down.

'Look,' she says. 'I know you must have a lot of questions, but I only know the answers to some of them. You have had visitors, but I couldn't tell you who. I'm sure they'll be back as soon as they can. Your next of kin will have been informed that you're awake.'

'But that's David,' I say, my voice little more than a whisper.

'Your friend has been in several times,' she says. 'Dee, is it?'

*Dee.* The relief of hearing her name. 'Yes, Dee. When will she come in again?'

'I don't know that.'

And just then, there's the sound of someone clearing their

throat at the other side of the curtain, and Angela pushes it back again, and there's a man standing there. I know he isn't staff because he's dressed in jeans and a tired-looking T-shirt. Angela smiles at him and then notes down my blood pressure on the iPad she's holding and hurries away.

'Hi,' he says.

I look at him. He's a bit scruffy, his hair slightly too long. Tall and a bit squashy, like he'd be nice to cuddle. He brushes his hair out of his eyes and smiles, and I notice that one of his teeth is at a slightly strange angle and, for some reason, it ups his attractiveness. It's strange, thinking about whether or not this man is attractive, because he is nothing like David. My husband is all sharp lines and angles, smart clothes and haircuts every four weeks.

'Hi,' I say, because it's been too long since he spoke and he's looking a bit uncomfortable.

He looks down at the floor.

'Are you...?' I'm not sure how to finish the question. What could he be? Not a doctor or a nurse, not a cleaner, I don't think, or one of the catering staff.

'I'm a volunteer,' he says, taking a step closer to me. 'Matt.' He holds out his hand.

I don't shake it, and when it becomes obvious that I'm not going to, he drops his and does a funny sort of cough to cover his embarrassment.

'What sort of volunteer?' I ask.

'Um, I just come and chat to people, bring them a hot drink or a snack. That sort of thing.'

'Milk and two sugars,' I say.

'Sorry?'

'Tea. You said you bring hot drinks. Could you get me a tea?'

'Oh, yeah, sure. Milk and...'

'Two sugars.'

He shakes his head very slightly and I wonder why he's bothered by how many sugars I take.

'If it's too much trouble...' I say, and then stop, because I can't finish that by saying I'll get it myself. It's clear that I can't.

'No,' he says. 'It isn't. I'll get it now.'

He's only gone for about five minutes and when he returns, he's holding one of those small plastic cups you get from a machine and two KitKats. He puts the cup down on my tray table and holds one KitKat out, inviting me to take it. And I want it. I can imagine how good the chocolate would taste, how well it would go with the hot, sweet tea, but I don't know who this man is or why he's bringing me things. I shake my head, and he shrugs and puts it down on the edge of the table.

'Maybe later,' he says.

I take a sip of tea and it's too hot and too sweet. When I asked for two sugars, I was imagining a mug.

'Is it awful?' he asks. 'I don't drink tea, but I know the coffee you get from machines like that is usually pretty dire. I always think hot chocolate is the safest bet in those circumstances.'

'I should have asked for one sugar. Small cup. You don't drink tea?'

'No. I don't like it.'

I can't imagine getting through the day without tea. That first one in the morning that I drink in bed if I have the time, or standing at the kitchen counter if I don't. The one I have mid-morning while I'm buzzing around, doing jobs around the flat. The one I have with my lunch, just before I open up. And the one I have at the end of the night, when my feet are aching and I'm tired of making small talk and I want to curl up in a ball and go to sleep.

'What kind of a person doesn't like tea?' I ask.

And he laughs, and there's something about the sound of it. It's rich and warm and it makes me want to laugh, too.

'I get that a lot,' he says. 'So, you haven't told me your name.'

Something clicks, and I realise what this is. He must be part of some charity that is kind to people who don't have any visitors, any friends or family. Is that me? Shelley Woodhouse, queen of the Pheasant, everyone's favourite landlady. How is my only visitor someone who's taken pity on me? Someone who made a new year's resolution to do something for the community, or some such bullshit?

'Guess,' I say.

'Guess? Your name?'

I nod, slowly.

'Sarah.'

'No.'

'Eleanor.'

'No.'

'Catherine.'

'No.'

'Charlotte, Lisa, Mel, Claire, Lucy, Andrea, Rosie, Anna, Fay.'

I shake my head, over and over. Then I stop, because it makes me feel a bit sick.

'I give up,' he says.

'Shelley,' I say.

He tilts his head slightly to one side, keeps his focus steady. 'Shelley,' he repeats.

'Those names, all those names you listed. Are they exes?'

'Why would you think that?'

'You just came up with them all so quickly.'

'They were all girls in my class at primary school.'

I smile then, can't help it. I imagine him as a young boy. Probably Matthew, then. Grass stains on his trousers and his hair untidy, just like it is now.

He's been standing up to now, but he goes over to a chair in the corner of the room and sits down, opens his KitKat.

'Is this okay?' he asks.

'Is what okay?'

'Me, sitting here for a few minutes, having a snack. I've been on my feet all day.'

'Don't you have other people to get drinks for?'

'Not just now. I'm going home after I leave you.'

I wonder where home is. Whether it's a flat he shares with a friend, or a girlfriend. Whether he has a wife and child. I can't ask. And why do I want to know, anyway? We're quiet for a couple of minutes as he eats. I take another sip of the tea. It's cooled down now but it's undrinkable.

'My husband tried to kill me,' I say into the silence.

He coughs, a sort of choke. Recovers himself.

'I'm so sorry to hear that.'

'It's okay,' I say.

But it isn't, is it? It's awful. For someone who is supposed to love and protect you to do something like that. Before I realise it's happening, I'm sobbing, my hands over my face because I'm embarrassed to break down like this in front of a stranger.

He comes a little closer, clearly unsure. 'Should I get someone? A nurse?'

I shake my head. 'Go,' I say.

'Go?'

'Leave.'

'Oh,' he says, clearing his throat and backing away. 'Sure, of course. I'll come back tomorrow, see if you need anything.'

It's on the tip of my tongue to say thanks, but I don't do it.

Instead, I wait until he's been gone a minute or two and then tear into the KitKat, taking big bites until it's gone. And then, as a distraction, I let myself slip back into my childhood. To Granny Rose. But it isn't until I'm there that I realise this memory isn't so soothing.

# 6

### THEN

I look over at Granny Rose and see a tear tracking down the lines of her face. It's fascinating to watch, like a tiny river overcoming obstacles and seeking out the low ground. I squeeze Granny Rose's hand and swallow back my own tears. We are in my bedroom, lying side by side on my bed, which is where we come to escape. Outside the room, down the stairs, there are muffled thuds. Mick and Mum, arguing. I remember something a teacher said once after a playground scuffle. *We don't argue with our fists.* Mick does.

It doesn't give me any pleasure that I was right about Mick. I would much rather have been wrong. If he had proved himself as a good boyfriend for Mum and a good stand-in dad for me, then I would have gladly let myself love him, and we would have laughed about that night when he first came round for tea and I'd barely talk to him, refused the present he brought. But that isn't what happened. Instead, there were a few months of fresh flowers and fancy chocolates, toys and magazines for me, and then he was staying over a few nights a week, and then, almost without me noticing, he moved in.

And soon, so soon after that, it started. The fits of rage, the bruises, the thuds and crashes of things breaking. I hate him. I lie in bed sometimes, thinking of things I want to do to him, if only I was bigger and stronger. I imagine him getting run over by a bus, or simply floating away on the breeze, like a balloon. I imagine us getting our lives back, the ones I didn't know to treasure until they were gone.

Suddenly, silence. I feel a shift in Granny Rose, a slight loosening of her arms around my small body. There's a pattern to this. When it is over, Mick leaves the house. Sometimes for an hour or two, sometimes for a day. Once, for a week. I hope it will be a long time. Just as I think this, I hear the bang of the door slamming. Granny Rose stands up.

'I'll go down, check on her.'

She looks so sad and I think I understand why. Once, Mum was a little girl like me and Granny Rose was her mum and she loved her and did everything she could to keep her safe. And now Mick has come along and made everything feel brittle and dangerous.

'Can I come too?' I ask. I don't want to be on my own.

'No, love. I'll come back. I won't be long.'

I know that Granny Rose doesn't want me to see Mum if it's really bad. I know I am being protected, but there's a part of me that feels shut out. Before Mick, we were always a trio, a little team, me and Mum and Granny Rose. And now I'm on my own in my bedroom, hoping they don't need to take Mum to hospital, and I hate Mick for that. Hate him, deep in my bones. It makes me want to throw things, and the only thing that stops me is picturing that tired expression Mum wears when I make everything worse by playing up.

It feels like a long wait, because I don't want to pick up a book or play with my Barbies. How can I, when anything could be happening downstairs? Could Mum be dead? It's something that's never occurred to me before, but recently I walked into the lounge when Mum and Granny Rose were watching the news and I heard something about a woman being killed by her husband. I don't understand why people would hurt the person they're supposed to love, but I know it happens. I know it's not only in my house.

Granny Rose appears at the door, her expression hard to read. 'She's okay, love. Do you want to come down?'

I nod and follow Granny Rose down the stairs. In the kitchen, Mum is facing the corner, lifting the kettle that is just coming to the boil. I want her to turn, and at the same time, I don't. But she does, and there is nothing to see. Just eyes that are red from crying. I blink away the thoughts I had of bloody noses and black eyes. I run across the small room to Mum and wrap my arms around her.

'I'm sorry,' Mum says. She whispers it into my hair. 'I'm so sorry, baby. You don't deserve any of this.'

I want to say it isn't her fault, but I find that I can't. It's suddenly clear that if I say a single word I will crumble to dust here in the kitchen. So instead I just hold on to Mum as tightly as I can.

Mick doesn't come back that evening, and the three of us have spaghetti Bolognese for tea, and it is my favourite because Granny Rose finds it hard to suck up the strands of spaghetti and always ends up getting sauce splattered across the tablecloth, and it makes me laugh. It is so strange, I think, to be laughing so soon after that awful clutch of fear. Barely an hour after I sat in my bedroom wondering whether my mother might be dead. But we all are, and I see, but don't yet fully understand, that this is how life is. Tragedy pushed up against comedy like strangers sharing a bus seat.

At bedtime, it is Mum who sits beside the bed and reads me a story, and I am so grateful for that, but it isn't something I can convey, or understand. Mum isn't going to the pub tonight, it's one of her nights off, and I think that after I'm in bed, Mum and Granny Rose will sit together in the living room watching that programme they both love about a hospital and Mum might open a packet of fancy biscuits for them to share. I wish I could be with them, but I know I can't. I lie back in the bath, submerge myself and hold my breath, and then I burst up through the water and Mum pretends to be shocked, and we both laugh again.

When Mum is tucking me in, after three stories, I gather the courage to say what I have wanted to say all afternoon.

'I don't like him. Mick.' As if Mum could have possibly misunderstood.

Mum takes a deep breath in and when she lets it out, it's quivery. 'It's complicated, Shelley. He does love us, you know.'

This is what she always says. But it makes me want to scream. Granny Rose loves us, and she would never hurt us. And we love each other, and wouldn't hurt each other. It isn't complicated, not to me. It isn't.

'We were fine, before,' I say.

'I wasn't.'

I look up at Mum, shocked, and wait for her to speak again.

'I was lonely, Shelley. Your dad left and there'd been no one else since, and then Mick turned up and he thought I was pretty and he wanted to listen to what I had to say, and I hadn't realised how much I'd needed that.'

*But then he hurt you*, I think. *And you didn't make him stop so he did it again. He isn't good, or kind.*

'I'm scared,' I say.

'Monsters?' Mum asks. 'Witches, ghosts? I've shooed them all away, my love. There's nothing here that can hurt you.'

But it isn't true, because Mick could return at any time. Some nights, he comes home after hours in the pub and he's loud and silly, and other nights it makes him sullen. I always pull my duvet cover right up to my nose and stare at my door, but he's never come in. He's never taken his anger out on me. Sometimes I wish he would, because surely then Mum would see that he was bad.

Mum sits on the edge of my bed for a while. She doesn't usually do this. I pretend to fall asleep in the end, because I know that will please her. I let my breathing slow and deepen, and keep my eyes shut tight. Still, Mum sits there, holding my hand. I want to open my eyes and sit up and ask for an extra cuddle, but I don't want Mum to know I've been pretending, so I just wait, and after a while I hear a sound that I think is soft crying. I am trapped, able to hear Mum but unable to comfort her. And after what feels like a really long time, Mum gets up and leaves, pulling the door closed gently behind her.

The next morning, Mick is back. I don't look at him as I carry my cereal bowl carefully over to the table. Mum and Mick are both smoking, sitting opposite one another, like they've just happened to find themselves here and they don't know each other. Granny Rose is making my packed lunch, slicing the cheese for my sandwich as thin as possible and choosing a packet of crisps from the Sainsbury's bag in the cupboard. I feel a bit sick, but I don't say anything. When I was younger, before Mick, I would sometimes say I wasn't well so I could spend the day with Mum and Granny Rose fussing over me. But now, I'd rather be at school. I hope Annabelle will be in one of her good moods. I won't tell her about what happened. I never tell her. I keep it all locked away, my secret shame.

# 7

---

NOW

The night is long. I thought I knew long nights, long shifts at the pub, Christmas Eve and New Year, when everyone wanted to celebrate and no one wanted to go home, but they were long in a different way. Exhausting and busy, all that rushing about and trying to keep everyone happy despite long waits, and ignoring the odd minor sexual assault. But here, there is nothing. Low light, footsteps tapping along corridors, people coughing, or shouting, some distance away. But no one to actually talk to or engage with. I am checked fairly regularly, my observations (or 'obs', as they all call them) taken. Pulse, blood pressure, temperature. The nurses are quick and efficient. I couldn't exactly ask them to stay. And besides, I didn't want to. I didn't know, yet, who was on my side. I slept in snatches, always waking a little cold and a little afraid.

So when the lights come on and the shift changes and someone comes in to ask me about breakfast, I am relieved. Because I didn't think I was scared of anything. I've walked down dingy alleyways alone at night, and let fairground rides swing me high in the air, and I once held a snake on a school trip to the zoo when no one else would do it. But it turns out that's not true. I'm not scared of any of the obvious things, perhaps, but I'm scared of being alone in the night.

I order toast and tea, and then a nurse comes over and it's Angela, and I realise she's had her time off, while the night shift worked, and now she's back.

'How are you feeling?' she asks me.

I do a quick check in with my body. Are the pains the same as yesterday? Are they worse, or better?

'Where would you put yourself on a scale from one to ten, if one was no pain at all and ten was excruciating agony?' she tries.

I think of the worst pains I've ever felt. I've been lucky, really. A jellyfish sting, period cramps, that time I fell off the low branch of a tree and broke my wrist.

'Five?'

I say it like it's a question, because I want her to tell me what's reasonable.

Angela puts the blood pressure cuff on my arm. It's only day two of me being conscious, but we've got this down. When I see her approach with it, I hold my left arm out. Then I give her my finger for the thing that checks my pulse.

'Five's pretty good,' she says. 'Do you have children?'

The question throws me. How is it relevant? And also, what if I did? Who would be looking after them?

'Er, no.'

She pulls a pen from her breast pocket and writes something down on my chart.

'Are they okay?' I ask. 'My obs?'

'Fine. Blood pressure is on the high side of normal, but it's nothing to worry about.'

'Why did you ask about children?'

I am thirty, and female. I get asked a lot about children. And while it's a great conversation starter if the answer is yes, because people can ask follow-up questions about gender and names and ages, it's a different story if you say no. It feels too abrupt to just offer the honest truth, so I find myself trying to explain. Sometimes I say that I'm not ready, or I'm not sure, or, if they don't know enough about my circumstances to know it's a lie, I say I'm single. Once, I asked David if anyone ever asks him whether he has children. He gave me a funny look, like it was a strange question, and said no.

'Oh,' Angela says, 'just because it tends to skew things on the pain scale front. Women who've been through labour tend to class other pains as lower, because they have known pain that's pretty bad.'

'Oh,' I say. 'Right.'

* * *

I've not long finished breakfast when a short, wiry man with a mop of very thick, very dark hair puts his head around the curtain.

'Hi,' he says, holding up a hand in a kind of wave. 'I'm Dr Ali. Or you can call me Hamza. I'm one of the psychiatrists here. Would it be all right to sit and talk to you for a while?'

I don't know what to say. Part of me is terrified of opening up but the rest of me is bored shitless and desperate for a conversation of some kind.

'Sure,' I say. 'Why not?'

He drags a plastic chair to the side of my bed. It makes an awful screeching sound and I wince.

'Too close?' he asks.

'No, it's not that, it's... It was loud, that's all.' I remember that the doctor said I should report any headaches. Is this the start of one? It's hard to tell.

'Oh. Sorry.' He sits down, and I notice that he doesn't have anything with him. No notebook or pen.

'This isn't a proper session,' he says, as if he can tell what I'm thinking. 'I just want to get to know you a little bit and assess whether we need to spend more time together. It's nothing to worry about. I talk to everyone who's been through this kind of ordeal.'

What does he mean by 'this kind of ordeal'? Everyone whose partner has tried to kill them? Or everyone who's been hurt badly enough, by any means, to end up in a coma?

'Is there anything you want to ask me, before we get started?' he asks.

My mind is blank. I've never had any kind of therapy, never felt I needed it, so I don't really know what to expect.

'No,' I say.

'Great.' He clasps his hands together on his lap. 'Why don't you tell me a bit about yourself. Your name, how old you are, where you live, what sort of job you do, that kind of thing.'

I reach to pull my hair into a ponytail. It feels lank and greasy – when was it washed? I don't like people seeing me like this. I'll have to ask Angela if we can wash it somehow.

'I'm Shelley,' I say. 'I'm thirty. I run a pub called the Pheasant and I live in the flat above it with my husband, David.'

Hamza looks quizzical. 'The Pheasant in Loughborough?'

I nod.

'I know it,' he says. 'You might even have served me an orange juice once or twice. Tell me, do you have a sense of what time of year it is, and what year, in fact?'

Angela asked me this yesterday. It strikes me that it's possible I've been in a coma for longer than I thought. Maybe it's October already? But no, didn't Fern tell me I've only been in here a few days? There's no window in the room to look out of at the weather.

'Well, when this happened to me, it was September 2017. But I don't know how long ago that was.'

'I see. And when you say when this happened, could you tell me exactly what you think happened to you? What led to you ending up in hospital with these injuries?'

'Yes,' I say. Now we're getting to it. This must be what he wants to hear about. The attack.

He waits, crosses one leg over the other, clears his throat. I can tell he's working up to speaking again when I finally find my voice.

'I'd been working, like every night. I came up to the flat an hour or so before closing. David was in our bedroom, waiting for me.'

I pause and look at him, and he nods politely, urging me to go on. But it's so hard to know how much is too much, how much is enough.

'He was all worked up. I know what it's like when he's like that. The best thing to do is just lie low and try to let him calm down.' I'm back there, in sensation and in fear. I don't have to close my eyes. And I know that I'm here, in this bed, on this safe hospital ward with this gentle psychiatrist, but I'm there too. I think perhaps a part of me always will be.

'Why haven't the police come?' I ask, my voice cracking.

He doesn't show any confusion about the interruption to my story.

'I don't know anything about that, I'm afraid,' he says. 'But I can talk to someone about it for you.'

'Yes. Thanks. Sorry. So there was this muscle twitching in his jaw, and I knew it meant trouble. He was furious about something and all I could do was wait to find out what, and how bad, it was.'

'Shelley,' Hamza says, 'is your marriage physically abusive?'

You tell yourself stories. Lies, I suppose. You tell yourself it's just this one time, and it was an accident, and he was under a lot of pressure, and he didn't mean it. He was sorry. This wasn't the real him. All of those things. But sometimes you wake up in hospital and you have to face up to the truth, no matter how ugly it is.

'Yes, it is.'

He nods, and I wonder how you learn to be neutral in the face of that kind of admission. He doesn't look like he's judging me, but he doesn't look like he's pitying me, either. He's just gathering facts so that he can help me.

'Thank you. Go on, about that night.'

'Well, it turned out he'd been down to the bar for a quick drink. It was so busy I hadn't even noticed him, but he'd seen me, and he'd got it into his head that I was flirting with this guy who comes in once or twice a week. I've known him for years, this guy. Liam, his name is. And even now, thinking back, I can't imagine what he saw or heard that made him jealous, but anyway. As soon as I got close enough to him, he punched me, broke my nose, I think. And then he was on me, punching and kicking and... It was the worst it's ever been. It was like he'd completely lost control of himself. I remember thinking that this was it. That I was going to die, at the hands of the person who was supposed to love and support me. Like so many women do. And I was so furious about that. In the past, I'd been angry with myself, I think. That I'd stayed, that I'd let it go this far, that I'd put myself in that position. But that night, I was just furious with him. That he would do that to me. That he would purposely hurt me. I swore to myself that if I survived, that would be it. It would be over.'

Hamza keeps his gaze fixed on me, his eyes giving nothing away.

'And here you are,' he says.

'Yes, and I'm sticking by what I said. My marriage is over. And I'm going to report this to the police, if I can ever get hold of them.'

He shifts, uncrosses and then recrosses his legs the other way. For a moment, he doesn't make eye contact, but then he does.

'Tell me, have you ever experienced any problems with your memory?'

I'm not expecting this, and I'm caught off-guard. Is he questioning my recollection of what happened? Because if he is, how dare he? I've just told him the hardest story I've ever had to tell, and he follows it up by suggesting that it's not true? If I wasn't in a hospital bed, I'd be tempted to get up and walk away, to storm out.

'No,' I say instead. 'Why do you ask?'

'Shelley.' He steeples his fingers. 'I'm just trying to explore various avenues to assess the level of damage to your brain.'

'Brain damage?'

It's a terrifying phrase. So much scarier than hearing you've broken bones.

'You were in a coma, Shelley. You were very badly hurt. And there's a small bleed on your brain.'

'I know!' I don't mean to raise my voice, but I do. The frustration is bubbling up and it needs to escape somewhere.

'I think we should leave it there for today.'

I nod, my throat suddenly dry and my eyes full.

'I'll come back another day,' he says. 'Thanks for talking to me.'

And then he gets up and slips through the curtain and it's like he was never there. I close my eyes and sink back into the past.

# 8

## THEN

I wince as Annabelle drags a brush through my hair.

'Shit, am I hurting you? Almost done.'

I keep quiet. I know, by now, that there is no stopping Annabelle when she's in the middle of something. It's not worth saying that it hurts, or that you're not sure, or that you are sure and you don't want to. I'm starting to understand that our friendship works, at least in part, because of my meekness and willingness to do what she says.

Annabelle dressed this up as a sleepover, but as soon as I arrived, she whisked me upstairs and started preening us both. Now, I'm shivering in a glittery top passed down from Annabelle's big sister, Tammy, and she's wearing mascara for the first time.

'I didn't tell you,' Annabelle says, as if I have asked, which I have, but only internally, 'because I knew you'd be like this. You're so scared of everything, Shelley.'

I consider this. Am I really? Yes, it's true that I'm not keen on Annabelle's plan for our evening, which seems to involve going to the park to smoke cigarettes and drink vodka stolen from

Annabelle's mum's drinks cabinet, while not wearing enough clothes. But that doesn't mean I'm scared of everything, does it? I think of the things I can do, the things I'm proud of. Swimming a mile, playing 'Chopsticks' on the piano in the music room at school, making cakes that everyone says are amazing.

But while, in the past, Annabelle's interests were similar to mine, over the last six months or so, it's all changed. Annabelle is obsessed with boys. I, too, am very interested in boys, but not interested enough to go to all this trouble, I think. And then I let out an involuntary yelp because Annabelle has got some kind of heated contraption for my hair and she is wielding it dangerously and it just touched my scalp.

'Ryan Benson is going to be there,' Annabelle says, almost as if it's new information.

'I know,' I say. 'But he's not going to fancy me if I have burn marks all over my face, is he?'

Ryan Benson is a boy we have known forever. But at primary school, he was short and very skinny and kind of annoying. The change had happened gradually, and one day, about a year earlier, I had looked over at him in Maths and seen an entirely different boy from the one who used to pick his nose in the playground and wipe his finger on girls' cardigans. He'd grown up, filled out, got taller. He'd grown into his face, that was what it was. And from that day on, I had been thinking about him, talking about him (only to Annabelle) and imagining our future together.

Annabelle turns off the straightener and does a 'ta da!' gesture with her hands. 'What do you think?'

I look at myself. I look the same but different, like my own older sister or something. I feel a familiar prick of pain, the one that comes when I see siblings joking together, or even arguing, sometimes. Being an only child is hard. I pretend for a minute that I am looking at my older sister in the mirror, try to imagine what that sister would say to me. But it's too hard. My only experience of this sort of thing comes from TV shows and books. It isn't real.

'It's good,' I say, touching my poker-straight hair and lifting my jaw to check for unsightly foundation lines.

'Ryan is going to love it,' Annabelle says. 'You look like a different person.'

There's an insult sitting inside that compliment, I think, but I can't be bothered to pick Annabelle up on it.

There's a knock on the door and then Annabelle's mum's face appears around it. She does a sort of double take when she sees me.

'You two look very glamorous for a film night at Shelley's,' she says.

Annabelle rolls her eyes. 'We're just practising so we're ready when we're finally allowed to go anywhere.'

'Okay, well listen, I'm heading out in ten minutes. Don't forget to lock up when you go. And have fun, both of you.'

When she's gone, I notice an instant change in Annabelle. A frostiness. I don't ask about it; I know there's no point. I assume Annabelle's mum is going on a date. Annabelle's dad left a year ago and her mum has recently started looking for a new man. Out of nowhere, I remember the day Annabelle told me I couldn't play because I didn't have a dad. And look where we are now. Not a dad between us. I think about saying something, making a joke out of it, but Annabelle's moodiness stops me.

Annabelle is wearing a tiny black skirt and top with a plunging neckline. We stand side by side in front of her full-length mirror, assessing. I think we look a bit silly, like we're trying way too hard, which of course we are. I know the boys, if they even turn up, will be in jeans and T-shirts. I know they won't have thought about it. That they might have even spilled tomato sauce on their tops and not bothered to change them. That is how it is for boys.

Ryan Benson is there, as promised. Annabelle takes hold of my arm as we approach the group of boys, a couple of whom are smoking, and a couple of whom are messing about with a football. Ryan is doing neither. He is standing still, looking over at us as we get closer. For a moment, I allow myself to believe that the makeover has really changed something. That Ryan has noticed me the way I noticed him in that Maths lesson. That this evening is going to be the start of the rest of my life. I picture the magazines me and Annabelle have pored over, with step-by-step instructions on how to French kiss. I might finally need that knowledge.

'Hey,' Ryan says when we are close enough to hear him.

He is looking at Annabelle, and when his eyes flick over to me, they don't stay on me for long. And I see it, then, how the evening is going to go. At some point, glassy-eyed with drink, Annabelle will come to me and say that Ryan has told her he likes her and she has refused to kiss him because she knows how I feel about him, but really she'll be silently asking for permission, and she'll kiss him later on, whether she gets it or not. I feel cold and stupid, and I take the water bottle from Annabelle's hand and take a long swig of vodka and Coke. It warms me immediately.

'Hey,' Annabelle says, her voice light and airy, like she's holding back a laugh.

I can't watch it. It's one thing knowing it's going to happen, but I can't watch it unfold. But before I can do anything about it, before I can think of a way to extract myself from the situation, Josh Landers is approaching me. Josh is Ryan's best friend, and he's funny and not bad looking and really clever but he's not... Well, he's not Ryan. I see it all for what it is. Josh has been dispatched to distract me so that Ryan is free to make his move on Annabelle.

'Hi,' he says.

His voice is kind and I can see that his heart's not in it, but it's what you do, isn't it? It's what you do for your friend when they really like someone.

'I have to go,' I say, pushing past him and forcing myself not to break into a run. I need to be as far away from this scene as possible. But I can hear Annabelle calling my name. I stop, wait for my friend to catch up. We are out of earshot of the boys now.

'What's going on?' Annabelle asks, breathless. 'Where are you going?'

'He likes *you*,' I say, my voice not much more than a whisper. 'I can't believe I didn't notice it before.'

'Who?' Annabelle asks. 'Do you mean Ryan?'

She's a passable actress, I think. She is not about to admit that she knew the way this was going to go.

'I want to go home,' I say.

And I leave a space before moving again, a space for Annabelle to say she will come with me, to link my arm and say who cares about boys anyway? A space for my best friend to promise me the films and popcorn we were supposed to be having. But Annabelle leaves it empty, and I feel the crack in my heart grow a tiny bit wider.

Annabelle shrugs. 'Go, then,' she says.

And there's nothing more to say after that. I turn and walk away, fighting back tears because I don't want my mascara to run in inky streams down my face. At home, Granny Rose opens the door. Mum is working, like always.

'Oh, love,' Granny Rose says, knowing immediately that something is wrong but not asking what it is. She pulls me in close and we rock from side to side a bit. Then Granny Rose pulls away and puts her hands on my shoulders, assesses me at arm's length. 'Do you want to talk about it?'

'No,' I say.

Granny Rose nods, quick and firm. 'Go and get your pyjamas on, then, and we'll see what's on TV.'

It is just what I need, this kindness, this generosity. Ten minutes later, my face clear of makeup, my fleecy pyjamas on, I cuddle up next to Granny Rose on the sofa, and she flicks through the channels, looking for something to distract us.

# 9

NOW

I must have fallen asleep because I suddenly snap awake with Dee's name on my lips. Angela said she'd been in a lot, but I've been awake for twenty-four hours now and I haven't seen her.

I've known Dee for seven years. She was at the Horse and Wagon when I started there, and I eyed her from afar, all that gorgeous nut-brown hair, all glossy and looking like it had just been cut and blow-dried. She was tiny, with sort of elfin features, a slightly pointy chin and eyes that looked big in her small face. As girls, we're taught to be suspicious of other girls, to feel threatened by them. And Dee was so achingly pretty that I wanted to hate her. I tried to hate her. But halfway through my second shift, I came out of a toilet cubicle to find her standing at the sinks, washing her hands. She smiled at me in the mirror and I found myself smiling back.

'Watch out for Jim,' she said.

'Jim?'

'Old guy, sits at the bar most nights. Actually, there are two of those. But the bald one is Derek and he's a sweetheart. Jim's the one with the bad toupee. He looks harmless and acts all butter-wouldn't-melt, but I can guarantee that he'll try to grope you before the week's out.'

And with that, she fluffed her hair and swished out, back into the rowdy bar.

And sure enough, later that same night, I was walking past Jim with a tray of empty glasses when his hand darted out and brushed against my bum. I think if Dee hadn't said anything, I would have thought it was accidental. Two days later, when he tried it again, I dodged out of his way. Back on my side of the bar, I motioned for him to come closer and I leaned in.

'I think you and I might have a little problem,' I said.

'What?' he asked, all innocence.

'Well, I'm going to be spending my evenings walking around this pub for the foreseeable future and you seem quite fond of sitting on that barstool, all of which is fine, but if you touch – or even try to touch – any part of my body again, I'm going to make sure you never get served in this place for the rest of your sorry little life.'

I said it quietly, and there was music playing and groups of people talking. So I didn't think anyone else would hear. But when I looked up, away from Jim, who was spluttering and trying to come up with something to say, I saw Derek smiling, and I saw Dee looking at me. She looked impressed. Later, when we'd locked the doors and were cashing up, she brought it up.

'No one has ever put Jim in his place like that. You know, you should be a landlady with that kickass attitude.'

I knew right then that we'd be friends, but I didn't know yet that I would go on to run a pub of my own.

Jim never touched me after that. He didn't touch Dee either. He must have seen us together, laughing at something Rob, the land-lord, had said, or passing glasses to each other from the dishwasher. He must have seen us getting close. Anyway, whatever it was, he still came in, he still sat there at the bar, still drank half pints of lager shandy, but he kept his hands to himself.

Meanwhile, what Dee had said started to take root and grow. I loved being a barmaid, but did I have it in me to run the show? Maybe I did. By the time David started coming in, it was a solid ambition. On one of our early dates, he asked me where I'd like to be in five years, and I said 'running my own pub'. He sulked for hours because he'd expected me to say something that involved him, but he didn't question it as a career goal. And that's how ambitions become reality, at least sometimes. Someone believing you can leads to you believing you can. Two years ago, when I was twenty-eight, I went for the job as manager of the Pheasant. And I took Dee with me.

I look up and Fern is approaching the bed, all smiles. For a minute, I can't remember what it is she does, and then my brain makes the connection. Physio Fern.

'How are you doing today?' she asks.

It's such an innocuous question but I don't know how to answer it right now. I'm so lost and confused. Automatically, I go to ask her one of my questions. When can I go home? Or why haven't the police been? But they are getting me nowhere, so maybe I need to do things a different way.

'I'm all right,' I say.

She nods and takes hold of one of my hands, looking at me for silent permission to touch my body, and I give it. She works quietly, asking me whether anything hurts and whether I can stretch a tiny bit more. But there's no chit-chat, and that's fine with me. She's brisk and efficient, and I appreciate it. When she's finished, she smiles at me, and it feels like an invitation.

'What's the weather like?' I ask her.

There are no windows in this ward and it adds to my disorientation. I don't know whether it's night or day, and I don't know whether it's raining or sunny.

'Blowy,' she says. 'It's mild, but when the wind gets up it feels quite chilly. Bright, though. Not many clouds.'

I close my eyes and picture it, imagine myself breathing in air that hasn't been recycled and watching the clouds drift along. 'Thank you,' I say. And then she's gone.

I lose track of how often Angela comes over to take my obs. Sometimes it feels like it's every ten minutes, and other times it feels like hours go by in between. She makes sure I always have a jug of fresh water, pours me some into plastic cups that look scratched and like they've been through the dishwasher too many times. She offers to adjust my bed, sometimes gets me to lift my head a little so she can plump my pillows. She never leaves without asking if there's anything I need, and there's just one thing, but I can't say it. I always want her to stay.

Every time the door goes, I look up, hoping to see Dee or even my mum. But it's never them. Always someone else's relative or loved one. Because I don't have any of my own, I listen in to other people's visits, catch little snippets of conversation.

'Of course, Aunty Beryl was having none of it.'

'Shall I bring you some of those mints you like?'

'Well, I said I'd be back in on Tuesday but it's hard to know, isn't it?'

'Maya misses you.'

'They've called her Erin.'

'I was so weary last night, I ate a bowl of cereal for dinner and was in bed by nine o'clock.'

And then, at some point in the afternoon, when I'm waiting for dinner because there's nothing else to mark out the time, she comes. Dee. I start crying before she's even reached my bedside.

'Your hair,' I say.

And she does that thing where she puts a hand to it as if it might have changed or disappeared without her realising. Her long hair is gone, replaced with a neat bob. It's still shiny and silky and gorgeous.

'Never mind my hair, Shelley. How are you feeling?'

She pulls the plastic chair a bit closer to my bed so she can sit down and also hold my hand. I feel like it's going to undo me, that touch. Since I woke, I've been touched by many hands, but all of them were doing a job, and Dee is being a friend.

'Dee,' I say, looking her right in the eye. 'What's going on? Where's David? He did this, and I keep telling them, and the police haven't come to talk to me about it.'

'I can't talk to you about all that,' she says, not quite meeting my eye.

'Why not?'

'Because... you asked me not to. You made it very clear that you didn't want me to.'

I'm stunned. What does she mean? I haven't seen her since the accident, have I?

She must realise I'm confused. 'You've been coming in and out of consciousness for a few days now. We've been trying to fill you in on everything, but you didn't believe what we told you, and then you got really angry and asked us to just let you regain your memories on your own.'

'Did I?'

'You did. And I get it, Shell. David used to fuck around with you, try to make you think things were different from how you remembered them, so it's bound to be scary for you to be told things you don't remember.'

What don't I remember? 'Okay,' I say. 'Who's we?'

'What?'

'You said *we* tried to fill you in.'

'Oh, me and the medical team. Dr Jenkins and Angela and Dr Ali. Everyone here.'

'So everyone knows not to answer my questions?' It's unbelievable, like some big conspiracy.

'For now,' she says. 'You wanted to remember on your own. So we're all giving you a chance to do that. I think it's for the best, Shelley, I really do.'

I sink back against my pillows, unsure of what to say next.

'Are you looking after the pub?' I ask.

She pauses, then nods. 'Yes. Don't worry, the pub is fine.'

'And what about Whiskers?'

Whiskers is my cat. She usually sleeps on my feet and will only eat one particular brand of cat food. I'm so worried that she'll be pining and on hunger strike.

'Whiskers is fine too. Please, Shelley, try not to worry. Everyone here wants the best for you and is working to make you better. Please believe me.'

And it's frustrating, but what choice do I have? I trust this woman more than anyone else, and she's telling me to be patient, to wait. So that's what I'll do.

'Do you know where my phone is?' Surely that's safe enough to ask about.

'Oh, it's broken. Did you have insurance?'

Broken. In the fall? 'No.'

'We'll sort it out. Do you want me to get you one of those cheap Nokias so you can make calls and send messages in the meantime?'

'Can you still buy those?'

'Yes, my mum has one.'

'Yes please. Where are my flowers?' It's a message, a signal that I'm doing what she has asked. Because this is how we are with each other. Not polite and reserved.

She grins. 'I didn't think this was bad enough for flowers.'

'What, a coma? What do I have to do for a bunch of tulips?'
She laughs, but I am suddenly elsewhere. The word 'tulip' was
a trigger, a key. It's unlocked something. I can see a bright
kitchen, a vase of tulips on the wooden table. Purple and red.
But it isn't a room I know or can remember. And then it's gone,
and I'm back in the hospital bed. I look at Dee, and she has
her head tilted to one side, like she's concerned, so I smile
at her.

'Tell me stuff,' I say. 'I need gossip and stories.'

Gossip and stories aren't why I went into pub work, but they're
an inevitable by-product. Always a steady stream of people, and
half of them drunk. 'Loose lips sink ships' and all that. I've lost
count of the number of strangers who've trusted me with their
sadness and secrets. The affairs and the family feuds and the
regrets. They are endless. And it could be depressing, always
hearing about things going wrong, but I've never seen it that way.
Because I always try to help, try to point out the other person's posi-
tion, try to steer people back to one another. I'm like an agony aunt,
but on the ground.

Dee puts one finger to the side of her lips, to demonstrate that
she's thinking.

'How's Derek?' I ask.

When I left the Horse and Wagon to take over the Pheasant, it
wasn't just Dee who came along with me. Derek moved from one
barstool to another, and he's barely moved since. Dee likes to joke
that he's in love with me, and I say he's in love with her.

She rolls her eyes. 'You know Derek. That last stool on the right
is never going to get cold while he's around. Oh, here's something.
He brought a woman in.'

'No!' I clutch at my chest as if to show I'm heartbroken.

'Yes. He didn't introduce her. And he sat in his usual spot, of
course, and she sat next to him. She matched him drink for drink,

though she was on halves. When they got up to leave, she was a bit unsteady on her feet, and he linked her arm.'

'Well,' I say.

Just then, Angela comes over, wheeling her machine. Dee stands up to make sure she's not in the way.

'I'd better go,' she says.

It feels like she just arrived, and I want to ask her to stay a bit longer, but I couldn't bear it if I asked her and she said no.

'If the police talk to you, about David, will you tell them I want to give a statement?' I ask her.

She flicks her eyes towards Angela and then back to me. 'I will.'

'And, will you come back?'

She nods, and I know what that means. She's trying to hold back tears. She leans forward and gives me a kiss on the cheek, and the smell of her is so familiar that it calms me. Floral and light. She smells like home.

'Tomorrow,' she says. 'Or the next day. Soon.'

I wait until she's gone before repeating that word back to her. 'Tomorrow.'

I lie there, thinking about David for a while. How he wasn't the first man to hurt me.

# 10

THEN

The first time Mick hits me, my overriding reaction is to be surprised that he didn't do it sooner. I am sixteen, in that strange, in-between space between childhood and adulthood. Old enough, according to the law, to have sex, to smoke, to leave education, to get married with a parent's permission. Old enough to make some very adult decisions, then. But not legally an adult. Like every teenager that went before me, I think that everything is unfair and that the world is conspiring against me.

I am in my room, the radio turned up loud. I am experimenting with my hair, which is long and thick, and which I spend a lot of time plaiting in elaborate ways. I am trying to decide whether or not to lose my virginity to Mark Riley, who I've been seeing for about a month. Annabelle says I should, that he won't wait around much longer if I don't, and I know that's probably true but there's a part of me that wants to save this for someone who would wait around. And for someone I would find it impossible to keep waiting. There's nothing wrong with Mark Riley, per se, but I recognise that he is a school boyfriend, that whether we have sex or not, we will not stay together more than a couple more months at most.

When we first got together, at someone or other's sixteenth birthday, he pushed me up against a tree and told me he'd fancied me for weeks and I was flattered. And drunk. When he kissed me, I liked the laziness of it, the way he took his time, when other boys I had kissed were in a hurry and lacked any kind of technique. And that is enough, at sixteen, for the two of us to be a pair. But is it enough for me to do this huge thing with? I know that I will always remember the name of the person I lose my virginity to. Do I want it to be Mark Riley?

When Annabelle comes in, I jump.

'Sorry,' Annabelle says, but straight away she negates the apology with a shrug. 'I knocked. You've got this too loud.' She crosses my room and turns the volume down a few notches. She doesn't like the same kind of music I like. I know that after one or two more songs, at most, she will bossily put a CD on.

'Who let you in?' I ask.

'Mick.' Annabelle makes the face she always makes when we talk about Mick.

She knows I can't stand him but I haven't told her why. Not the full story, anyway. If she knows, she's pieced it together herself, because I have never said out loud that Mum is regularly assaulted by her boyfriend. If I told someone, wouldn't it seem strange that I hadn't done anything about it? I have wanted to do something about it. But what? I am powerless.

'I didn't know he was here,' I say.

Mick is usually at work at this time on a Friday. He's a hospital porter and he works long days, comes home wanting a fight. By the time he does, I'm usually long gone. To Annabelle's, or another friend's, or out somewhere, like the Bells, which is the only pub in town that doesn't seem to care how old you are when you go in and try to look as grown up as possible and ask for a vodka, lime and soda.

'Is tonight the night?' Annabelle asks, sitting down on the edge of my bed and looking at me in the mirror as I unravel one tiny braid after another. 'With Mark?'

The addition was unnecessary. This is Annabelle's favourite question, has been for weeks, ever since Mark and I got together. Sometimes I wonder why Annabelle is quite so invested in my relationship. She has a boyfriend herself. He's called Tom and he's a couple of years older. When he is around, Annabelle rolls her eyes a lot, as if the rest of us are way too immature for her and she doesn't know what to do about it. Tom is doing A Levels in Business and PE and Annabelle gets really sniffy if anyone asks why he's only doing two, and I have kept it to myself but I'm not sure what kind of career that might possibly lead to.

'I'm not going to tell you when it's going to happen,' I say, reaching for a pair of tweezers and attacking my already-thin eyebrows. 'It's gross. I'll tell you after.'

Annabelle sighs, flops backwards. 'You need to get a move on, Shelley, because...'

'I know. He won't wait around much longer. Tell me again. It's so romantic.'

'Your problem is, you expect life to be the way it is in films and books, and it just isn't. Chances are, your first time will be pretty shit, but at least it will be over with then.'

'You know, you're really not selling this,' I say.

I wouldn't admit it to Annabelle, but I do expect a bit of romance. For it to feel natural and right. Last time I was with Mark, in his bedroom while his mum did the ironing in front of *Casualty* downstairs, he had stuck his fingers inside me and asked me whether I liked it. And I hadn't known how to say that I didn't. That it had come as a shock, and been a bit painful, and hadn't made me feel special at all.

No, I think, shuddering at the memory. I will not sleep with

Mark. I will finish things instead. I know Annabelle won't under-
stand, because she seems to think that any boyfriend is better than
no boyfriend, but I have not yet given up on the kind of love we
used to see in Disney films, before everything got so complicated.

Annabelle gets up and puts a CD on without asking if it's okay.
She chooses Beyoncé and it's not my favourite but I sing along to
'Crazy in Love' anyway, and by the end of it, I feel sort of giddy, and
I'm not sure whether it's the song or the decision I've made.

And then I hear it. Mick's voice, loud and low. How long has he
been shouting for? I go to my door, open it, and move towards the
stairs. He is in the hallway, hands on hips. Clearly furious about
something.

'What makes you think you can just ignore me?'

'I wasn't ignoring you. I... I didn't hear you.'

He hates being contradicted; I know this. It doesn't matter who's
right. It's safer to just go along with what he says.

'Come down here,' he says.

And I do. As I walk reluctantly down the twelve stairs, I think of
Mum, already at the pub because they open in the day now, and
serve food. And I think of Granny Rose, who meets her friend Eliza-
beth on Friday afternoons. They drink tea and eat scones, or they
go to the cinema, and she always comes back full of laughter and
joy and says she feels like she's been recharged. I am used to having
the house to myself after school on Fridays. Why is he home?

'I wanted toast,' he says. 'And what did I find?'

I have no idea. Are we out of bread? If we are, it isn't down to
me. I eat porridge every morning, snack on apples and biscuits and
sometimes crisps after school, but never a sandwich. Never toast.

'I don't know,' I say.

'You do know, because when I had toast this morning for break-
fast, there was plenty of peanut butter left, and now...'

Ah, this *is* down to me. I sometimes spread peanut butter along the inside of sticks of celery. I remember doing just this when I first got home, throwing the empty jar in the bin without a thought.

'Oh, I finished it. I didn't know…'

He hits me, then. A fast, sharp slap across the face, and the sting of it lingers like a shock. But I am not shocked. Because I know this man; I know who he is. He has always been this way, and it's only been a matter of time, and there's almost a sense of relief now that it's finally done, because the anticipation of it, stretched over months and years, has been terrible.

And I hate him. Truly hate him, with everything I have. Because he's not my dad, not even my stepdad. And this is not his house. And yet, here he is, in this space that worked so well when it was filled with three generations of women and no men. Too big and too angry and too fucking awful. We stare at each other, and I am thinking about what my mum will say if I tell her. And I think maybe he is thinking the same. Because he takes a step backwards, looks at his hand as if he has no idea what happened, as if he has no control, and then he turns and leaves the room. I hear him pulling his shoes on, his coat, and then he's gone. This is what he does. He hurts people, and then he leaves.

I cry in the kitchen. It is a quiet kind of crying. I make cups of tea for me and Annabelle, giving myself time to try to pull myself together. I practise what I'll say when I go upstairs. 'Fucking Mick, always moaning about something.' I will say it without my voice cracking. I must. In the downstairs toilet, I examine my face. Brush away the tears. There is a red mark where his hand made contact with my skin, but if I can avoid Annabelle noticing, I will be able to cover it with makeup. Many times, I have watched my mother cover bruises and marks with makeup, and I always thought I would never let it happen to me. And here I am.

When I go back to my room with the tea, Annabelle looks at

me, eyebrows raised. I have unravelled the remaining braids and am using my hair like a curtain to cover my face.

'He just wanted to know where something was,' I say.

I hate myself for covering for him. Why am I doing it? I've always wished Mum wouldn't. But I can't face the way Annabelle would look at me. This is not who I want to be. How unfair, that I have no control over what I may or may not become, in this way. Annabelle seems to sense that I want her to go. She drinks her tea quickly, so quickly I think it must have burned her mouth, and then she says she has to go, that she's seeing Tom in a bit.

'Let me know if it happens, with Mark,' Annabelle says over her shoulder as she goes out of the door.

'You'll be the first to know,' I say.

And Annabelle goes, sees herself out like she always does. I turn off the Beyoncé CD. It hasn't quite finished and it strikes me as strange that I was one person when this CD started playing and now I am quite another. I sit at my desk and stare at myself in the mirror where I do my hair and makeup. The mark is fading already; it will be easy enough to disguise. But am I crazy for thinking that there's something in my eyes that will give me away? It's impossible to say, and there's no one I can ask.

Later that evening, I do have sex for the first time. Before the slap, I'd decided I wouldn't, but when I see Mark, I change my mind. What am I waiting for, really? Who am I saving myself for? Mark isn't someone I can see myself with long term, but he is kind and he knows I've been nervous about this. Better that than with some stranger after drinking too much cider at a party. It's just like Annabelle said. It's a bit shit, but then it's over with. Mark keeps smiling over at me, afterwards. Says that I look beautiful, and though I don't believe it, it's nice to hear all the same.

Something about the juxtaposition of the two events, the slap and the sex, makes me feel like I have lost sight of myself entirely.

There's a before and after. Before, my childhood. Not idyllic, certainly not that, but with a kind of innocence that is gone, after. And I think this is when I became an adult. It has nothing to do with laws or birthdays. It is when you cross over a line that you cannot cross back from. Or sometimes, two.

## 11

NOW

When the volunteer from yesterday puts his head around the door, I can't bring his name to mind. I look at his hands to check whether he's brought me another KitKat. Empty.

'Shelley,' he says. 'Can I come in?'

I nod. I was rude to him yesterday, and I don't know yet whether today will be any different. I'm so lost, stuck in hospital and with a husband who might or might not be my husband any more. I look at him as he ambles into the room. Matt, I think. His name is Matt. I'm not sure I would have come back, if I were him.

'Do you have any news?' I ask.

He looks surprised. 'What sort of news?'

'Anything. I've barely moved since you last saw me. What's happening in the world?'

He smiles, looks a little unsure. 'It's just another day on the wards. I've been called a stupid twat and asked to take in someone's dog if she doesn't make it out of surgery.'

I don't know whether or not he's joking, but I smile anyway.

'And now I'm here, hoping not to make you cry this time.'

I nearly say that it wasn't his fault, that he didn't make me cry, that I'm fragile, scared of everything. But I don't know him, so I don't. I don't say it's good to see him either, but it is. He looks so solid and dependable, like he'd stand steady through a hurricane. Like he'd stand by you, no matter what. Why am I thinking about these things?

'The police still haven't been,' I say, as if it's something he can help with.

He pulls a chair over so it's closer to my bed but not too close, and then he sits down and rests one ankle on the other knee. And all the time he's doing that, he doesn't talk. But once he's settled, he does. 'I spoke to the nurse.'

'About me?'

'Yes, she wanted me to reassure you that you're safe. You don't need to worry about anything.'

'That's what everyone keeps saying, but I don't know how it can be true. He tried to kill me, Matt, and no one is listening. What if he's out there trying to kill someone else? What if he's successful this time?'

Even as I'm saying it, I know this isn't likely. Women are killed by men they know, by their partners, predominantly. David wouldn't do this to anyone else. But still, he should face the consequences, shouldn't he? He should at least do that.

Matt just absorbs my storm of words. 'I'm sorry,' he says. 'I just get the tea.'

'Well, could you maybe do that, then?'

He laughs, and there is something familiar about it. Who is it he reminds me of? While he's gone, I run a list of TV people through my head, trying to find a match, but come up short.

'Here,' he says. 'Tea, one sugar.'

It's sweet that he remembers. I take it from him and try to smile.

'That's quite the shiner you have there,' he says, pointing to his own eye to show me what he means.

'Oh,' I say, touching it. It's faintly sore. 'I haven't seen it. I haven't been out of bed.'

He doesn't say anything, just sits down and looks at his shoes, rests his plastic cup on his thigh.

'Do people tell you that you look like someone?'

He looks up, meets my gaze. 'Um, I don't think so. Well, once there was this guy who was in EastEnders for a few months. He was, like, going out with one of the Slater sisters, or something. And a couple of people said I looked like him.'

It's the most he's said in one go. And it's about a soap opera I've never watched. I have no idea who the Slater sisters are.

'It's not that,' I say.

'Oh, then... no.'

'Why do you do this?'

He looks taken aback. Perhaps he's not used to people asking frank questions. But he doesn't look offended. He doesn't shut down.

'This... volunteering?'

'Yes. Do you have a paying job as well? Or are you a lottery winner or something, looking to do a bit of good? What's the story, Matt?'

He leans back, starts tipping on his chair, and it takes me back to schooldays, teachers giving warnings about possibly mythical children who had cracked their heads open and had to have them stitched back together. And I almost tell him not to do it, but then I remember that he isn't my pupil, or my colleague, or even my friend. Not yet.

'I work here, actually.'

'In the hospital?' For a moment, I think he's going to say that this is his work, that he's not a volunteer at all, that he's assessing me or something.

'Yes. I run the restaurant.'

'And you choose to spend your spare time here too?'

He smiles, and I can see he's not sure how to answer. 'Things are a bit strange for me at the moment. Quiet. I don't much like being at home. So I hang out here a bit, meeting people.'

There is so much that he's not saying. I think perhaps there is a wife or girlfriend, or there was. But I won't ask, not now. Not when he's picked his words so carefully to avoid disclosure.

'We're in the same line of work,' I say instead.

'Oh yes?'

'Yes. I run a pub.'

'Tell me about it.'

What is there to tell about the Pheasant? I tell him it's in town, that I live above it which is a blessing when you wake up on a frosty winter morning and don't want to step outside, and a curse when you lock up and want to get as far away from your job as possible. He nods, like he understands. I tell him that it was a bit of a dive when I took it on, that one of the barstools is moulded into the shape of Derek's arse. How I managed to keep him happy while also attracting a younger crowd with a new menu and a cocktail list. How I got a long line of chefs to cook dinner for David and me before finding Gabriel, who's Romanian and cooks like a demon while managing to be nice to the waiting staff.

'It means a lot to you,' he says.

It isn't a question. It's come through in my words.

'Yes.'

'Would you ever give it up?'

I wonder why he asks this particular question. When someone tells you about their job, or their hobby, or their relationship or whatever, you don't ask about ending it.

'I don't know. Would you give up the restaurant?'

'Yes,' he says immediately. 'It's just a job. It's not my whole life.'

Is the Pheasant my whole life? It's felt like it, at times. I live there, work there. David's always saying I don't have any time for him. But now, I don't have to think about what David wants, do I? I don't have to consider David in my future.

'I do have this one dream,' I say, surprising myself.

Matt crosses his arms and leans forward. 'Oh yes?'

'Well, pubs are all I know and now I have my own, it would be hard to walk away from it, but I have always had this idea that one day I'll do something that helps people. You know, work for a charity or something like that.'

He nods. 'You should do that. One day.'

We've both finished our drinks and he takes my cup from me and goes over to the bin. Will he go now? Is this conversation over? He doesn't sit down again, but he paces a little.

'Is there anything else you need?' he asks. 'Before I go?'

I need to know what's going on. Whether anyone's told my mum I'm here. Where David is. Why Dee didn't really tell me anything. But he can't help with any of that, so I shake my head.

'Tomorrow?' he asks, pulling on his jacket.

He's asking for permission to come again, and I want him to, because the hours are so long in here with no one to talk to and nothing to do. But I'm scared to say it.

'If you're passing,' I say.

And he nods and makes his way out of the room without saying goodbye. After he's gone, I wonder about the work I do, about how I ended up there. Was it all inevitable, from the days I would sit and watch my mother get ready to go to work behind a bar? Was I always destined to end up there?

# 12

## THEN

Before Mick hit me, I had an idea that I would go to university. I liked art, both the making of it and the learning about it. I thought I might try to make something of that. But that day, a flick switched in me and I started to see things differently, and my future was one of the casualties. There's a fuck-it attitude to me now, and it almost led to me leaving school straight after my GCSEs, but Annabelle talked me round and we are both taking A Levels – Annabelle's in English Lit, French and Geography and mine in Art, English Lit and History. Annabelle is talking about being a Geography teacher, and I don't say anything but I can't think of anything worse than signing myself up to a lifetime spent in school. Our own school's Geography classrooms, which had walls covered with maps and diagrams of riverbeds, and always smelled like no one had ever opened a window, had put me off the subject for life.

We both work in a pub, the Three Crowns, on Saturday nights and Sunday lunchtimes. We're not allowed to serve behind the bar, because we're still only seventeen, but it's legal for us to be paid five pounds an hour to wash dishes and serve food and clear plates. For Annabelle, it's strictly about the money. She is saving up for a dress from Topshop that her mum refuses to buy for her, and there are always things to be paid for – McDonalds milkshakes and makeup palettes and earrings and vodka from the cheap off-licence to replace what we've taken from Annabelle's mum's Smirnoff bottle. But I have started to think I like this life, have started to enjoy my hours in the pub more than my hours at school, where I have to sit still and pay attention while my young body wants to move and be free.

I'm getting ready for a shift. I'm wearing opaque black tights, a stretchy and short black skirt, and a white shirt which Mum makes me iron myself. I have three that I wear in rotation and I always leave the ironing of them until all three have been washed and I'm due to be at the pub in half an hour. There's no one at home so I'm ironing my shirts in my skirt and bra, singing loudly and out of tune to Girls Aloud's 'Love Machine', when Mick comes in. Instinctively, I hold up the shirt I'm currently ironing to cover my chest. It's too warm, and I feel sweat start to prickle under my arms. This is one of the difficulties of living with someone to whom you're not related and you don't love or feel comfortable with. Not being able to wander around in minimal clothing. Mick says nothing, goes to the fridge and takes out a beer. The hiss and fizz after he cracks it open makes me want one myself. But I never drink before a shift. Afterwards is another matter. Often, once we've locked the doors, Annabelle and I and the other staff put the Scissor Sisters or Eminem on the jukebox and dance and drink for an hour or two. When a shift feels long, or my feet are hurting, I look ahead to those times, to the vodka the landlord will turn a blind eye to us drinking and the sneaked cigarettes we will smoke.

There's a boy I like. He works behind the bar, and his name is Phil. Mark Riley, who I lost my virginity to, is long gone. Since him, there have been others. Jason, and Aaron, and Daniel. Now it's Phil, who hasn't shown the slightest bit of interest in me yet, but who my sights are very firmly set on. I've heard he's staying behind tonight, and all through my shift I practise lines I might use, ways I might look. When the last revellers are being ushered out of the door, I sneak to the toilets with my makeup bag and do what I can to undo the toll the shift has taken on my face. New mascara, powder to cover the sheen of sweat, a spray of that citrussy perfume I love. I pull the band out of my hair and shake my head. I'd put it in a bun when it wasn't quite dry, and now it's falling in loose curls, just the way I'd hoped it would. I look okay. No, better than okay. I look good enough.

On my way out of the toilets, I'm in a hurry. I can almost taste the sweet sharpness of the vodka, lime and soda I'll drink. The first one is always the best. The way it warms me, loosens me up. The way it calms me. I don't see Phil until we've collided, and I step back, stunned, muttering apologies. Phil smiles his easy smile, the one I see him flashing to customers left, right and centre, which does something to my insides, and I feel my face flushing.

'No harm done,' he says. 'Are you staying? There's a drink on the bar with your name on it.'

'Yes,' I say. 'I'm staying.'

'Oh good, it's just...'

'What?'

'You look nice. I thought maybe you had other plans.'

I know it is silly to be this pleased that he's noticed the way I look. But I am. 'No, no other plans.'

'I'll see you in a minute then,' he says, jerking one thumb in the direction of the door to the Gents.

Annabelle is already draining her glass when I get to the bar. There's a small crowd, everyone in good spirits now the work is over and it's time to spend our tips on getting drunk.

'Is this for Phil's benefit?' Annabelle asks, looking me up and down.

I nudge her, hard, and grab my drink from the bar. I know that by the time I have finished this drink and one more, I won't care what Annabelle says, how obvious she makes it that I am interested in Phil. I've been hoping he'll notice me for weeks, and I've decided tonight is the night. If he doesn't kiss me tonight, I'll move on.

He does though, kiss me. We've been drinking for a couple of hours, have been getting more and more flirty. Annabelle has left us to it, is round the corner playing cards with the guys who work in the kitchen. And I find I am sitting on Phil's lap and don't remember how I got there when he leans in, and we are kissing, and our remaining colleagues are jeering. I don't care, but Phil whispers something about going outside, and I follow him, our fingers linked, and he kisses me again by the wall just outside the door, his hands roaming my body. Presses himself against me, slides a hand beneath my skirt.

'Come on, let's go to my car,' he says.

I am drunk, my movements slow. 'No,' I say.

Phil has hold of both my hands, is pulling me. 'Come on, I'm so fucking turned on right now.'

I shake my head. I don't feel like I'm in danger. In the future, I will be in situations like this and I will be scared. But I am still young and I still believe in the good in people. At least some people.

'I don't want to. I'm going back inside.'

Phil shakes his head, like he's mirroring me. 'What the fuck, Shell? I thought you wanted this.'

I am a few feet away from him now, and I pause. I did want this, didn't I? But it was his attention I wanted, his kisses, his touch. Not a quickie in the backseat of his car with the chance of any of our colleagues catching sight of our pale, naked bodies. I wanted him to ask me to go out for a drink. I wanted romance, and phone calls, and the way my insides melt when he smiles at me a certain way.

'I don't,' I say.

'Then why did you come out here with me?' He's angry, making big movements with his arms. He might not be conscious of it, but he's showing me he's the bigger, stronger one. 'You're a fucking prick tease.'

I want to say that I can kiss a guy, can come outside with him, without committing to having sex with him in his car. But the back door to the pub opens then, and Annabelle comes out. She looks from Phil to me and back again.

'Are you okay?' she asks me.

'Yes, I was just coming back inside. Are you leaving?'

'Not yet,' Annabelle says.

I know that Annabelle knows something is wrong. That in the time I've been outside with Phil, something has shifted between us. It's in the air, the disappointment and the resentment. Hanging.

'Are you going home, Phil?' Annabelle asks.

It's only then that I notice he has his car key in his hand.

'I guess I am,' he says. All bravado gone.

Annabelle puts an arm around me and guides me to the door. 'See you, then,' she says over her shoulder. I say nothing.

Back inside, we get another drink and find a quiet corner.

'What happened?' Annabelle asks.

'He was just a bit handsy. And he tried to get me to go to his car for a quick shag.'

Annabelle rolls her eyes. 'Men. Was he pushy about it?'

'Not really. Just trying his luck, I think.'

'Well, fuck him,' Annabelle says, downing her drink. It must be her sixth or seventh, but we don't count. We just weave our way home when things get too blurry and we've run out of cigarettes.

I don't have another drink, though I wait until Annabelle is ready to go home. We live within a five-minute walk of each other, and we always walk home together when we're both working. While Annabelle drinks and flirts and smokes, I think about Phil, about how it went so wrong, so fast. From him saying something nice about how I looked outside the toilets to calling me a prick tease in the car park a couple of hours later. I wonder, sometimes, if there's something I give off, some kind of impression of being easy, or up for it. Because I want what all girls I know want. A boyfriend who is nice to me.

On the walk home, Annabelle is too drunk to walk in a straight line. She keeps taking my arm and then almost dragging me into the road. If I was just as drunk, I would find it funny. But there's nothing like being insulted to sober you up, and I stopped drinking a good hour ago, and now I feel clear-headed and hurt. When we get to Annabelle's street, she wraps her arms around me and both of us nearly tumble to the ground.

'Forget about him,' she says.

I nod, bite my lip.

'He's a prick.' And with that, Annabelle turns and makes her way up her street, and I wait until she gets to her front door before walking away.

At home, I try not to make too much noise, but just as I'm walking through the kitchen, Mick says my name. I jump. The room is in total darkness, but now I can make him out, standing by the sink, a glass in his hand.

'Where have you been, until this time?' he asks, his voice low and dangerous.

I have learned to recognise when he's spoiling for a fight, and this is one of those times.

'At work,' I say.

'It's one o'clock in the bloody morning. I bet you've been with some boy or other.'

'I haven't, I...' I don't finish. It's better to ignore him, I remind myself. I turn away and go up the stairs. But not before I hear him speak again.

'You're a little slut.'

And then, unexpectedly, there is another voice, coming from the stairs, loud in the dark and quiet room.

'No!' It's Granny Rose. 'You don't talk to her like that, you bastard. This is her home.'

'And mine, too,' he says, and there's a sneer in his voice.

'Well, it's been hers a lot longer. Come on, Shelley. Let's get you upstairs to bed.'

Like I did when I was a child, I let Granny Rose lead me up the stairs. On the landing, we hug, and I do not dissolve into tears, but it takes a lot of effort.

I crawl into bed without taking my makeup off or cleaning my teeth. I feel emptied out. Too tired to cry. What do they want, these men? Because in one night I have been insulted for not having sex and for having too much of it. And neither of these things are reflective of the truth. Is this how it will always be? When I talk about it with Annabelle, she insists that there are good men out there, that we will find them and marry them and have gorgeous babies, but I'm not so sure these days. Because it's a long time since I've been made to feel good, or even just about okay, by a boy or a man. And there are only so many times you can be called hideous things before you start to wonder if they might be true.

# 13

NOW

I wake with a jerk, with my heart thumping. I'm on high alert, as if I'm in danger, and it takes me a while to locate myself. I'm in the hospital. I'm safe. It must have been a dream. I close my eyes and try to remember it, but there's nothing to cling on to. It's completely disappeared at the moment of waking. It's not yet morning, the lights in the unit are still low, and the nurse who's buzzing around nearby is Harry, my regular night nurse, so Angela hasn't come on shift yet. I reach for my cup of water and take a long gulp, but it's warm and doesn't quench my thirst. Angela said that she and Fern are going to try getting me up and out of bed today, and I'm more than ready. I don't think I've been as still as this, for as long as this, in my entire life. I shuffle around a bit, try to get comfortable. There's no clock in here, and I don't have a watch, and it could still be the middle of the night for all I know. I should try to go back to sleep; everyone keeps telling me that rest is healing. I've just drifted off when I wake again, and this time I remember what it was I dreamed about. Or perhaps it wasn't a dream, but a memory.

I feel sure, suddenly, that David is out of my life. Could he be dead? It would fit with the fact that the police haven't come, that nobody seems to be treating what happened with any urgency. Because there's no case to try if the accused is dead, is there? I sit with it for a few minutes, the idea of him being gone. I let it settle. It's so hard to pinpoint what I would feel. Sadness, of course, but also relief, and hope, and worry. They're all mixed in with one another and I can't separate them, can't pull at any of the threads to see what comes loose.

I must eventually settle back to sleep, because the next thing I'm aware of is Angela wrapping the blood pressure cuff around my arm and smiling at me.

'Is my husband dead?' I ask her.

She takes a step backwards, widens her eyes. 'Your husband?'

'David. Is he dead? Do you know?'

Angela puts a finger to her lips while the cuff inflates. She's told me before that if I talk while she's taking my blood pressure, it can skew the results. It feels like an eternity, but eventually she jots down the numbers on my chart and pulls off the Velcro cuff.

'Whatever made you think that?' she asks. 'No, no one is dead.'

It seems a strange thing to say, because of course there are people who are dead. But I find it's mostly a relief to hear that David isn't among them.

Fern arrives then, all neat and smiley, and asks if I'm ready to have a go at standing up. Angela slowly raises the bed until I'm sitting upright.

'How do you feel?' she asks.

'Fine.'

It isn't true; I feel a bit dizzy. But I don't want to give them an excuse to give up on this for another day. I'm desperate to be on my feet.

'Well, your blood pressure is a bit on the low side, so let us know if you start to feel funny. Okay?'

She eyeballs me and I feel like she knows. 'Promise,' I say.

Slowly, slowly, they help me to swing my legs round until they're off the side of the bed, and then Angela uses the remote control to lower it until my feet are touching the ground.

'Remember,' Angela says. 'We can take this as slowly as you like. If this is enough for today, that's fine.'

'No,' I say, because it isn't enough. It isn't nearly enough. I want to be walking up and down the corridors. 'I'm good. I'm fine.'

Fern stands to one side of me, Angela to the other. They take an arm each and I stand, a little clumsily. It's a bit scary, and I want to ask them not to let go, but I don't want them to think I'm not up to it. And they don't let go, anyway. I'm standing, for the first time in... how long? A long time.

'Do you want to try taking a step?' Fern asks, and Angela gives her a bit of a frown, as if she's suggested a spot of skydiving.

I nod, eagerly. And it's only then I notice that there are tears streaming down my face. Happy tears. I take one step, then another. They keep hold of me.

'Right, now stand still,' Fern says.

I do, and she lets go, goes across to get the chair Matt sits in when he visits and pushes it over to where I'm standing. They help me ease down into it. And then they both take a step back.

'Now then,' Fern says, 'how's that?'

And I can't speak, because it's incredible. And I never would have imagined that sitting in a chair would feel like an achievement, but right now I feel like I've climbed a mountain or swum the channel or something. Exhausted, and proud.

'Can I stay here for a bit?' I ask.

'Of course,' Angela says. 'I need to fill out some paperwork but I'll be back to check on you. You just let me know when you're ready to get back to bed.'

'I will.'

She goes to the nurses' station, but Fern stays where she is. She's looking down at her shoes, and then she looks up at me, and her eyes fix me to the spot.

'It might not always feel like it,' she says, 'but you're doing really well.'

I don't know what to say. Usually, she is all business, which means this unexpected praise means a great deal. And still, she doesn't go. She sits down on the very edge of my bed, tilts her head to one side, as if trying to decide whether or not to say anything.

'I was married, once,' she says.

She only looks about thirty, like me. It surprises me a bit that she's talking about her marriage being in the past, at her age. And then I realise that I'll be doing that, too, so I'd better get used to it.

'He was violent, my husband,' she says.

I'm shocked. Not Fern, who is so put together and ordered. I cannot imagine her standing in front of a mirror, trying to use concealer to cover up the marks of a home life in disarray.

'I'm sorry,' I say. What else do I have to offer?

'I don't usually tell people, especially not patients. But I wanted you to see that there's something beyond it, something on the other side of it. When I was in it, I couldn't see that. But hopefully you can see me, and see that I'm well and reasonably happy, and know that that will be you, too.'

It's like a present she's given me, and I don't know what to do with it.

She looks at her watch, glances so briefly at me that I can't read what is in her eyes. 'I have to see another patient. I'll see you later, Shelley, all right?'

And she's gone, her neatly braided hair swinging behind her. She doesn't look like a victim. Do I?

In the end, I sit in the chair for about half an hour. When Angela comes back and asks me if I'm ready to get back in bed, I surprise myself by realising that I am. I'm shattered from the effort of it. It's a reminder that none of this is going to be easy.

'Reckon we can do this, just the two of us?' Angela asks.

I nod. I do. She holds out an arm and I cling on to it while I stand, and then we do what we did before in reverse. Over to the bed, swing the legs, adjust the bed until I'm more horizontal. And I must fall asleep almost immediately, because I don't remember her leaving my bedside.

* * *

There's a voice, calling my name. I blink a few times and look up. It's Dr Jenkins.

'Sorry to wake you,' she says, not sounding remotely sorry. 'I've arranged for another scan. We need to see whether that bleed has stopped.'

I feel disoriented, the way you do after a daytime sleep. A bit cold, too. I try to sit up, but I feel dizzy.

'Take your time,' Dr Jenkins says. 'Angela's on her way to help, and there's a porter coming with a wheelchair.'

And I know, as soon as she says it. I feel hot, prickly, like my skin is too tight.

'No,' I say. 'No.'

Her brow furrows. 'What is it? Are you worried about something? Because I can talk you through the process, and it really isn't anything you need to...'

He arrives, then. Pushing a wheelchair. Older, of course. His hair white and his body heavier. Mick. I haven't seen him since Granny Rose's funeral. I freeze, waiting to see if he'll recognise me.

'Ah,' Dr Jenkins says, 'here we are. The patient's just a bit nervous, aren't you, Shelley?'

His head snaps to attention at the sound of my name, and

there's a horrible moment when we make eye contact. *You little slut.* I remember that first slap, and the ones that came after. Always when my mum wasn't around. His mouth drops open and Dr Jenkins sees that there is something between us, some kind of history, and she looks back and forth from me to him, unsure.

'I can't go,' I say, surprised by how calm and strong my voice is. 'I won't. Not with him.'

# 14

---

THEN

It's hot for September, and I am at Annabelle's, waving her off to university. When we hug, I can feel that she is scared.

'I wish you were coming with me,' she says.

'Me too.' I say it automatically, but it's not really true.

I am aware that my relationship with my best friend has been equal parts supportive and toxic, and I don't think it's such a bad thing that we're going to be in different places, meeting different people. But there is definitely a sense of being left behind. Annabelle is moving away, moving forward, and what am I doing? I have half-decent A level grades but I am too restless to spend another three years studying before starting my real life. I want to start it now. I want, if possible, to have started it already. Since our exams finished, I have been putting in upwards of forty hours a week at the pub, and I'm going to carry on with that. I need money, because going to university isn't the only way of getting out. I want to move out of home, want to cut all ties with Mick and, if necessary, Mum, and I want to do it as soon as possible.

'Come on,' Annabelle's mum says. 'We need to get going if we want to arrive by lunchtime.'

It is an hour's drive to Nottingham, where Annabelle is going to study Geography. I was at work last night until gone midnight, and I got up earlier than I usually would to be here for this send-off.

'You'll be so great,' I say. 'They're going to love you.'

I know this is Annabelle's greatest fear; that she won't be loved. Even worse, that she won't be noticed. So while I don't have any idea whether what I'm saying is true, I know it's the kind thing to say. That it will put Annabelle's mind at rest a little.

'You'll visit soon, won't you?'

'Of course.' I will, later this same month, but I won't enjoy it, and Annabelle will spend the entire weekend with the new friends she's made, and I'll feel left out. After that, we will mostly see each other when Annabelle is home for holidays and looking to pick up shifts at the pub to earn some extra cash.

But for now, neither of us knows how that will go, and I stand in the street with one arm in the air until my friend's car is out of sight. I feel a hollowness that comes from not having had enough sleep, and not knowing what the future will be like. All I know, about my future, is that I want it to be as different as possible from the life my mum has led. A nagging voice asks why I am following my mum into bar work, if that's the case, but I push it down, like I always do. This is the work I know, the work I'm good at. People like me, at the pub. People want to know how I'm doing and whether I'll be around for a drink later. It is at home that the problems lurk.

I have something to do, something to say. I've been building up to it, and I promised Annabelle, and myself, that I would do it by the time Annabelle left. So I can't put it off any longer. I am moving out of home. I am leaving Mum and Mick and Granny Rose behind. Mostly I feel great about it, but I still long for those days when it was just the three of us, when the love was uncomplicated, when I wasn't afraid. The truth is, Mum has turned a blind eye to Mick's treatment of me. It's not possible that she could live in the same house and not know. So I feel let down by the person who was supposed to protect me. I know Mum loves Mick, for some reason, which muddies things. But I can't forgive it.

On the walk back home, I run over different ways to bring it up. I'm going to sit them all down, do it in one go. But when I get there, I find I can't, because Mick isn't at home. Mum says he's 'gone to see a man about a dog'.

'Okay, well, I'll just tell you two then,' I say.

I've successfully rounded up Mum and Granny Rose, and we are all in the kitchen. I have lined up three mugs and the kettle is whistling to a boil.

'I'm moving out,' I say, not looking at them. Looking, instead, at the mugs of tea I'm making.

'Where are you going?' Mum asks.

'There's a room in a house in town. I went to see it and I've put a deposit down. It's mine from next week.'

There is a moment of stillness, of silence. I know that there is nothing they can do to stop me, and I'm not sure they'd want to, anyway. I am eighteen years old, an adult. But I am changing the dynamic that has been in place for a number of years, and I am nervous about it. To my knowledge, Mick has never been violent towards Granny Rose, but what if he starts, once I am gone?

When I turn, a mug in each hand, I see that Granny Rose is sitting quite still, but there is a tear tracking its way down her cheek. It's just like all the times the two of us hid away in her bedroom, when Mick was in one of his tempers. I feel like I can't bear it, like it's too hot suddenly. I take off my jumper but it's not enough – I want to claw off my skin.

'Don't cry,' I say.

I know it's a ridiculous thing to say, and yet it is the only thing I can think of. I sit down, watch the way the steam rises from our mugs. None of us reach out for them.

'Well,' Mum says. 'It's your decision, of course. I'm happy for you. And I'm glad you're not going too far.'

I nod, wait for my grandmother to say something. Anything. And then she does, but she's not talking to me. She's looking directly at her daughter, so there's no confusion.

'If you let her go, you're choosing him over her,' she says. 'Your own daughter. You've been doing it for years, but you could stop it, right now. You could kick him out, and she would stay. Wouldn't you, Shell?'

Hearing Granny Rose's pet name for me undoes something inside me. Sometimes, on trips to the beach when I was a child, Granny Rose would say 'She sells seashells on the sea shore' and pull me to her and kiss the top of my head, and I hadn't realised it at the time, but I recognise now that I felt so protected and loved in those days, and I haven't felt that way for a long time.

Mum stands. 'She didn't say that, Mum. She didn't say that's why she's going.'

But we know, all three of us, that it is. That it doesn't need to be said. Mum can pretend all she likes, but she knows.

'I'm going upstairs,' I say, because suddenly the room is too airless and I don't know where to look. I pick up my tea, but then Mum puts a hand on my arm to stop me, and it makes me spill a bit, and Granny Rose gets up to fetch a cloth.

'Is it true?' Mum asks. 'Is it because of Mick? Because of the things he says and does to me?'

Granny Rose snorts. 'It's not only you,' she says.

'What do you mean?'

'God, open your eyes. You're not the only one trying to cover up bruises with cheap makeup and hiding away the emotional scars.'

Mum looks shocked, and I can't believe it. How? How can she not know?

'Is that true?' she asks.

I nod, the gesture swift and small.

'What about you?' Mum turns to Granny Rose.

Granny Rose snorts. 'Not me. He'd rather pick on a child.'

'I'm not a child,' I say.

'No, but you were, when he started.'

'Why didn't you tell me?' Mum asks. 'Why didn't either of you tell me?'

I don't know how to answer that, but luckily Granny Rose does.

'Because you taught her not to, love,' she says. 'You taught her, from the very first time that man laid a finger on you, that what you do in that situation is cover up and pretend it's not happening. I've thought about getting us all out, so many times, about scraping together enough money to rent somewhere. But I was scared that you wouldn't come, that you'd still choose him over her. I couldn't bear that.'

And then none of us says anything for a while, because it is so obvious and true. And I wish we'd had the courage to have this conversation years ago, when it first started. How different things might have been if we had. But we didn't. And while having it now is better than nothing, it's done some damage that can't be undone; I know that. I don't stand up for a long time, because I know that I will never again have this honesty with these two women who I've always loved. The ones I am leaving, because they failed to protect me.

## 15

---

NOW

It takes Mick a few seconds to recognise me, but when he does, I see it click. He says something to Dr Jenkins, about how we knew each other a long time ago, and god knows what she makes of that, but she lets him go and says we'll sort out the scan later. Leaves me with Angela.

I feel panicky and frightened. Angela doesn't ask me any questions, she just rubs my back in circular motions as I take deep, gulping breaths and get myself under control. It comes back to me, at that moment, that I once told my mum I might like to be a nurse, when I was nine or ten or so, and she said she didn't think I had the right qualities for it. And she was right. These men and women, who are paid pretty appallingly, are sometimes required to hold a person's hand, or just sit in companionable silence with a stranger, or to rub the back of a woman who is scared and alone, and I'm not sure I would have it in me. But I'm glad Angela does.

'Do you want a tea?' she asks when I'm calmer.

'Yes please. What about the scan?'

'Oh, the scan can wait. Don't worry about it.'

While she's gone, I think about the commotion I caused, how

uncommon that must be here in Intensive Care, where everything is so still and serious, where people are too ill to make a scene. It makes me wonder something.

'Here you go,' Angela says, putting a hot mug of tea on my tray.

'When will I go to a normal ward?' I ask.

'Oh, quite soon I expect.'

I nod. I'm getting better. I've been out of bed, sat in a chair, and while that's not a huge thing, it's a lot more than most of the inhabitants of this unit can manage. I will miss Angela, I think. She is so kind, so caring.

'Thank you,' I say.

She doesn't ask what for. It must happen a lot, this. She just nods slightly and gives me a smile that crinkles her eyes and asks if I've looked at the dinner menu yet today. And I'm exhausted suddenly, like the run-in with Mick has taken every last ounce of energy I had. I feel my eyelids starting to droop, and I fall asleep to the sound of Angela's chatter.

* * *

When Matt appears, I'm disorientated. Before, he's always come in the evening, but I haven't eaten dinner yet. It must still be mid-afternoon.

'It was quiet in the restaurant,' he says, as if he can read my thoughts. 'Thought I'd pop up for a few minutes, see my favourite patient.'

He must say that to everyone. But it's nice to hear, all the same.

'How are the customers today?'

'Oh, the usual. Mostly a delight, but the odd one, Jesus.'

'There's always one. It's the same at the pub.'

'Tell me your worst.'

I let out a small laugh, and it feels good. 'It's mostly just men who are too drunk and want to fight or think they're entitled to the attentions of women who aren't interested in them.'

'At least we don't have drunkenness to contend with here,' Matt says.

'What's your worst?'

'Today, or worst of all time?'

'Today.'

'Well, today hasn't been so bad. There was a guy who insisted I remove the pepper from his sandwich, stood there with his hands on his hips, as if that's a thing you can do.'

'What did you do?'

'I had to chuck it away and start again.'

'Right. And worst ever?'

'Well, that's a story. Are you sure you're ready for it?'

I nod and smile. I love a story. I wriggle down a bit in the bed, arrange the covers over my legs.

'Well, there was this guy, a couple of years ago, used to come in every day. Now, I always try to be mindful of the fact that our customers either work here, in which case they're in uniform, or have a relative or friend who's in hospital. People aren't always at their best when their loved ones are seriously ill, so I give them more leeway than I would normally. But this guy was a serious pain in the arse. He used to ask for a cappuccino and then, when we gave it to him, he'd say he'd asked for a latte. Ask for a jacket potato with extra cheese and then say why was there so much cheese, he'd asked for no cheese. He did it with all the staff, not just me. I couldn't work out why it was happening. It was the same every day. We'd check and recheck his order, and it was always the same. He'd say "This isn't what I asked for. I need to speak to the manager." I kept telling him I was the manager and he wouldn't have it. Said I looked like I was barely out of short trousers.'

I laugh properly at that, and it makes him smile.

'Me!' he continues. 'I'm about to turn forty.'

Forty, I think. Ten years older than me. And then I'm not sure why my brain has made that connection.

'So what happened?' I ask.

'One day, after this had been going on for weeks and weeks, he just blew up and said he was going to find somewhere else to have his lunch. I thought, good luck with that, because it's the only restaurant in the hospital. He'd either be getting a stale sandwich or he'd be back. But he never came back. It was a bit of a mystery. We'd talk about him sometimes. Funny how someone can be the bane of your life and then, when they disappear, you can sort of miss them. Anyway, months later I ran into him on the street outside Tesco. I said I hadn't seen him at the hospital for a while and I hoped that meant that whoever he'd been visiting was better. He gave me this funny look and said he hadn't been visiting anyone in hospital, he'd just liked the food.'

Two things happen. One is that we both laugh, and it feels so good, to be in on a joke together. To feel happy. And the other is that I have this odd sense of déjà vu. I didn't know how the story was going to end when he was telling it, so why do I feel like I've heard it before now it's finished? I put it down to the brain fog I've felt since waking. Remind myself that my body's been through a lot.

I notice that it's gone quiet, and Matt's shuffling around a bit like he's wondering whether it's time to go. He probably needs to get back to work. Or to sit with someone else. I can't be the only patient in the hospital who's short on visitors.

'Listen,' he says, standing up.

I look at him, notice how he smooths down his jeans and sweeps his messy hair off his face.

'I have to go, but I could come back a bit later, if you're not totally sick of me.'

'I'm not,' I say.

'I can always go, if someone else comes.'

'No one else comes. Well, my friend Dee has been once, but no one else.'

He looks a bit pained at that. And no wonder. You should have at least two or three people in your life who will come to see you in hospital after your husband tries to kill you. If you don't, it seems like maybe you've gone wrong somewhere along the way. Did Dee say when she'd come back? I'm not sure she did. But here is this man, a stranger, who always offers to come back, and does.

'Sorry,' I say, 'not your problem. I'll maybe see you later.'

'Can I bring you anything?'

I don't have to think. 'Another KitKat, if that's all right? I'll give you some money.'

He smiles and nods, waves his hand to signify that it doesn't matter about the money, and turns to go.

The man in the next bed has his mother beside him, holding his hand. She is here every day, for hours, though he's rarely awake. Angela comes to do my obs and I ask her something without realising I'm going to.

'Can you help me to call my mum? I'd like to see her.'

In raking over old memories, I'm getting further away from her. From my mum. Closer to David. Is that where everything went wrong?

## 16

### THEN

I'm taking glasses out of the dishwasher, drying them, lining them up, upside-down, behind the bar. Dee is giving the tables a wipe, putting out cardboard beer mats that we will find, shredded and damp, later on. This is my favourite time of day, just before the doors open and people start piling in. It feels like the shift could go any way, at this point. Like it could be one of those magical ones where everyone stays on the right side of the happy–sad drunk line, and no one throws a drink at their boyfriend, and no one sits in a corner alone for an hour before accepting they've been stood up. Sometimes, standing behind that bar pulling pints and pouring wine, we get to see the very best of life. People falling in love, people celebrating promotions and engagements and new jobs with their friends. Friendships forming, people transitioning from colleagues to friends, from friends to lovers. And sometimes we see the worst, but I don't like to dwell on that. I'm a romantic, always hoping for the best. I don't know, can't know, that today is the day I'll meet the man who'll become my husband.

'Time to open the doors?' Dee asks, and our boss, Rob, gives her the nod.

Dee is small, and she has to go up on tiptoes to undo the bolt, but for some reason it's almost always her who does it. She flips over the sign from Closed to Open. And then she comes and stands near to me, behind the bar, and we chat about this and that. Dee had a date the night before, and when I ask her whether she's planning to see him again, she screws up her face and says she doesn't think so. Men come and go in our lives, and while both of us would claim to have been in love, neither has felt the full force of a broken heart.

Derek's the first one through the doors, and I am halfway through pouring his first drink by the time he's settled himself on a barstool and thought to ask for it. Not for the first time, I ponder the fact that this place is like home, to Derek. At home, I know, he is alone. But here, there is always someone to talk to, for the price of a couple of drinks. I can't imagine being so alone in the world. Having to buy company like that. But when I've raised it with Dee in the past, she has said she doesn't think it's quite like that. She just sees Derek as a man who's retired and enjoys spending his days in our company. She doesn't read so much into it. She's easy like that, Dee.

When David comes in, I am in the thick of it, small sweat patches under my arms and a glass in each hand, and I've momentarily forgotten what drinks I'm supposed to be getting. I look at the woman who just gave her order, give her an apologetic shrug.

'Two vodka and slimline tonics,' the woman says, annoyed.

Of course. Now I remember. I get the drinks and take the woman's money and say 'What can I get you?' and when I look up, I see David, who looks out of place, with his suit and his smart haircut.

'A pint of lager, and whatever you're having,' he says.

His voice is crisp, clipped. Scottish accent. I notice that because it is different.

'You're not from round here.' It is a clichéd thing to say and I sort of hate myself for it immediately.

'No,' he laughs, looks me right in the eye. 'But I'm here now. Fancy showing me around?'

I am used to being propositioned. It's part of the job. I barely notice it now. But for some reason, David's question makes me flush a little. I see him noticing.

'I spend practically every night in here,' I say. 'I wouldn't make a good tour guide.'

'What about days?'

He's persistent, and I like that. It makes me feel important. Most men, they try it on as if it's a habit, and when I turn them down, they just shrug and move on.

'Days I sleep.'

'Fair enough.'

When I have a minute with Dee, I ask her to serve him next time, to see whether he's the same with her, and I feel a rush of pleasure when Dee reports back that he was all politeness but no flirtation. But then I get caught up in an argument over whose turn it is to use the pool table, and there's a flurry of activity as lots of people come in at the same time, half of them wanting cocktails that take ages to make, and when I think to look over to where he was standing, he's gone. I don't know his name, and I feel a bit deflated, like I've missed out on something.

Dee picks up on it, teases me a little. 'Pining over the mysterious Scottish stranger?' she asks when we're clearing down and cashing up.

'No,' I say, defensive, though I'm not sure why.

The next night, I keep an eye on the door, and by nine, I've decided he's not coming. If he's new in town, I reason, he's probably trying out various places, trying to decide where he wants to spend his time. So I'm surprised when I hear his voice, hear that accent, when it's not far off closing time. I hope I look okay, that my hair and makeup have lasted the night.

'What can I get you?'

'A pint of lager and whatever you're having,' he says once again, looking me dead in the eye.

Has he already been drinking? If he has, it doesn't show in his speech or his movements. I know drunks, both habitual ones and those for whom it's a more occasional state.

'Did you find someone?' I ask, handing him his drink.

'Find someone?'

'To show you around,' I say.

'Ah, no. Not after you shot me down.' He clutches his heart as if it's been pierced with an arrow.

I can't help smiling. But then Derek leans across and asks me for a packet of peanuts, and as soon as I've given it to him and he's paid, someone else is asking for a bottle of Merlot, and I don't get to speak to David again until he orders another drink.

'What's your name?' he asks.

'Shelley.' Sometimes, when men are trying it on, I give them a false name. But it gets confusing, trying to remember who you've told what. And everyone in here knows I'm Shelley. All he would have to do, if I didn't tell him myself, is ask around.

'I'm David,' he says.

All the Davids I have ever known have called themselves Dave. There's something appealing about him using his full name. It seems to fit with the idea I'm building of him. Smart and clean and confident.

'Can I get you another drink, David?'

'Yes please. And I'd like your phone number, too, if that's all right.'

I'm not quite ready to give that up. Not so soon.

'Nice try,' I say.

He shrugs, as if it doesn't matter to him one way or the other. But then, when he's drained that second drink and is leaving, he leans across the bar.

'I'll change your mind,' he says.

It makes my heart pound. I am young, and I want this. Want someone to fight for me, to persuade me. And so, though I don't give my number to him for another week or so, my mind has already changed. In some small but oh-so important way, I am already his.

# 17

NOW

Things move slowly in this place. Sometimes you ask for water and you're still thirsty an hour later, so I don't know when Angela will take Mum's number from me, but at least I've set something in motion. I want to get this done before I can change my mind.

I'm surprised when Angela brings me a notepad and pencil on her next visit to check my obs.

'Want me to write it?' she asks.

'No, I want to try.'

She puts the paper and pencil down on my tray table and pushes it so it's in the right position over the bed, then uses the remote control to move me into a sitting up position. I pick up the pencil and my hand feels clumsy, like I've got pins and needles or I'm wearing a massive glove. It takes me longer than it should but I write the number down, the digits big and uneven on the page. It's one of the only phone numbers I know off by heart – the landline at my childhood home.

Angela takes it from me and then surprises me again by pulling up a chair and sitting down by my bed. I've only ever seen her standing or walking around.

'You know, we see a lot of mothers in here. When people are very ill, it's the mothers who come, first and foremost. We thought perhaps you didn't have one.'

'Everyone has a mother.'

'You know what I mean, though.'

I do. She assumed my mother was dead, because what other reason could there possibly be for a mother to stay away, when their child is close to death?

'We're not close. We haven't always got on.'

Angela nods. 'I've got a daughter. Fifteen. First ten years of her life, she would hardly let me go to the toilet in peace. Would have come to work with me and slept in my bed if I'd let her. And now, she barely speaks. Just asks me for money and to take her places. We don't argue, so much. It's more that she treats me like I'm a stranger.'

'It wasn't like that,' I say.

'Oh gosh, I wasn't suggesting that. Just chatting.'

'Oh.' I feel wrong-footed, like I've jumped to the wrong conclusion and run. Still, she doesn't get up to go. And I find myself wanting to talk, wanting to tell her. 'I never had a dad, so it was always me and her, plus her mum. I thought that was what family was.'

'And it can be. There's no right way to be a family.'

It's true. The other families I saw, growing up, they were all a bit different and the ones that looked like the families in books – the ones with a mother and a father and two children and a dog – they weren't necessarily the ones that lasted, or were happiest.

'But then my mum met someone, and he came to live with us, and it all changed.'

She gives a slow nod. Does she know, I wonder? Does she make the connection between this story and the panic I felt earlier when Mick turned up to wheel me to my scan?

'It must have been hard to adjust, when you were used to it being the three of you.'

'It was.'

I could tell her, about the nights curled up with Granny Rose, listening to Mick throwing words and sometimes physical objects at Mum. The way Granny Rose would cry, completely silently, and I would feel like I was the loneliest person in the world. And then, later, about the times it was me on the wrong side of his anger. She would be sympathetic. I can see that in her. But it's just, that isn't how I want to be seen. I don't want to be a victim. I want to be me. And as soon as I share that story, I'm something else.

'I moved out when I was eighteen,' I say. 'And we just... lost touch.'

She doesn't challenge it, but we both know you don't just lose touch with your own mother. Those words – losing touch, drifting apart – they are for old colleagues and acquaintances and distant cousins. They don't fit here.

'Well,' Angela says. 'I'll try her. I'm sure she'll come, when she hears.'

It's my turn to nod, though I don't know whether it's true. The truth is that Mum chose Mick over me when I was a child and teenager, and I've chosen David over her as an adult. What fools we have both been.

\* \* \*

I'm just finishing dinner, a tasteless chicken curry, when Matt comes for the second visit of the day.

'KitKat?' he asks, holding one out.

I smile, and it's the first genuine smile for ages.

'I should bring you up some proper food,' he says.

'I would really like that.' It's true what everyone says about hospital food. Sometimes it's cold and often it's stodgy and always it's disappointing. 'What do you serve down there anyway?'

'Well, mostly it's sandwiches and salads, but we have a fresh soup every day...'

'What was it today?'

'Cream of celery.'

I screw up my nose.

'Not a fan of celery?'

'Not really. It's so stringy.'

'I mean, I'm not sure how familiar you are with the concept of soup, but we don't usually get accused of stringiness. Tomorrow it's butternut squash.'

'Now you're talking.'

'And we have some hot food, too. Fish and chips and lasagne are our standards, plus a daily special. Fish pie today.'

'Telling me what you had today is a bit "Here's what you could have won",' I say.

He laughs, and there's a small satisfaction in having amused him.

'Tomorrow is chicken tikka masala. Shall I bring you some?'

I think about food, about flavour, about how it was missing from the curry I just ate. About the curries David and I would order in and the brilliant pasta dishes Dee would make for us, sometimes at the end of a long shift. I think about cake, about pastry, about chocolate. I haven't realised, until now, how much the bland food has been getting me down. And Matt must see the enthusiasm in my eyes, but then I remember.

'I don't have any money,' I say. 'I mean, I do, I have money in bank accounts and all that, but I have nothing here with me. I'll ask my friend to bring me some.'

It's disconcerting, not having access to my things. Embarrassing, too. I look away from Matt's piercing gaze. He strokes his jaw, which is a bit stubbly. I imagine I know how it feels, the prickliness of it, but how could I? David is the only man whose face I've touched for years, and he is always clean-shaven.

'Leave it with me,' he says.

'Where was the last place you went on holiday?' I ask, desperate to get off the awkward subject of money.

He doesn't look surprised, and doesn't pause, either. 'Greece,' he says, like it's nothing. 'Have you been?'

'No. Tell me what it was like.'

The truth is, I haven't been anywhere, even though I've always longed to travel. As a child, I used to ask Mum and Granny Rose to get holiday brochures for me and I would spend hours cutting and gluing photos into a scrapbook. Places I wanted to go. Things I wanted to see. How have I reached the age of thirty without once flying on a plane?

'It was gorgeous. White-sand beaches, clear sea, houses built into hillsides, and the food. The food was incredible. I've never known salads like them.'

I close my eyes, try to picture it. And I feel like I can. Must be all those hours spent flicking through brochures. For a second, I can feel the hot sand on the soles of my feet, but then it's gone, and I'm back.

'I'd like to go,' I say. 'One day.'

'Where else?'

'Italy, and the south of France, and pretty much everywhere in Asia, and maybe Canada and some parts of the US.'

'Where will you start?' he asks.

I'm a bit surprised, because I expected him to ask where I've already been, but he doesn't, which means I don't have to admit that I've been nowhere further than Edinburgh.

'I don't care,' I say. 'Anywhere. There's nothing like being stuck in a hospital bed for days on end to give you itchy feet.'

'Any news on when you might expect to escape?'

I feel a slight pang, but I ignore it. 'My nurse, Angela, she thinks I'll be moving to a normal ward soon, but no one's mentioned anything about going home.'

That word, home. What will I find there? Do I even have one? And because it's too painful to think about the end of my relationship with David, I wait until Matt has gone and then I go back to the beginning of it instead.

# 18

## THEN

I am applying mascara when the doorbell goes. I answer with the wand in my hand. It's David, his face hidden behind an enormous bouquet of flowers.

'For you,' he says.

'God, why?'

'No reason. I just... wanted you to have something beautiful, that's all.'

I feel like I can't believe my luck. Those awful years with Mick, those feelings of being worthless... they were all leading me here. To this rented flat, which is small and a bit worse for wear but all mine and Dee's, and this man. How refreshing it is to be with someone who adores me and doesn't try to play games or make me suffer for it. Who picks up flowers just because and often calls into the pub with a piece of my favourite carrot cake from the deli up the road.

I have cooked for us. Dee is working, so we have the place to ourselves. Though we've been seeing each other for a few months now, this is the first time I have made him dinner, and I'm strangely nervous about it. It isn't like serving him drinks in the pub. It feels intimate, and like I'm showing him something of myself. And besides, I'm better at baking than I am at cooking. I've spent half the day poring over recipe books and have come up with this: a beef bourguignon, bubbling away on the hob, rice ready to go on. And in the fridge, individual strawberry mousses, and plenty of wine. I take the first bottle out now, and David goes to the cupboard where I keep the glasses, and it is oddly satisfying that he knows his way around my place. For a second, I imagine us living together, sharing the making of dinner. Working around one another, like a team.

'This all looks great,' David says, gesturing with his hand to take in the food cooking and the table I've set for two. 'Thank you.'

'You haven't tasted it yet,' I say.

But I know, really, that I've pulled this off. I look at him properly, then, for the first time, and see the way he is looking at me, like he almost can't believe it, and it makes me feel all soft and shiny. He's leaning back against the kitchen worktop, a glass of wine in his hand, raising it in a toast. And I go over to him, take the glass from his hand, go up on my tiptoes, and kiss him. I try to show him how I'm feeling, try to let him know that I am happy. I put a hand on the crotch of his jeans, suggestive. But after a minute or so, he pulls away, puts his hands up as if in surrender.

'Woah, Shelley, hold on a bit, can't you?'

I am taken aback. It isn't as if we haven't slept together yet. We've had sex countless times, and he's always seemed keen. So why the reluctance? I turn away from him so he can't see my hurt, flick the kettle on for the rice.

Before the kettle starts to make a sound, it is too quiet. I hear David swallow. And then, suddenly it is too loud and I feel like an idiot. I am wearing new underwear and my favourite jeans, the ones he says my arse looks amazing in. How have I got this wrong?

'Shelley,' he says, reaching for my hand. 'I just... I thought we were having dinner.'

'We are having dinner.'

'But it seemed like we were about to take things into the bedroom, and...'

I wait, because what is the end of that sentence? I have never met a man who has had a problem with skipping dinner for sex.

'That's not the kind of girl you are, that's all.'

I am confused. I turn my back on him, stir the rice. And then it hits me. Is it the first time I've been the one to initiate things? Is that what the problem is? I go back over previous times we've been in this flat, and yes, it's always been him, reaching out, determining the flow of things.

'I haven't seen you for a few days,' I say, trying to keep my voice from cracking. 'I thought you'd want to.'

'And I do, but not like this. Not some sordid, groping-in-the-kitchen thing. We'll have dinner, and then we'll go to bed, and we'll do things properly.'

Already, I am wishing I'd never made a move. I feel foolish, rejected. I watch the bubbles form in the water, watch the rice start to expand. I feel like asking him to go. But I won't.

'Let's start again,' he suggests. 'Come here.'

I go to him, and he puts his arms around me and gives me a chaste kiss on the lips, and I feel like things are ending. Like he'll walk out of here after dinner, decline my invitation to stay, and I will never see him again. I can't bear that.

'Has something changed?' I ask.

'No,' he says, cradling my head in his hands. 'Look at you, so worried. We're fine, Shelley. I'm sorry, I guess I wasn't expecting that and I handled it badly. But we can fix it. Let's have this delicious dinner you've made.'

I have no appetite. I serve the food and David tucks in but I push mine around the bowl, taking big gulps of wine between tiny mouthfuls. David opens a second bottle, and I pour myself a big glass. I can feel myself unwinding, becoming looser, caring less about what happened. I know that my voice is getting louder, my gestures bigger, and then I see David frown and know I've somehow messed things up again.

'I think you've probably had enough to drink, don't you?' he asks when I reach for the bottle to top up my glass.

The words are like a slap. Every day, I tell people they've had enough, that I don't think they should have that next shot or pint or glass. But that is when they are falling over, slurring, obviously drunk. I am just a bit pissed. Why does he care?

'No,' I say. 'I don't.'

We are at a stalemate and he is standing up now, crossing the room and heading for the kitchen, putting the bottle back in the fridge.

'David, what's going on?'

He comes back to the table, pulls out his chair.

'Nothing's going on,' he says, but there's an edge to his voice. 'I just don't want you to make a fool of yourself, that's all.'

'Why would I make a fool of myself?'

'Because you've had too much to drink and not enough to eat, and you're getting a bit... silly.'

I have no idea what is happening, but I want him to go. I wish we could go back to the moment he arrived with those beautiful flowers, but we can't. It's ruined, somehow. I stand and clear the plates, despite the fact that neither of us has finished eating. I open the fridge to take the strawberry mousses out, and then close it again. Return to the table.

'I've got a headache,' I say. 'I think we should call it a night.'

He doesn't make a move to stand up. 'Are you sulking, because of what happened in the kitchen? Or because I said you've had enough to drink?'

'David, I think you should go,' I say.

He stands, wipes his mouth on a napkin, then pushes his chair back underneath the table, as if he's determined to be as polite and courteous as possible.

'I think you're making a mistake,' he says, his voice calm. 'I think we just got off on the wrong foot and now...'

'I've got a headache,' I repeat.

We look at each other and neither of us moves. David nods, as if to show that he understands, and he walks out without kissing me goodbye or saying he hopes I feel better soon. And I scrape the uneaten food off the plates and into the bin, and eat both of the strawberry mousses with another glass of wine in front of a soap opera I'm not following.

When Dee comes back, just before midnight, I am still on the sofa, and Dee knows, like she always does.

'Has something happened? Did David not come?'

I reach for the remote control and turn off the TV. Realise I don't even know what I've been watching for the past hour or more.

'He came, but everything went wrong, and then he left again.'

'Break it down for me,' Dee says, kicking off her shoes and sitting down at the other end of the sofa, stretching out her legs.

I take Dee's feet in my hands and rub them. This is something we do for each other, after long shifts. Dee closes her eyes and waves her hands to invite me to speak. So I tell her, about the flowers, and the strange reaction to me initiating things in the kitchen, and the monitoring of my drinking. When I am done, I stop rubbing Dee's feet and wait to hear her response. But I'm in a no-win situation, because I want Dee's sympathy, for Dee to tell me that he was being an idiot, but I don't want anyone picking holes in what I thought was a good relationship.

'Men are such twats,' Dee says.

And I find that I am laughing. Dee can always make me laugh.

'It sounds to me like he was having an off day,' Dee says. 'It doesn't sound like the David I know. But where a woman would probably own up to that and apologise, or even call off the dinner in advance if she knew she wasn't in the right headspace, men just go about their business, making women miserable.'

I think this over. It's been all hearts and flowers so far. We have watched each other's favourite films and gone to each other's favourite restaurants and there has been no conflict. And while that's been lovely, I know it isn't realistic to expect it to last forever. Perhaps how we react to this setback will determine the kind of couple we are, more than the gifts he brings me.

'I hope that's all it is,' I say.

I don't have to tell Dee that I really like him, that I think I'm falling.

'Shall I make us hot chocolate?' Dee asks.

She makes the best hot chocolate. Always keeps squirty cream in the fridge and mini marshmallows in the cupboard ready.

'Yes, and tell me about work. What did I miss?'

Dee goes through to the kitchen but keeps talking, her voice raised.

'This group of middle-aged women came in and sat on that massive table in the corner, near the toilets. There must have been about fifteen of them. They all pulled the same book out of their bag. I thought, huh, book club, okay. Expected them to be quite quiet and timid, but once the wine was flowing, they were savages.'

'What was the book?'

'No idea. Looked dull. But seriously, it was getting feisty.'

She comes back into the room, puts two mugs down on the table. She's found a KitKat somewhere and she breaks it in half, gives two fingers of it to me.

'God bless the inventor of KitKats,' she says.

'I want to hear more about these book clubbers,' I prompt.

'Oh yes. Well, there was this woman called Jane who was sort of in charge, and she thanked them all for coming and asked them to go around and say their names and a bit about what they thought of the book as there were a couple of new people, and it was all very civilised. But next thing I knew, one of them was standing up and waving her arms around. Saying, "I understand what you're saying, Liz, but I don't see how you can possibly conclude that from what the author's written. I think you're missing the whole point."'

Dee is standing, fully taking the part.

'And then Liz got up too and she had the book in her hands, like she was holding it up as proof, and she said, in this crisp voice, "Carol, you're not the authority on this or any other book, you know. Just because you work at a library. We all bring our own experiences to the table and, as far as I'm concerned, it's quite obvious that he's in love with her from the outset." Well, Carol was fuming. I thought she was going to throw a drink or something. Poor Jane was trying to calm things down, and it seemed like she'd managed it for a while but then Liz told Carol she clearly knew nothing about the industrial revolution and that was it. Carol stormed out, but not before making a speech about how she'd been coming to this book club for seven years and she'd never been so insulted. After she'd gone, they all put their books away and just carried on necking the wine. Ordered a shedload of crisps, too. We had to kick them out in the end.'

I laugh. 'Whoever would have thought book club would get so heated?'

'Not me! It's making me question what my mum was getting up to all those evenings when I thought she was just sitting around having boring discussions about imaginary people. I hope they come back.'

By the time I go to bed, I am feeling much better. And then he messages me and I feel better still. He says he's sorry, that he doesn't know quite what happened, that he's miserable. Can he see me tomorrow? Can we forget about it? I think about making him wait until the morning, but I can't make myself do it. I say I am sorry too and we chat, back and forth, for about an hour. The last message I read before falling asleep reads:

You are everything to me, Shelley Woodhouse.

## 19

NOW

I'm moving out of Intensive Care and onto the Brain Injury Unit, Angela tells me when she does my first obs check of the day. My first thought is that it's a step towards getting out. And my second is that Matt won't know where to find me.

'We'll miss you up here,' Angela says. 'But it's always good news when we lose a patient to another ward.'

The way she phrases it makes me think of the alternative. I wonder what the ratio is of people who leave to go to another ward and people who go to the morgue. The thought makes me shudder.

'When will I move?' I ask.

'As soon as I've done my rounds. There's a bed ready and waiting for you.'

I feel a bit lost, then. It's not like I've bonded with the people who are sharing this unit with me. The beds are too far apart for patients to have a conversation and half of them aren't conscious, but I have a bit of new-girl anxiety about being in a new bed, surrounded by new people.

'You know that volunteer, Matt, who's been visiting me?' I ask.

Angela smiles and nods.

'Will you tell him where I've gone, if he comes again? It's just, he was going to bring me some food from the restaurant...'

'Oh, it's his food you're interested in, is it?' Angela says. 'Yes, I'll tell him. Of course I will.'

I don't know what to say, so I'm silent while she checks my temperature and writes it down on my chart. Because she's implying that I fancy him, isn't she? And what am I supposed to do with that? When she walks away, saying she'll be back soon and giving me a cheery wave, I try to examine my feelings for Matt. When he visits, I get a squirmy kind of feeling, the good kind of squirmy, but I thought it was because I'm bored and alone here and he's funny and nice. Or did I? Did I know there was actually more to it than that, and pretend I didn't? It's too confusing. Too much to hold in my damaged head.

Before the move, Hamza comes to see me. 'Do you remember me? I'm the psychiatrist.'

'Hamza,' I say, to prove that I'm with it, that I know what's going on.

'That's right. Wow.'

'What?'

'Well, no one ever remembers my name.'

'I have to remember a lot of names in my line of work. If people come in once and introduce themselves, and then they come in every week for five years, they get annoyed if you don't know their name, and they rarely tell you a second time, so I've got good at storing that kind of information. Names, favourite drinks, that sort of thing.'

'My favourite drink is...'

'Orange juice,' I cut in.

He looks astonished.

'You said you knew my pub, the Pheasant. Last time you were here. You said I might have served you an orange juice.'

'Okay, well I think we've established that some parts of your short-term memory haven't been affected,' he says, pulling up a chair and sitting down. He crosses one leg over the other and then behind the first, so his legs are curled like a corkscrew.

'My memory is fine,' I say. 'Both long and short-term.'

And it is, isn't it?

'What are you thinking about?' Hamza asks.

'Just, what happened. It doesn't matter. What did you want to talk to me about today?'

He clears his throat, looks a bit wrongfooted. Perhaps he doesn't like the patient trying to take control. Perhaps he doesn't like a woman being in control. Men don't, do they?

'What did *you* want to talk about?' he asks, throwing it back to me.

'My mum's partner,' I say. I've never called him my stepfather.

He doesn't seem fazed by this but I am. Mick's been on my mind, of course, since I saw him for the first time in years, but I didn't know I was going to bring him up.

'Tell me about him,' Hamza says. 'When did he come into your life?'

'When I was nine,' I say.

'And what was he like?'

'He was a violent bastard.'

He nods, and I see that this is the way he is. He must hear all sorts. He doesn't look shocked, like a friend would. Of course he doesn't.

'Did he hurt you?' Hamza asks.

'Yes, but not at first. He started out hurting Mum, and I would lie in my bedroom listening to it, too scared to go down and help her.'

'Do you blame yourself for that?'

I do, I know I do.

'Because his violence is only down to him. You were a child, Shelley. And even if you hadn't been, it wouldn't have been your fault that he was hurting your mum. Do you see that?'

I do. It's clear and logical, what he's saying, but it doesn't change the way I feel, the way I've always felt. Like I let her down, and then she let me down right back.

'When I was a teenager, he started hitting me too. Apparently Mum didn't know. I thought she did. I moved out as soon as I'd scraped enough money together.'

'Do you ever see them?'

I shake my head. 'Never. My grandmother died when I was in my early twenties, and I wondered whether that might bring Mum and me back together, but it didn't.'

'I understand. So do you think, on some level, you ended up in a violent marriage because that's the kind of relationship that was modelled to you when you were a child?'

I feel like he's pushed me off a cliff, like I'm freefalling. But also like I can see clearly for the first time in a long time. I remember a documentary I watched once, about domestic violence, about it being a cycle, about the pattern repeating. But how could I have known, when I met David? He wasn't violent for a long time. But could it be that he could sense that vulnerability in me?

'I saw him, yesterday,' I say, the words tumbling out and my heart racing even though I've barely moved. 'My mum's boyfriend. He works here, in the hospital, as a porter.'

'That must have been very distressing for you,' Hamza says levelly. 'I can put something in your notes, if you like, to make sure that situation doesn't arise again.'

'Please,' I say.

It undoes me, this gentle and sensible offer. It makes me start to cry. Hamza doesn't look uncomfortable, and I wonder how many women have wept in his sessions. He gets up and goes to the nurses' station, and when he comes back, he's holding a box of tissues, and he passes them to me. His mouth is a straight line, but there's compassion in his eyes. I think, again, that he must hear awful things every day. How does he get it out of his system, stop it from keeping him awake at night?

'One of the nurses, Angela, I've asked her to call my mum,' I say.

He nods again. 'Just be aware that seeing her might bring up a lot of feelings. Give yourself time to process them. And take it slowly. Rifts like this can't be healed overnight.'

It's all wise, sensible stuff. And when he says that's enough for today, I'm almost sorry to see him go. Perhaps I would have benefited from seeing someone years ago. Perhaps I would have been able to avoid ending up here in a hospital bed, my brain and body broken. But it's too late for might-have-beens. I thank him, and he goes, and I'm alone again.

* * *

An hour or so later, Angela comes with a wheelchair and helps me get into it.

'There's not much to pack up, is there?' she asks.

'No,' I say. 'Not much.'

'Right then, let's get this show on the road.'

As she wheels me past the man lying in the bed next to the one I was in, he lifts one hand in a wave, and I wave back, and it makes me laugh a bit. Being pushed around and waving at people like I'm the queen or something.

'What's it like, where I'm going?' I ask Angela, because I know I'm going to miss the sound of her voice.

'Oh, party central on the Brain Injury Unit,' she says, and we both laugh.

'Is there anyone else there like me?' I ask.

'What do you mean, like you?'

I'm not sure what I mean. Young? Abused? Alone in the world? 'I mean, have the others had accidents or been attacked?'

'People are there for all sorts of reasons. Attacks, like you say, car accidents, strokes. You name it. They'll look after you, Shelley. Try not to worry.'

I'm glad I'm sitting in front of her and she can't see my face, because I find it hard to accept kindness, sometimes, and I feel like I might cry.

We go in a lift with a couple of doctors who are talking about a football game, and then we're there, at the Brain Injury Unit, and Angela's handing me over to a nurse who introduces himself as Jamie, and together they are helping me into my new bed.

'She's a real handful,' Angela says.

'Looks like it,' Jamie says.

They move away and I expect they're talking about me, about how I ended up here. Then Angela comes to say goodbye.

'Did you try my mum?' I ask, remembering.

'I did. I forgot to say. No luck, I'm afraid. I called a few times and it just rang out.'

'Oh.' I feel deflated. I shift around, trying to get comfortable. And for the first time in a long time, perhaps because I've been talking about it, I remember the time after Granny Rose died.

## 20

---

### THEN

David holds my hand, and I feel quite sure that if he let go, I would come completely unravelled, like a poorly knitted scarf. It is a blustery March day and we are standing outside a church, and I want it to be time to go in, and also don't. Granny Rose. When I was a child, I thought that Granny Rose would live forever, because there was just so much of her. Not in terms of physical size, more her love and her personality and her support.

The cancer took hold of her quickly. By the time it was discovered, it was already everywhere. Already too late for surgery and fighting. I met her for a coffee in town, for the first time in ages, and when Granny Rose told me the news, I just refused it. Chased the crumbs of my chocolate cake around my plate like nothing had happened. Because it couldn't be true. Because if it was true, and I was going to lose this woman who'd been such a mainstay in my life, who'd been everything to me, and with whom I'd foolishly missed out on the last few years, I would never get over it.

I started going back to the house, though I had to take deep breaths as I approached it, and I was still too angry with Mick and Mum to do more than exchange quick hellos. I spent hours by

Granny Rose's bedside, trying to catch up on everything we'd missed. Trying to fill her in on the life I had built for myself. David, and the flat with Dee, and the pub. It didn't sound like much, when you listed it out like that, but it felt like enough. Granny Rose listened and held my hand. She didn't say much. She didn't ask why I had cut ties with her when she hadn't done anything wrong, but I apologised for it anyway. Over and over. And then, one morning, I went round and Mum was weeping in the kitchen, Mick's arm wrapped tightly around her. And Granny Rose was gone.

'Thanks for coming with me,' I say.

And David screws up his face. 'Shelley, I'm your partner. I would never leave you to do something like this on your own.'

Sometimes, he says all the right things. We've been together a little over a year now, and I am trying to focus on things like this, and not on the side of him that makes me worry. The side that is controlling and wild.

We go into the draughty church, at last. I see Mum and Mick in the front row and go to join them. I hadn't been sure whether I would, but Mum looks broken, and the decision is made. As we slide into the pew, Mum turns to me and reaches out, grips my arm.

'Oh love,' she says.

And there are a few seconds when it is only the two of us, and these men we've chosen don't matter, and we have lost the third point of our triangle. I know that if I start to cry, I won't be able to stop. So I hold it in, but it takes everything I have.

David holds my hand through it all. The hymns and the prayers and the readings. And afterwards, when everyone trails out and clusters in small groups outside to talk, he doesn't let go. A woman approaches us. She's a similar age to Granny Rose.

'Shelley,' she says, holding out her hand. 'I'm Elizabeth. I was a friend of your grandmother. She was a wonderful woman.'

'She was,' I say. We've met before, and I don't know whether she doesn't remember or assumes I won't. Elizabeth and Granny Rose used to go out for drinks and gossip.

'What she did for you and your mum, well. I don't mind telling you that I advised her against it, moving in like that when your dad left. I knew it would be a full-time job taking care of the pair of you, and I thought she deserved to live a bit, you know? But she wouldn't hear it. Stubborn as a mule, as I'm sure you know. Anyway, I just wanted to say that. She loved you very much.'

I don't speak. Cannot. David steps in and says something polite to Elizabeth, and she moves away. But I am caught on those words, about Granny Rose's sacrifices for me and Mum. I never thought. You don't, as a child, but even as an adult I didn't put the pieces together and realise that Granny Rose had effectively saved us. And what had I done to repay her? I had walked away.

'I want to go home,' I say.

David looks surprised. 'What about the wake?'

'I can't face it. I want to go.'

David pulls the car keys from his pocket and we start to walk away, but then someone calls my name, and it's Mum. I turn.

'Are you leaving?' Mum asks. 'We're going to the pub, you know, the Oak, for some sandwiches and drinks. Will you come?'

Mick is standing behind her, his hands on her shoulders, and I want to scream at him to let her go. Why can't he let her go, for one minute?

'I can't,' I say. 'I have to go to work.'

It is a lie, and when I look at Mum, I see that we both know this. We stand there for another half a minute or so, and it's like we're drinking each other in. I am the one who breaks the spell, who walks away.

I've taken the whole day off, and David has too, so we go back to my flat and I open a bottle of red wine.

'Bit early, isn't it?' David asks.

I look at him, and there's a challenge there. 'I just said goodbye to my grandmother.'

And David holds both hands up in acquiescence. An hour later, our teeth are stained and we are listening to Queen, Granny Rose's favourite band, at an unholy volume. I feel untethered. The fact that I'd barely seen Granny Rose these past few years notwithstanding, knowing she was there, in the world, was like an anchor for me, and I didn't even know until it had come loose. I am telling stories about Granny Rose, and David is listening, nodding, not saying much, which is exactly what I need him to do. When I get up to get another bottle, he follows me into the kitchen and grabs me from behind. He turns me around and pushes me gently up against the fridge. Kisses me, his hands in my hair.

I am surprised at the tug of desire I feel. We haven't had sex since Granny Rose's death, and today is the last day I would have expected to want him. But I do. We go through to the bedroom, and David is sweet and complimentary, whispering in my ear how beautiful I am and how mad with lust I make him. For a while, I forget my sadness.

* * *

It's about seven o'clock when Dee gets in. David and I are on the sofa, limbs entwined. I have the beginnings of a headache, from daytime drinking, and I've been crying again, and the news is on but neither of us are really watching it.

Dee comes over to give me a hug from behind. Her hair tickles my cheek and it is comforting.

'Hard day?' Dee asks.

'I'll leave you girls to it,' David says, dropping a kiss on the top of my head and going through to my bedroom. He's good like that. Knowing when to stay, when to step away.

'I didn't think to miss her,' I say. 'All those years when I barely saw her, because I guess I just thought she'd always be there. And now I miss her so much.'

Dee understands about complicated relationships. She has a brother she loves to distraction but can't be in the same room with, a sister she isn't all that close to.

'How was seeing your mum?' Dee asks.

'Hard. And kind of good, too. She's the only one who loved her as much as I did. There were some good years, before Mick came on the scene.'

Dee has heard about Mick, too. About the violence and the fear and the way things were for me growing up. She has things to say about men like that.

'He was there, then?'

I nod. 'It was a nice service.'

'Good hymns? I love a good hymn.'

'"Abide With Me", at the end.'

'"How Great Thou Art",' David says, from the doorway.

I hadn't realised he was standing there.

'What?' I ask.

'It was "How Great Thou Art", not "Abide With Me".' He comes over, ruffles my hair with his hand. 'You're confused. It's been a long day.'

I don't say anything, but in my head I hum both hymns. Is he right? I'm not sure. And it doesn't matter.

'I'm hungry,' I say. I haven't eaten since breakfast, other than a packet of crisps.

Dee and David look after me. Dee makes me cheese on toast while David runs me a bath, and by nine we are all on the sofa wrapped in a blanket, watching old episodes of *Friends*. It doesn't stop the hurt, about Granny Rose, but it makes it more bearable.

# 21

---

## NOW

I wake from a dream with that strange, unsure feeling, and I close my eyes and try to piece it together. Dee was there, with me, and we were shopping, but she was pregnant. I remember touching the bump, feeling the baby kick, and it felt so real. But Dee has never been pregnant. I make a mental note to tell her about it when she comes in.

And as if I've summoned her, she turns up after lunch. It's only a couple of days since I saw her but I've forgotten about the short hair again and have to adjust to it.

'I dreamed you were pregnant,' I say.

I think she'll laugh, but she doesn't. 'Really? Who was the father?'

'No idea,' I say.

Dee and I talk about babies, sometimes. About whether we want them, and when. I've never told her outright that I know I can't bring a child into my marriage with David, but she knows. And she is single, but adamant that she will have a baby by her mid-thirties, whether that means a whirlwind romance or going it alone. I've always found it so brave, that she's so sure about that.

'What else happened?' she asks.

I didn't expect her to take such an interest. I thought she'd just laugh at the idea of it.

'We were shopping, and you were wearing these denim dungarees, and you stopped in the middle of the street and grabbed my hand and put it on your bump because the baby was kicking. That's all, I think. You know how random dreams can be.'

She looks a bit tearful, but not unhappy. Isn't it always on her mind, to a greater or lesser extent? Her singleness, her being in her thirties, her biological clock?

'Anyway, enough of that,' I say.

She blinks a few times, and I know she's trying to stop herself from crying.

'Dee, what is it?' I reach out a hand, and she comes closer so she can take it.

'Nothing. I'm so happy you're getting better, Shell. It's just all this, seeing you in here, like this...' She doesn't finish. Doesn't need to.

'I've had an upgrade, though,' I say. 'Intensive Care to Brain Injury. Next stop home.'

She nods. And I think about home, again. About the pub, and David. I can't go there.

'Dee?'

'Yes?'

'Can I stay with you, while I find my feet?'

She looks a bit confused. Have I asked too much? But all those times, she's offered to take me in.

'I'm not going back to David,' I tell her. 'So I'll need to get somewhere of my own, or get him to move out. Probably that, since I'll still be running the pub so it makes sense for me to be the one living there. I just know I need to make a clean break. If I go back, even for a couple of days, he'll try to persuade me to stay.'

Dee squeezes my hand and I look down at it. Wonder, absently, where my wedding ring is. Not that it matters. It's now a symbol of something that's broken.

'Yes,' she says. 'Of course you can stay with me. It will be like old times.'

We lived together for years, Dee and me. When I took over at the Pheasant, we moved out of the flat we'd been sharing and into the one above it, where I live now. And then she moved out, without any fuss, when David and I were ready to live together. Turns out I would have been better off sticking with her. Is it a step backwards, to move in with a friend in your thirties? But what does it matter, really, if it means you're happy and safe?

It crosses my mind to ask Dee about the police again. But then I remember how adamant she was that she couldn't talk to me about it all, and I don't.

'How did you know I was here?' I ask then.

'At the hospital?'

'No, on this ward. Did you go to Intensive Care first?'

She looks down and I know, deep in my bones, that she's going to lie. And I don't know why.

'Yes, I went there and they pointed me in this direction. Why?'

She can't look at me as she says it. Why would she lie about that? And how else could she possibly have found out?

'It's just, there's this volunteer. He's been visiting me, and he said he'd bring me some food from the restaurant, and I was sort of hoping he'd be able to find me.'

Dee's hands fly to her mouth. 'God, I'm so stupid! I can bring you things, Shelley. Anything you want. While you were in Intensive Care, I thought you probably weren't up to reading or doing crosswords or anything like that, and you're not allowed to take flowers in. All I brought was pyjamas and a wash bag. But now you're here, just make me a list and I'll bring you things.'

If things were completely normal between us, she would definitely have asked this volunteer's name. Probably would have teased me about him. She's being overly careful with me, and it's fair enough. She could have lost me, and that kind of thing makes you think. But I'm sure, once I'm out of here, we'll get back to where we were. Talking in shorthand, leaving each other little notes written on Post-its and stuck to the kitchen worktop. I've missed living with her, I realise.

'Can you bring me my purse, next time? And a KitKat?' I ask.

She laughs, a proper laugh that bursts out of her like she's not expecting it. 'I can bring you as many KitKats as you can eat, Shell. And yes, purse. Of course.'

Then I look up and Matt is walking over. He makes some kind of gesture and I think he's saying he'll come back when I'm free, but I wave him over. I want to introduce him to Dee.

'This is Matt, who I was talking about,' I say. 'And this is Dee.'

Dee looks at him, and he looks at her, and they both smile politely.

'Hi, Matt,' she says, shaking his hand.

'Hi, Dee.'

'Dee's my best friend,' I say.

It's quiet, verging on awkward, and Matt clears his throat and then hands me the carrier bag he's holding.

'I brought you these,' he says.

Dee helps me unpack the bag. There's a polystyrene container with a generous portion of chicken tikka masala and rice, which smells so good when I open it that I actually start salivating. Another container with a wedge of cake. And there's a book and a couple of magazines, and a lip balm and some moisturiser. I don't know what to say.

'You didn't have to do this,' I say eventually.

'I just... You said you didn't have any things, so I thought about what you might need. Shall I get you a fork?'

I nod and he disappears. I look at Dee, wondering what she'll think of all this.

'Can you believe this?' I ask, gesturing to the bits and pieces that are all over my tray table.

'It's lovely,' she says. 'Really kind.'

But there's a tightness to her smile, and I realise she probably feels bad about turning up empty-handed when this near stranger has brought me so many things, so I change the subject. We chat about the pub, and she tells me about a night out she had, and a film she saw, and then she gets up and says she's sorry but she has to go. I don't ask her why. When she leans in to kiss my cheek, she smells faintly floral.

'New perfume?' I ask.

'Oh, yes. Birthday present.'

I put a hand to my mouth. 'I missed your birthday.' It was the day after I fell. At home, under my bed, there's a bag I chose for her, wrapped up and tied with ribbon.

'It doesn't matter,' she says, and there are tears in her eyes. 'Please, Shell, just concentrate on getting better, okay?'

She's gone by the time Matt returns with a fork in one hand and a small tray with two steaming plastic cups in the other.

'She had to go,' I say when he raises his eyebrows to ask what's happened. 'And... you don't have to do all this for me, you know.'

'Getting a fork?'

'Not just getting a fork. The tea, and the food, and the magazines and all that. It's so kind.'

I must be gesturing with my hands when I talk because he puts one of his hands on mine, and it's warm and smooth.

'It's all right,' he says. 'I wanted to do it.'

He sits down, blows on his own drink to cool it. When he looks up again, I notice that he looks tired, and I want to ask whether things are all right. But I'm not sure what the rules of this relationship are. We're not friends, are we? This is a job, for him. One he volunteers for, but still. It's not a natural situation, like meeting someone in the pub and getting talking.

'So,' he says. 'Brain Injury Unit. You'll be swanning into the restaurant soon, buying your own curry.'

I picture it for a second. Being up and out of bed, able to go where I like. And the idea of me choosing to go to the hospital restaurant makes me laugh.

'I feel better,' I say.

'You look better.'

I realise I haven't looked in a mirror in all this time. Jamie said earlier that they're going to take my catheter out, so I'll need to start getting up to go to the toilet. What will I see, when I look at my reflection? I'm a bit scared to find out.

'If we're being honest,' I say, 'you look sort of tired.'

He runs a hand over his face, shakes his head a little. 'I'm shattered.'

'Not sleeping?'

'Not really. Things are sort of strange for me, at the moment. At home.'

I don't say anything for a moment, because we've never really gone into any detail about his life outside the hospital. I don't know whether he's married, or has children. I've looked for a ring, and there isn't one, but that doesn't mean anything.

'Do you want to talk about it?' I ask at last.

'I'm not sure. It's really complicated.'

'Does it involve a woman?'

'It does.'

'Aha. I knew it.'

My tone is carefully light but there's disappointment in my face and I just hope he doesn't see it. It's silly, these feelings I've developed for him. It's like a schoolgirl crush. I think about school, about Annabelle, who I haven't seen for years, about the boys who I felt so strongly for. I wonder where they ended up, all of them.

'I'll tell you all about it sometime,' he says. 'But not today.'

And I long for and simultaneously dread that day arriving. I try to think of something to say, but he beats me to it.

'How's your food?'

'So good. I've remembered I have tastebuds.'

He laughs. 'Well, I'm glad. I'll be sure to tell Jonny.'

'The chef?'

'Yes. He's a wizard in the kitchen but he doesn't come in for much praise, because people who dine at our establishment tend to be pretty distracted.'

'Tell him the woman in the Brain Injury Unit salutes him.'

'I will,' he says, gentle and kind.

And the way he looks at me, I could almost think that he feels something for me, too, and I have to look away because I can't let myself hope. He's made it clear that he has someone, or at least that there's someone on the scene. All I can do is enjoy his visits and be grateful for the spare time he's giving up for me.

'Hey, guess what?' I ask, suddenly remembering I have some news for once.

'What?'

'I had a scan today and my brain has stopped bleeding.'

'Well, that's great news.'

'Yeah. I don't think they'll keep me much longer.'

'How do you feel about going home?'

It's a simple question, but I know he's asking about so much more. The state of my marriage. Where I'll call home.

'I don't know,' I say. 'I'm trying to stay positive.'

He nods, then gives me the saddest smile and looks away. And then he drains his plastic cup and gets ready to leave. And though I don't want to, I go back to the start of my marriage in my mind.

## 22

---

### THEN

It is three days after our wedding when it happens. I still feel high from it – all the dancing and the beautiful, three-tiered cake and everyone I know telling me that I look beautiful. We're not having a honeymoon, because the wedding cost us pretty much every penny we had. We're saving up, planning to go away somewhere in a few months, or a year. I still haven't been anywhere, really. Just the Isle of Wight, and rainy Wales. I long to go to France or Argentina or Japan – anywhere. But David says we have to be sensible. We closed the pub for a couple of days after the wedding, and we've been lazing around, eating sandwiches and opening cards and telling each other about the day, because there was so much packed into those hours, and I don't want to lose any of it.

But today we're opening the doors again. David isn't back at work until tomorrow, so he's offered to help. I have mixed feelings about this. Occasionally, David collects glasses or wipes down tables and very occasionally, like the time Dee had to go home with food poisoning and my new barman didn't turn up, he's served a few drinks. But he's not at home behind the bar the way I am. I prefer it when he's on the other side, chatting to the regulars and making me laugh whenever I have a minute between customers. But when he offered to help today, I didn't want to seem ungrateful. And I am a man down – my latest recruit, Jon, has asked for a night off.

So here we are, at noon, Dee breezing in and unlocking the doors and David and me standing behind the bar. Dee tells him he looks like he's concentrating, like he's getting ready to catch a ball, and David says it is a bit like that, for him. That he's not a natural like the two of us. Can't make a cocktail with one hand and give someone their change with the other, while taking an order from a third person.

'Why don't you just do a couple of hours?' I ask, flicking him gently with the tea towel I've been using to dry glasses. 'Dee and I will be fine.'

'Let's see how busy it is,' he says.

And he puts a hand on top of my head, pulls me in and kisses me on the cheek. I smooth my hair down, pretend I'm a bit annoyed that he's messed it up, but I feel warm inside. Dee asked me, before the wedding, whether I thought it would change anything, and I said I wasn't sure. We were already living together, already committed. But I do feel different, in a way I can't quite define. I think perhaps his jealousy will be curbed, now I've promised myself to him forever.

The next few hours rush by in a haze of foaming pints and glasses hot from the dishwasher and condensation on the side of wine bottles. Laughter and questions about the wedding from regulars and snippets of gossip, and when I look at the clock, it's coming up for six, and I'm hungry. When the evening staff arrive, I send Dee on a break, tell her to take her time because she hasn't stopped since she arrived. And once she gets back, me and David go upstairs for something to eat. I'm so focussed on the pasta I'm going to make, can almost feel the warmth of it in my mouth and the contrast of the sharp tomato sauce, the salty cheese, that I don't notice the atmosphere until we're standing in the kitchen, the kettle boiling.

'Thanks,' I say, easing off my shoes. 'You really didn't need to do all afternoon. When I go back, you stay up here and relax a bit.'

'So you can flirt with the customers without me seeing?' he asks.

I turn to look at him. I don't know where this has come from, but I know it's nothing good.

'I don't know what you mean,' I say. I mumble it, my head low.

'I saw you down there, winking, touching customers' arms, acting like you're anyone's for the taking.'

I go over the day, sure at first that I haven't done any of those things. But is it possible I did? I am friendly with the customers, always have been. It's not out of the question for there to be the odd touch or wink. So I don't say anything.

'You're my wife now, Shell,' he says, waving his arms around, all tightly wound fury. 'Christ, I thought it would stop.'

'David, it's my job. I'm just friendly, chatty. I'm not flirting with—'

But I don't get to finish that sentence, because he moves across the room, so swift and light on his feet that I'm astonished by it, and slaps me across the cheek. Afterwards, we stand a couple of feet apart, him breathing heavily and me trying not to fall apart.

How is it possible that just three days ago we were standing in a cold church, promising to love each other forever, and now we are here, in the kitchen, and I am holding my face where the imprint of his hand is forming? It's a line he hasn't crossed before, but now that he has, it's like I can see that perhaps it was always heading in this direction. Had I known? Had I been aware of the type of man he was and married him anyway? I am a fool.

'Shell, I...'

I don't rescue him. What can he possibly say? In the past, when he has hurt me with words, he's been reluctant to apologise, to step down. He's good at twisting the things he said, and the things I said, to make it seem as if we were equally at fault. But this is clear-cut, something he can't possibly deny. Isn't it?

'I'm going out,' he says.

And it's the last thing I expected, so by the time I'm ready to say anything, to ask him where, he's already gone. I don't make the pasta; I've lost my appetite. I stand in the kitchen, going over the small steps that led me to this place. Where was it that I went so wrong? When I feel strong enough, I go into the bathroom to look at my face. It's a bit red, but I can cover that. I can finish my shift. And I do, just like my mother before me. I use concealer and powder, the way I learned from sitting next to her in front of her dressing table. And I go back down and act as if I'm the blissful newlywed that my customers think I should be.

'Where's David gone?' Dee asks. 'He came through with a face like thunder just after you'd gone on your break.'

I haven't prepared a lie, so I fumble for one. End up saying that we needed some things from Tesco, and I can see that Dee doesn't believe it. Dee knows how David can be. A week before the wedding, she took hold of both of my hands and asked me if I was absolutely sure I was doing the right thing. But she doesn't know about this, about the slap. If she knew about this, she would be upstairs with me right now, instructing me to pack a bag. And to hell with the fact that we've only just got married, to hell with what people will think. To Dee, it's black and white.

He comes back as I'm closing up. He's been drinking. It strikes me as funny, in a way, that I run a pub and we live above it and he's gone elsewhere to drink. I tell Dee to go home, and she looks at me and then at David, trying to work out what is going on between us, and because she doesn't know, she agrees to go.

'Tomorrow,' she says, one hand up in a wave as she opens the door we've just closed on the last customers.

'Tomorrow,' I say.

And then she's gone, and it's just the two of us, and I am determined I won't speak first. I carry on with what I was doing, wiping and sweeping and clearing, and I turn at the sound of him crying.

'I'm sorry,' he says, reaching forward and taking the cloth from my hands before holding them in his. 'I'm so sorry, Shelley. I don't know what happened. I promise you, I'll never let it happen again.'

Tears prick at my eyes. 'I didn't know whether you were coming back.'

He holds me at arm's length, shock on his face. 'Shelley, I adore you. And we're married. I don't take that lightly. Of course I was coming back.'

For the first time since I took over the pub, I go upstairs without finishing the clearing up. I'm weary. He follows me, and we get ready for bed without saying much. I think about my mum, and Mick, about me and Granny Rose cuddled up in a single bed with a faded pink cover, listening. I have ended up in the exact place I didn't want to be, and I don't know how. Once we're in bed, David reaches for my hand and then kisses me. Not a leading kiss, but a heartfelt one.

'I'm so sorry,' he whispers in the dark. 'Please forgive me. I will never, ever do anything like that again.'

And when I wake up the next morning, there are flowers in a vase on the kitchen side, and he is making pancakes.

## 23

NOW

I'm not expecting to see Matt again so soon. He comes to the side of my bed, asks if I fancy some company.

'Isn't it Saturday?' I ask.

'It is.' He nods, slowly.

'When do you ever take a break?'

He doesn't answer that. I notice that he's holding something in his hands, some booklets or brochures.

'What's that?'

He looks down, as if he's completely forgotten he's holding them. 'Oh, I thought, well, you mentioned that you're interested in travelling, and obviously you can't really do that at the moment, but I thought we could take a look and maybe plan a trip for you to take when you're back on your feet.'

It's a stack of holiday brochures, from a travel agent, like the ones I used to cut up and stick into scrapbooks as a child. And the idea of him doing this, actually going into a shop and asking for these, for me, is a little overwhelming.

'We've got a bit of everything here,' he says. 'Beach holidays in

Spain and Greece, European city breaks, safaris in South Africa. Where would you like to start?'

It's then that he looks at me and sees that my eyes are full of tears, threatening to spill.

'Oh shit,' he says. 'Have I done the wrong thing? Does this just remind you of everything you can't have at the moment?'

'No, no, it's not that, it's just...'

It's just so thoughtful. Why didn't I choose a man who brings me holiday brochures to plan a future trip when I'm recovering in hospital, instead of one who puts me there in the first place? That's really the question, when I get to it.

'Do you want me to go? Or start again, without the brochures? It was just supposed to be a bit of fun, but I can make them disappear. Or I can get tea? I know how you like it now.'

I find that I'm laughing, and I brush away the tears. 'It's fine. I just wasn't expecting this, that's all. You've already done so much, and you can't possibly do this for all the people you visit here.'

'Well, I'll let you in to a little secret,' he says. He lowers his voice, leans in. 'You're my favourite.'

'Oh yes, and who is my competition?'

'There's Fred on Ward Seven,' he says, 'who likes talking about the different breeds of dog he's owned over the years, and Marjorie on Ward Fourteen, who seems to think I'm her grandson and is always trying to give me Fruit Pastilles.'

'And I'm your favourite, even though I don't have Fruit Pastilles?'

'You are,' he says solemnly.

It feels like flirting, and I'm like a bottle of pop that's been shaken up. I feel like a teenager, all giddy and light. And that's what makes me think of Annabelle.

'Do you think it's normal to lose touch with your best friend?' I ask.

He shakes his head slightly, as if adjusting to the topic swerve.

'Dee?' he asks, looking confused.

'No, not Dee. Dee's my grown-up best friend. But my childhood and teenage best friend, Annabelle, we don't talk now. There was no argument or anything, just a gradual decline.'

Matt considers this. 'To be honest, I think it's more strange when childhood friendships last into adulthood. Most of them are based on things like whether you preferred Spiderman or Superman or what your favourite colour was. If you get to be adults and you still like each other and have things in common, that seems like a bonus to me. But I don't think you can expect it.'

He's right, I think. Annabelle and I made friends because we had the same lunchbox. Care Bears. And that was it; we were by each other's sides for the next decade. More.

'Are you still friends with anyone from your childhood?' I ask.

'Just my brother and sister.'

I laugh again. 'What are they like?'

'She's great. She's a social worker, really cares about people. He's a bit of a dick, if I'm honest. Really tall, handsome. That guy who women think is sweet and sincere, because he is. Clever, too. It was pretty hard to follow him through school, I have to say. Teachers would say 'Oh, you're Michael's brother, are you?' like they couldn't quite believe it was true. He went to Oxford and he's a management accountant for some big City firm and he has an incredible wife and twin baby daughters.'

'Wow,' I say. 'That's... a lot.'

And then something occurs to me, and I'm not sure I want to know the answer, but I can't stop myself from asking.

'Do you have any?'

'Any?'

'Kids?'

'Oh, kids. No.'

He looks at me for a long moment, and there's a tinge of something that might be sadness and might be wistfulness, but I don't know him well enough to know the difference.

'Do you?' he asks, and his voice is a bit thick, as if he needs to swallow.

'No.'

I'm not sure how things have gone from light and playful to intense, but I know I need to cut through it somehow. To steer us back to where we were before.

'Shall we have a look at these brochures then?' I ask.

He looks relieved. 'You start looking. I'll get the tea.'

I get lost, over the next half an hour, in daydreams of white sand beaches and cloudless skies.

'Where would you go?' I ask Matt. 'If you could go anywhere at all.'

'Money no object?'

'No object.'

'I'd really like to do a road trip across North America. You know, Route 66, all that. New York at one end, California at the other, and a whole lot of nothing in between. I'd eat greasy burgers in roadside diners and paddle in the ocean and everyone would think I was cute because I have an English accent.'

I try to picture it. I close my eyes and see us in a car, together, me at the wheel and him leaning back in the passenger seat. It's a convertible, and the wind's whipping through our hair, and I have never felt more alive.

'Wow,' I say.

'What?'

'You really sold it. I closed my eyes and felt like I was there. Have you been, to the States?'

'Yes, a couple of times. But there's so much of it to see, you know? And it's so vast that it has a bit of everything. Beaches and mountains and desert and cities.'

'I hope you get to do it,' I say.

'Me too.' He takes a deep breath, says that he needs to get going, asks if he should leave the brochures here with me.

'Yes please,' I say.

I'm not sure how to tell him that they're the best thing he could have brought. So I say nothing, just goodbye.

Just after he leaves, Jamie comes over to check my temperature and blood pressure.

'He's a good one, isn't he?' he says, jerking his head in the direction that Matt just wandered off in.

'Seems to be,' I say. 'Is he... I mean, does everyone in the hospital know him?'

'What do you mean?' Jamie asks, frowning as he wraps the blood pressure cuff around my arm.

'I just wondered whether he's volunteered here for a long time.'

Jamie stops what he's doing and frowns at me. 'I've never seen him before in my life. I thought he was a friend of yours. Or more than a friend, if I'm honest. I thought he might be your partner.'

I feel the redness creep up my neck and onto my cheeks. I laugh, but it sounds fake. Hollow.

'He visits people,' I say. 'People who don't have many visitors.'

'Oh,' Jamie says. 'Well I never. And is he whisking you away on some big trip?'

'What?'

He nods towards the brochures, then inputs some numbers on his iPad.

'Oh, no, he just... He brought these for me to have a look through. So I could plan a trip for, you know, when I'm better.'

Jamie catches my eye and doesn't look away. After a full minute has passed, I break the stare-off by looking down at the small pile of brochures.

'Seems above and beyond the role, if you ask me,' Jamie says, and then he wheels his equipment away, his shoes tapping on the vinyl floor.

That afternoon, I drift in and out of sleep. And I dream of being far from the hospital, far from the Pheasant, far from David. I am with Matt, rubbing suncream on his shoulders, taking a forkful of his dinner to try, passing him his book from the bag I'm carrying. We are looking up at the Eiffel Tower, and asking someone to take a photo of us by the Colosseum, and going into a chocolate shop in Brussels. And when I wake up, because my dinner is being brought in on a tray, I feel like I've been all over the world, when really I have been nowhere at all. Because of him. Because of David.

## 24

### THEN

David brings flowers – lilies, roses, hydrangeas. He brings chocolates. He comes home with something for me more often than not, even if it's just a scribbled love note on a piece of his estate agency's headed paper. The notes are my favourite, actually, because I can keep those, can look through them when I feel unsure. He showers me with love. More love than I know what to do with, sometimes.

The moments when he loses control are few and far between, and he hates himself afterwards. I can see it in his eyes: the shame. I tell myself that no marriage is perfect. I believe that.

I am in the pub, behind the bar. This is where I feel completely safe, and that's something I don't examine too closely. Dee is sitting on a high stool, and there are only a handful of customers, and she is telling me about the latest in a series of bad dates.

'And then,' she says, 'he asked me if I would consider joining his cosplaying group.'

'His what?' I ask.

'Cosplay,' Derek says. 'Dressing up as characters from books or TV shows, isn't it?'

I look at Dee and cross my eyes to make her laugh. We didn't know Derek was listening, but we can't really object, since we're having this conversation in public.

'That's it,' Dee says. 'They all get together and dress up like characters from *Lord of the Rings* or... what's it called?'

'*The Hobbit*?' I suggest.

'No. Well, yes, that too, but I meant the one with the little furry bastards.'

I raise my eyebrows.

'Ewoks,' Derek says, draining his pint and sliding it across the bar to indicate that he wants another. '*Star Wars*.'

I pull him another pint of lager.

'Yes!' Dee says. '*Star Wars*. Seriously, why me, Shell? Do I have a sign on my head that says "Freaks and weirdos welcome"?'

'No, but we could make you one,' I say.

Dee pulls the tea towel from where it's hanging on the dishwasher handle and throws it at me. And I catch it and throw it back, and it lands on Dee's head, and Derek slaps the bar and almost falls off his stool laughing.

'I miss the days when you and I could go out together on the hunt for men,' Dee says. 'I can't believe you got married and left me without a wing woman.'

'I miss those days too, sometimes,' I say.

And then I turn and see that David's come down the stairs and is standing by the door to the cellar, looking at me. I go back over what I just said, how he'll have heard it. And I know that tonight will be one of the bad nights. I look up at the clock. Gone ten. I will time to slow, so I can stay down here with these drunks and misfits and friends and not go upstairs with my husband to face his fury.

'Hey,' I say to him, keeping my voice as light as I can. 'Can I get you something?'

'Can't I even come downstairs now?'

Dee looks from David to me and back again.

'Of course you can come downstairs. I just... wondered whether you were looking for me, or for something?'

'It was clear from your conversation that you weren't expecting me,' he says coldly.

He moves towards me and for a split second I think he's going to do it now, in front of everyone here. But he reaches past me for a glass and holds it up to the optics, helping himself to a whisky. Neat, no ice. He drinks it, leaves the glass by the dishwasher, and disappears again. For a few seconds, no one moves or speaks. It's like they've been paused, and I can't bear it, so I go to rinse the glass and then ask a woman who's just approached the bar what I can get her, and that gets things moving again.

It isn't until we're closing that Dee brings it up. 'What was that all about earlier, with David?'

I have told Dee certain things. That David can be jealous, possessive. That we argue sometimes. Nothing about the violence. But I have often wondered whether Dee knows, whether she's guessed. David is careful never to leave a mark on my face or my arms. But there was that time we went to a spa and I thought Dee had seen the bruises on my ribs when we were changing. And Dee is sharp; it's hard to get things past her. Twice now I have tried to organise a surprise party for her at the pub and she's guessed weeks in advance.

'You know what he can be like,' I say. Even to my own ears, my voice sounds weak and a bit fragile.

'I'm not sure I do,' Dee says.

We have finished collecting glasses and wiping down the tables and we're both standing behind the bar. I pick at my nails, unable to look at my friend. I feel as though I might crumble to dust if Dee sees the truth in my eyes.

'Do you want to come with me, stay at mine?' Dee asks.

I know that would make things worse. That it would only delay the punishment that is coming.

I shake my head. 'Why would you ask me that?'

We are skirting around the subject, and I need us to get to the heart of it. Even if it means I crumble. It is time.

'Because I think maybe he hurts you,' Dee says, and her voice cracks on the word 'hurts'.

I don't look up, but I sense Dee moving closer to me, and when my friend is only inches away, I risk a glance.

'Does he hurt you, Shell?' Dee asks.

And I nod, quick and slight. Someone who wasn't paying attention might have missed it. But not Dee.

'Fuck,' Dee says. 'I knew it. I wish I'd said something earlier. I wish...'

'It's not your fault,' I say.

And without a beat or pause, Dee replies. 'And it's not yours.'

I'm not sure what to do, because for the first time, someone in the world other than me and David knows what is going on in our marriage. And I haven't crumbled. I am right here, with my friend at my side. And Dee doesn't think I'm stupid, or pathetic – doesn't seem to, at least. It's a position I've never considered, and I feel like I'm floating in the middle of an ocean with no land in sight.

'You can't stay here,' Dee says.

'Dee, it's not that simple. We're married, and he loves me...'

'No!' Dee is shouting now. 'No, Shell. That isn't love.'

And I feel as though my friend has set my whole life on fire with these words. 'You should go,' I say.

'What? No. I want you to come with me. I can't just leave you to go up there and face him.'

I walk over to the door, open it on the cool November night. 'You should go.'

Dee stands defiant for a minute or two more, and then she picks up her bag and coat and walks past me.

'Tomorrow,' she says. 'And Shell, I'm here. Whenever you're ready to leave. Okay?'

'Tomorrow,' I say. As if I haven't heard the rest of it.

Upstairs, David is waiting. I knew he would be.

'You took your time coming up,' he says.

He's on the sofa, his feet up, the TV off and no book or magazine in his hand. Has he just been waiting here for me since he came down?

'I was clearing up,' I say, my voice flat.

Sometimes, the attacks come out of nowhere, and I can't prepare for them. I prefer that. When I know it's coming, like tonight, the anticipation is just as bad as the actual beating. Sometimes, when it happens, I think of Mick. Wonder whether my mum is still living with this same thing. Whether it was inevitable, for me, once Mick had started things off in this direction, like a ball rolling down a hill, gathering pace.

'If you miss being single so much,' David says, 'why don't you leave?'

Why don't I leave? I think about the good days, which outweigh these awful ones. The way he looks at me with total adoration in his eyes when we're lying in bed side by side. The support, the companionship, the love. I still want those things.

'I don't want to,' I say.

'Well then don't' – he stands – 'fucking humiliate me like that.'

He pushes me, and I end up sprawled on the floor. I am so tired. From work, from life. I want to get into my bed and curl up. I want to be anywhere but here. He grabs me by the arms and pulls me up, and I know this is just the start of it. I go away somewhere, in my mind. To a white-sand beach, with the sea like glass and the sun warming my back. I stay there until it is over and I am slumped on the sofa, every part of me hurting, and he is gone.

# 25

---

NOW

Catheter out and I am finally free to roam. I have been back and forth to the toilets several times. Usually with Physio Fern on my arm. The first time, I didn't even need to go, just wanted to look at myself in the mirror for a minute or so. I looked older, more tired. A little broken. Today, Fern isn't working but she's suggested I try going a little further. She thinks I'm ready. And I am. I don't feel dizzy when I stand now. Dr Jenkins says my recovery so far has been nothing short of miraculous. I asked her about going home, and she said it wouldn't be too long now, and I was half excited and half filled with dread, about what it will be like, back out in the world. About whether I'll have to see David, and how that will go.

I hear the low drone of a TV and follow it to a waiting room. There are a handful of people looking sick with worry and pale-faced, like they haven't seen the sun in weeks, and there's a TV on the wall showing the weather. I stand in the doorway for a moment, pleased with myself for making it this far, and I see the weather segment end and a news section start. In the corner of the screen, there's a time and date: 10.22 a.m., 15 February – 2024.

I'm winded. What? It can't be 2024. I feel dizzy suddenly, and like I might fall, so I take a few steps and collapse into one of the chairs. The worried relatives look over and I hold up a hand to show them I'm all right. But I'm not all right. I look at the woman closest to me. She is a decade or so older than me, with a small face and big glasses.

'Excuse me,' I say, trying to sound as normal as possible. 'What year is it?'

She looks puzzled. 'It's 2024.'

I nod my thanks and stand up, desperate to get out of this room, now, where people are looking at me and my world has tilted slightly on its axis, but everyone else's has stayed the same. Because somehow, I have lost seven years of my life. I think about what Dee said, that they wanted me to work out for myself what's been happening. I thought it was all to do with David and the attack. I never imagined this.

When I get back to my bed, Jamie is there. He takes one look at me and knows something is very wrong.

'Shelley, what is it? Have you remembered something? Come here, sit down.'

Have I remembered something? So they know. They all know that I'm labouring under this illusion.

'It's 2024,' I say stupidly, as if he's the one who's confused. I remember looking in the mirror in the hospital toilet, thinking I looked older. Not even considering that I was.

'Yes,' he says. 'It is.'

I fire questions at him while he checks my obs, though he makes me stay silent while he does my blood pressure. It's hard, because my head is bursting. I'm making connections, understanding things. The incident with David happened seven years ago. Have I been in a coma for seven years? I feel cold, shivery, and I pull the covers up and around my shoulders.

'I'll get Dr Ali,' Jamie says. 'I'm sure he's around today. He's probably the best person for you to talk to.'

Dr Ali. Hamza. I rake back over my sessions with him, the things I said. And he knew. It's humiliating, isn't it? No, not quite that. Because these people who've been caring for me, they're not laughing. They're full of compassion. So perhaps it's just sad.

While I'm waiting for Hamza, I go over and over it. The argument with David, his push. It feels so fresh, so recent. But I have to get used to the fact that it isn't. So I need someone to tell me what happened next. And the only people who can do that are David, who's god knows where, or Dee.

'Shelley.' Hamza comes over to my bedside, a look of contrition on his face, my name a fact, a statement.

'I don't know what's happening,' I say. 'Have I been in a coma for seven years?'

'No.' He's clear and firm. 'No, you've been in two comas. One seven years ago, and one recently. And you seem to have lost your memories from the intervening years. We hope it's temporary.'

It's such a lot to take in. How can you lose time like that? Lose whole years? Anything could have happened to me in that time. Or, more worryingly, nothing. Am I still married to David? Still living that life of pain and punishment?

'Would you like to go somewhere a little quieter?' He looks around at my wardmates, who must have heard my conversation with Jamie. I haven't spoken properly to any of them, just the odd nod of greeting. But they've all had brain injuries too, of course. They could be in a similar boat. Still, talking in private, now that I'm free to move around, sounds like a good idea.

I nod, and Hamza waits while I get myself up, leads us down a corridor to a small, sterile room with a desk and two chairs in it. He gestures for me to sit, and I do. Hamza is settling himself, clearing his throat. What does he think of me, this serious, composed man? Am I the first person he's seen with this kind of memory loss?

'Tell me what you remember,' he says.

I rake my fingers through my hair, which feels greasy and lank. I'll ask Jamie to help me have a shower, after this. I'll wash my hair and my body and I'm bound to feel so much better.

'I don't remember anything,' I say. 'Nothing more than I remembered before. I just know that everything I think just happened actually happened seven years ago.'

He nods his head in acknowledgement.

'How can that happen?' I ask.

'Shelley, your brain has suffered a huge trauma. And it's a complex organ, there's so much about it that we still don't know or understand. It might be that it's shielding you from your recent memories because it thinks they might be harmful to you...'

'More harmful than my husband trying to kill me?'

He tilts his head slightly to the side. All his movements are small and considered. His clothes free of creases and his shoes shiny. How does he work with all these broken people, when he's so together himself?

'I don't know,' he says, uncrossing and recrossing his legs. 'It's just a theory. Look, Shelley, have you heard the terms retrograde and anterograde amnesia?'

I shake my head.

'Retrograde amnesia is when you can't remember incidents that happened before the trauma that caused it. So in this case, you can't remember the last seven years. That's quite extreme, but not unheard of. But in addition to that, when you first woke up, you were displaying signs of anterograde amnesia, which is the ability to form new memories. Me and the nurses and doctors and your friends were telling you things about your life and you just refused to accept them. Every time I met you, you had no recollection of meeting me before. You got very agitated, and you asked us all, several times, to stop telling you things. To let you come back to your memories in your own time. We agreed to give you a week and see where things stood.'

It's so much to take in, but I don't stop to digest it. I go straight in with the questions. 'How far into that week are we?'

'Four days.'

'And I haven't recovered my memories, but now I know there are huge gaps to be filled. What if I never get them back? Is that possible? Could I never know what happened in those seven years?'

I know my voice is getting panicky, and he makes a motion with both of his hands to indicate that I should calm down.

'That is a possibility,' he says.

It hits me then, hard and fast. This injury he keeps talking about, this trauma. If it wasn't caused by David pushing me down the stairs, what was it caused by? 'Could you tell me what happened to me?' I ask.

'What do you mean?'

'I mean, how did I end up here, in hospital, in a coma, again?'

'Ah.' He pauses, and scenarios flash up in front of me. David, again? Another attack, something worse? Or a stranger, this time? 'You were in a car accident.'

A car accident. I let it settle. 'Was anyone else hurt?'

'I don't know, I'm afraid. I can find out for you. But, listen... You've had a shock, Shelley, and you need to focus on adjusting to it, which is going to take some time. Try not to let anything else get to you, all right?'

I nod, unsure what to say. I don't choose what does and doesn't get to me. Does anyone?

'Now,' he says, his expression shifting to one of apology, 'I have to go, I'm afraid. I have appointments and I can't push them back any further. But I'll come and see you again, when you've had a bit more time to digest this. And in the meantime, is there anyone I can call who you'd like to discuss these past years with?'

I want Dee. He says he'll ask one of the nurses to call her. And then we're up and walking back to my ward, my bed, and I feel hollowed out and scared. For the rest of the day, I drift in and out of sleep, waking when Jamie comes round to do his checks, but never for long. I miss lunch but I'm awake for dinner, which is a fish pie I don't remember ordering. There's a skin forming on the top of the mashed potato and the inside is bland and tasteless, but I eat it anyway, because everyone keeps telling me I need to get my strength up. I guess it's all caught up with me, and today my body has had enough. When I've eaten as much as I can, I push the plate to the far side of my tray table, take a few sips of water, and go back to sleep.

The next time I wake, Matt's sitting quietly in the chair next to my bed. He flashes me a gentle smile when our eyes meet, and I hope he hasn't been sitting there long, hope I haven't been snoring or dribbling. And then I remember, about the lost years, and realise none of that really matters.

'I thought it was 2017,' I say, my voice a croak.

He stands up, pours me a glass of water from the jug on my tray, and slides it closer to me. 'I know,' he says.

I wasn't expecting that. It must be clear to read on my face, because he goes on.

'One of the nurses told me. She said they were trying to let you piece things together for yourself.'

I think of all the people who were somehow complicit in this. Nurses, doctors, Hamza, Physio Fern. But him? He isn't part of the medical team. I get it, and I understand why he'd do as they asked him to, but it still feels like a bit of a betrayal. 'I don't know anything,' I say.

'What do you mean?'

'Well, I don't know what's going on in the country, or the world. I don't know about the latest celebrity scandals, which pop star is sleeping with which actor. I don't know what I don't know, because I don't know what there is to know.'

'Got it,' he says. 'I guess that must feel quite disorientating.'

That's exactly right. I feel like I'm locked out of a secret, like everyone's in on something except me. I always hated that feeling.

'Can I help?' he asks. 'I could answer questions. Or just tell you things?'

'Is Theresa May still the prime minister?'

'No. You've missed three prime ministers, actually. Boris Johnson, Liz Truss, and now Rishi Sunak.'

'Boris Johnson? God.'

'Yeah. Also, there's been a pandemic.'

A pandemic? 'Like the Spanish flu or something?'

'Kind of. It's called Covid-19. Thousands of people died. Hundreds of thousands.'

That term, Covid-19. It doesn't feel completely alien. It feels like something I've heard before.

What am I doing? The thing I really want to know is what I did with the years between David's attack and this one. Whether I got out. But Matt won't know the answer to that, will he?

'I need to know whether I'm still married to the man who tried to kill me seven years ago. I woke up so sure that I would end things, but now I find out that I'm seven years too late, and I don't know what I did or didn't do.'

'Shelley, your ex-husband is in prison,' he says.

I am very still, very quiet. Ex-husband.

'I feel like everyone has been lying to me. Letting me think he was still out there, that he might come here at any moment. The doctors, nurses, Dee. Even you.'

He stands, and his chair makes an awful squeaking sound as it pushes back across the floor. 'I'm sorry, Shelley,' he says. 'We all thought it was for the best, because you were so upset when we tried to tell you it was 2024.'

I try to reach for that. For them telling me, for me getting upset. But there's nothing there.

'I can see I've upset you,' he goes on. 'So I'll go now. I'll come back tomorrow, and you can let me know whether you want to see me or not.'

He doesn't wait for an answer, starts walking away. I watch his back. There's something about his gait. Resignation. Why does he care? Could it be that he's developed feelings for me, the way I have for him? And if David is in prison, and my marriage is over, has been over for years, possibly, I don't need to feel guilty about those feelings, do I? I am a free woman. I say it again, inside my head. A free woman. It's like a pair of jeans I'm trying on, checking the fit. And it's good. It's sweet. So perhaps there are some things to be grateful for, among all this mess.

## 26

### THEN

I'm getting ready to open up, Dee at my side. Something's shifted a bit between us, in the months since I admitted to the violence in my marriage. I feel like she's always watching me but, at the same time, she's keeping me at arm's length. We haven't talked about it again. She's tried, but I've always walked away or changed the subject. Sometimes I worry that we'll never recapture our friendship, the way it was. But tonight, I'm not thinking about any of that. Things feel easy. She's telling me about a date she went on last night, on her night off, with one of our regular customers, Liam.

'I was looking forward to it. I mean, he's a good laugh, isn't he?'

I nod my agreement.

'But he was so boring, Shell. I don't know what happened.'

'Boring how?'

'Like, every single thing that came out of his mouth was about his job or an article he'd read about climate change or something.'

'What is his job?' I'm surprised to realise I don't know.

'He's an IT consultant. God, I almost wish I'd been at work. At least I would have got paid for it,' she says.

'Don't go down that road,' I say.

And Dee realises what she's said, covers her mouth as if her small hand can contain her huge laugh.

'What are you going to say next time he comes in?' I ask.

Because Dee is at the Pheasant five or six nights out of seven, it's there that she meets the men she goes on dates with. There just isn't really the opportunity to meet them anywhere else. And when the dates are a disaster, which they usually are, she's on pins waiting for the men to come in again, and I find myself having to pretend Dee has food poisoning or that she left for another job when she's actually hiding in the cellar or crouched down by my legs, trying not to laugh.

Dee shrugs. 'Do you think he will?'

'Dee, it's Liam! He's been coming in every few nights for as long as I can remember.'

'Oh god, why do I always do this? He talked to me about mortgages.'

I laugh, because I know I am expected to, but I am thinking that Dee doesn't know how lucky she is. How I would choose boredom over terror any day. How I would always take a chat about mortgages with safe Liam over a shove or a kick from my husband.

'So what's the next instalment in Dee's Dating Disasters?'

'Who knows?' Dee goes over to the doors, slides the bolt across. 'Let's see who comes through the door, shall we?'

Derek appears as if he's been waiting there, which he probably has, and both Dee and I laugh so hard we're bent double for a while, can't even gather ourselves to serve him while he stands there saying, 'What's all this about, then, ladies?'

By the time Liam comes in, it's gone six and we've got our hands full. A group of drunk women staggered in an hour or so earlier, and they're drinking cocktails. I don't see him at first, with all the faffing about with crushed ice and sugared rims and slices of lime, and when I do, I realise Dee has disappeared and there are five drunk girls waving glasses at me, Derek looking ready for another pint, and Liam, a bit sheepish, holding a ten-pound note in his hand.

'Is Dee in?' he asks.

I'm not sure what to say. I've lied for Dee many times, but this is Liam, who I know and like, and I don't want to say no if Dee might suddenly materialise in front of us.

'Yes, but she must be on a break or in the loo or something.'

Liam covers his face with his hands, then drags them down as if trying to pull his features into something grotesque. 'I messed up last night. I'm sure she told you.'

I don't want to be in the middle of this, so I hold up a finger and go back to the cocktails, and when the rowdy group are all satisfied for a few minutes, I pull two pints of lager – one for Derek, who gives me a nod and slides the exact change across the bar, and one for Liam. Dee is still nowhere to be seen.

'I really like her,' Liam says, leaning in close. 'And I was nervous, so I was just saying whatever came into my head, and I could tell she was desperate to leave. She had one eye on the door the whole time.'

'She said something about mortgages,' I say.

'Mortgages! What the hell was I thinking? Is it too late for me to rescue this, Shelley?'

Dee chooses that moment to come up the stairs from the cellar, and I shoot her a look which I hope conveys both my annoyance at being left to handle all the customers alone and my reluctance to be having this conversation with Liam.

'Hi Dee,' Liam says.

Dee holds a hand up in greeting, and it's the most awkward

thing I've ever seen her do. But she looks sort of bashful, too. Is there actually something here, between these two?

I go over to the other side of the bar, because for the first time with Liam and Dee, I feel like I'm in the way.

It's later, maybe approaching ten, when I go upstairs to see David. He likes me to go up to the flat on my breaks, because I barely have time to say hello when he comes in from work and we never get to eat together.

I find him in our bedroom. Not in bed, just standing as if waiting for me.

'Hi,' I say.

I know from the way he's standing, from the tautness of him, that there is something wrong. I wish I'd stayed downstairs, but the drunk girls had left and Dee and Liam were flirting across the bar for ages.

David looks at me, and there is something like hatred in his eyes. I know this look. He has found or seen or imagined something, and then he's gone over and over it until it is the only truth in his mind. I think about turning around and going straight back downstairs, but it will be worse later if I do that. At least now he knows I have to go back down, so he'll have to be careful about what he does to me.

'Are you sleeping with him?' David asks, his voice cold.

'With who?'

As soon as I've said it, I realise my mistake. By asking who, I am perhaps indicating that I am sleeping with someone, or so David will say. He's a master at twisting my words and manipulating my actions.

'I'm not sleeping with anyone,' I say, before he can pick me up on it.

'Well, the two of you looked pretty cosy when I came downstairs.'

I try to work out who he means. Rake over the shift. Derek, the drunk girls, Liam. In between, there were other customers. But I can't remember anything that would have looked even remotely like flirting.

'David, I don't know who or what you mean.'

He takes a step towards me and I shrink back, can't help it. This is what our marriage has come to. We are like magnets, but I am turned the other way, so he repels me.

'Liam.'

'Liam? Liam went on a date with Dee last night!'

'Then why were the two of you whispering together at the bar?'

I track back over the conversation, remember Liam leaning in.

'He leaned in to tell me that he really likes her,' I say. 'Dee.'

'No.'

He says this when he doesn't like my reasoning, when he doesn't agree. It's so final, the way he says it, so menacing. He takes another step.

'David, I have to finish my shift. I have to go back down there.'

I am trying to remind him, and he's usually so careful, but there is something different about today. Maybe he's had longer than usual to wind himself up, or maybe he's just reached a point of no return, but I see in his eyes that he's not going to be stopped. He keeps coming towards me, but I stop going backwards. There's no point. He is bigger, stronger, faster.

And then something rises up in me, some latent instinct to survive, and I change my mind. Twist around and start moving away from him, towards the door, towards the stairs. If I can make it back down to the bar, I will be safe. At least for the time being. And then perhaps I can take Dee up on her long-standing offer to stay at hers. It's time for action. Something has to change.

I don't make it to the stairs, though. Not before he's caught me by the neckline of my top, ripping the fabric and pulling me around to punch me square in the face. I feel my nose crack and there's a warm wetness on my face. Blood. I keep moving, something compelling me. And then I'm at the top of the stairs, and I see, in an instant, that I am at once closer to safety and the closest I've ever been to real danger. And then he pushes me.

## 27

---

NOW

I've never been so relieved to see someone as I am when Dee's head appears around my curtain the next morning. Dee will fill in the gaps for me, with me. She'll let me know where I've been these past few years, and then I won't feel like I'm flailing, like I'm lost.

'I know it's 2024,' I say. 'Tell me everything.'

She wasn't expecting that, I can see. She's thrown, and she doesn't say anything for a few minutes. Of course, I think, the hair. I should have known from the fact that her hair was completely different. But people get haircuts, don't they? I have to stop blaming myself. I didn't remember, and that's that.

'How?' she asks, and it feels like she's trying to buy time. 'Did someone tell you?'

'I found out. It doesn't matter. Why has everyone been lying to me?'

'Oh, Shell. We haven't been lying. We've just been waiting for you to remember. You were so adamant that this was what you wanted.'

I start to cry. 'It was a shock. And I was on my own, in the family waiting room. I saw the date on the news. It was terrifying, Dee. I've never been so scared for my own sanity.'

Dee comes in close and holds me in a hug, but it's awkward, because she's leaning over and I'm sitting up, so she pulls away but keeps her face close to mine. She reaches out, brushes away some tears, but they just keep coming.

'I'm sorry,' she says. 'I'm sorry, Shell.'

I remember the dream, then. Out of nowhere. Dee, with a baby.

'It wasn't a dream, was it?'

'What?'

'That you have a baby. Do you have a baby, Dee?'

She nods slowly. 'Well, he's more of a child now. Callum. He's four.' She pulls her phone out of her pocket and finds me a photo, and I see a little boy with Dee's wild hair and her deep brown eyes and someone else's jawline. I think he looks a bit familiar but I can't be sure whether I just want that to be the case.

'Who's his dad?' I ask. And before she speaks, I know the answer.

'Liam.'

I think about that night, when David pushed me. When Liam and Dee had just been on a date, and he told me he really liked her. That was the thing that had pushed David over the edge, wasn't it? The leaning in, the whispering. Even though I know, now, that all that happened seven years ago, it's hard to adjust to that fact.

'Did you marry him?' I ask.

She nods again.

'Was I...?'

'There? Of course. You were my Maid of Honour.'

'Can I see a photo?'

She scrolls through her phone again until she finds one, and then she shows it to me. She is breath-taking in a champagne-coloured fifties-style dress with a full skirt, her hair big and bouncy, her eyes shining. And next to her, there's me, my dress electric blue, both of our bouquets in my hand, my eyes on her.

'Gorgeous,' I say, and there are tears in my voice.

'Does it make it worse, looking at photos?' she asks, putting her phone away. 'Or do you think it might help? That it might jolt something loose? Can you tell I have no idea how memory works?'

Through my tears, I smile. 'I have no idea either.' I consider her question for a minute. It's hard, seeing these things I can't remember, but it's great, too.

'Keep showing me things,' I say. 'But can we take it slow? It's a lot to take in.'

'Yes, I think that's plenty for now.'

'Tell me about your son.'

She looks up at the ceiling, as if reaching for information about him.

'His name is Callum. He's tall like Liam but cheeky like me. And his favourite things are Fireman Sam, the colour yellow, sausages and dinosaurs.'

'Those feel like the things you'd tell someone you've never met before,' I say.

She pauses. 'You're right. I'm sorry, Shell. This is hard. Let me think. He can't say lamppost. Says langhost. It's my fault because I think it's cute so I don't correct him. He's just started at school and his teacher says he's not great at sitting still but his imagination is incredible. He does these drawings – big scenes with stick figures and robots and funny-looking animals – they're all bright colours and strange shapes. He spends days on them. Doing a bit, then running off to kick a ball or play with his dinosaurs, then coming back. You have one on your kitchen wall. He's just starting to understand so many things about the world, and when I really think about it, it blows my mind. He wants to understand everything, and to see everything. It takes us forever to walk to school because he'll stop to look at a ladybird or pick up a stone or ask where Santa lives in the summer. He's been asking about you, and I had to explain what a coma is. He's making you a card. And he asked me to tell you that he will come in and play Snap with you when you are better enough. That's how he phrased it. I've been waiting to tell you that.'

She comes to an abrupt stop and I go back over everything she's said. Searching for familiarity, for recognition. And it's there, I think. It's cloudy, and confused, but it's there.

There's so much I want to ask her. About David, and the attack, and what happened after it. About the existence of my marriage. About my life since, my work, about the pub. About our friendship. She mentioned my kitchen wall. Does she mean the one in the flat above the Pheasant?

'What's happening in *Coronation Street*?' I ask instead, because it's easier.

And she smiles and tells me about unfamiliar character names and far-fetched stories, and I laugh, and it feels for a few minutes like an ordinary stretch of time with my best friend. If I can block out the surroundings, and the circumstances. And I think I can, for a little while. But when I can tell that she's getting ready to go, I force myself to ask her the most important question.

'Dee, is David really in prison?'

'Yes.'

'And do I – I mean, did I – go to see him?'

I feel like I can't breathe waiting for her to answer. I need to know I haven't spent the last seven years going to prison to visit a man who put me in hospital. Who hurt me, over and over.

'Yes,' she says again.

And I feel like I might break into pieces, just scatter on the wind. But she must see the pain on my face, because she holds up both her hands.

'You went once,' she says. 'I came with you. You wanted him to see the scar you have on your wrist, from where it was gashed open on the bottom step. And you wanted to tell him that you were seeking a divorce.'

I take a deep, shaky breath. It's over. My marriage is over. I look down at my wrist, run my thumb across the scar there, which is little more than a silver line. And it helps me, looking at that, to believe in the time that's passed.

'So I'm divorced?' I have to check.

'You are. And he's doing ten years.'

'People always talk about prisoners only doing half their sentences.'

'Yeah, I think that's often the case. But not when you lose your temper and attack a prison guard.'

I put a hand up to my mouth. I can't believe it. And at the same time, I can. Of course I can. I know that temper. I lived with that temper.

'I have to go,' she says, her face twisted into an apology.

I look at the clock on the wall. It's five past six in the evening.

'Home for bedtime?' I ask.

'Yep. He hates it if I'm not there. Apparently I'm the only one who gets the voice of his cuddly rabbit right.'

'Well, that sounds like a really important job.'

She gives me a hug, and it's one of those really tight ones where you feel like the life's being squeezed out of you. I think we both need it. She's almost at the door when I say her name and she turns back. 'I'm really glad you got to be a mum,' I say.

She blows a kiss and opens the door to leave. But I call her name, because something's just occurred to me.

'Do I still have Whiskers?'

She shakes her head. 'I'm sorry, no. He died a couple of years ago. Cancer.'

I nod, work out how old he would have been. Fifteen. A good age. Still, it hurts, somewhere deep in my ribs.

'Oh, I nearly forgot,' she says, reaching for her bag. 'I brought you a brick, until you can get a new phone sorted.'

She passes it to me and I look at it. It's like the first phone I ever had, as a teenager. I wonder whether you can play Snake on it.

'It's fully charged, and I've put my number in it, and Liam's.' She shows me how to get to the contacts, and I see their names there, and it's the saddest list of contacts I've ever seen. And then she leaves.

I sit up in bed for a long time, going over memories of me and Dee. They're all jumbled up, some from the Pheasant, some from the Horse and Wagon, some from the flats we've shared. My wedding, and then, I think, hers. I can picture us dancing, me in that electric blue dress and her skirt swishing against me as she moved. I could have conjured it up, after seeing the photo, but I don't think I have. I close my eyes and imagine Liam, and he's in a suit, standing at the end of the aisle, joking about how much he's sweating.

So Dee has a husband and a child. A happy marriage, I hope. And I have nothing. But I could have less. I could still be trapped in my unhappy marriage. I could still be letting David treat me like I'm less than him, less than anyone, barely a human being. David is in prison. I have to keep repeating it to myself, letting it fully sink in. I'm in hospital, in a Brain Injury Unit, but I won't be for too much longer. I'll be back to my life, whatever that is now. And he'll be alone, full of regret. Well, good.

My dinner is macaroni cheese followed by a sponge pudding with custard. It's all bland and stodgy, and I make a note to ask Dee to bring me a salad and some fruit next time she comes in. I've just brushed my teeth when Jamie comes to do his usual checks.

'Could you tell me stuff, when you come round?' I ask him.

'What kind of stuff?'

'Just things that might jog my memory. News stories from the last seven years, celebrity gossip, that sort of thing. Trump is gone, right?'

'Yes, but he didn't go gracefully. God, it's hard, this, when you're put on the spot.'

'Matt told me there's been a pandemic. That must have been hard for you, here.'

'Horrendous,' he says, and it's the most serious I've ever seen him. 'People were flooding in, and we couldn't help them fast enough. We lost so many people.'

'And is it over?'

'It is and it isn't. There's a vaccine. Fewer people are dying. But people are still getting it. Look, I'll try to come up with something a bit cheerier for next time.'

'Can you tell me about the car accident?' I ask him.

'What about it?'

'Well, now I know that's what put me in here, I just wondered if you could fill in any details. Whether it was my fault, whether anyone else was hurt, that sort of thing. I asked Dr Ali, but he didn't know.'

'I don't think you should be worrying about that. It won't do your blood pressure any good.'

What does that mean? 'Do you know, whether anyone else was hurt?'

'The driver of the other car had some cuts and bruises but nothing serious.'

I nod, and he finishes what he's doing and walks away. That night, I dream of car journeys. Where I'm a child, sitting in the back, reading a book with the window down and my hair blowing. Where I'm a teenager, in the passenger seat, blowing gum into bubbles and changing the CD. Where I'm an adult, stuck in traffic, sweat trickling down the back of my neck. None of them end in crashes, but I feel exhausted when I wake, like I've been alert all night long. I doze until breakfast, and even then I'm back in a car. And it's funny, because when I look across to the driver, I see Matt there, grinning at me. I shake myself awake. I'm so confused.

I think about the last memories I uncovered. David pushing me, the force of his hatred. It's time to think about the last time I was in here, the first time. I close my eyes and there's a rush of images. Angela, her hands on her hips, stretching out her back. A physio – not Fern – giving me a high five. I can smell antiseptic and recycled air. And there's pain. Sharper and cleaner than the pain I've felt recently. It's time to face it.

## 28

---

### THEN

I wake, panicked. I'm in a hospital, can tell by the smells and the sights, the distant bleeping noise and the feel of rough sheets against my skin. All I can focus on is keeping my eyes open, and I'm not entirely successful at that. My eyelids droop, fall. Open again. What happened to me?

As soon as I ask myself the question, I know. David. That argument, that push. I remember tumbling down the stairs, thinking clearly that these might be my last moments, that he might have actually killed me this time. Hoping, if he has, that he is made to pay for it. There are people moving around me, but they haven't noticed that I'm coming round. If I could just call out, they would turn and come to me, but my throat is so dry and my eyes are so tired.

Awake, again. I shake my head a little, feel at last like I'm properly conscious. A nurse comes into view, carrying a jug of water and a cup, and I smile at her because that's exactly what I need.

'Hello, love,' the nurse says. 'I'm glad you're back with us.'

I read her name badge. Angela. I take the cup of water she offers and drink half of it in one go. 'Hello,' I croak. 'Do they know? Do they know my husband tried to kill me?'

The police come that same day. Two officers, a short man called Webb and a tall woman called Persson. There's a strange dynamic between them, something in the air, and I wonder whether they're a couple, or about to become one. Persson takes the lead. Do they always send a woman, when it's male violence towards a woman? I don't know. I've never reported it before.

I take them through it, question by question. Every detail I remember. It's hard, but doable. It's the last question that throws me.

'Would you be willing to say all of this in court?' Persson asks.

Her expression is neutral, but I think she's probably kind. She's probably on my side. I picture going into a courtroom in smart clothes I don't yet own, looking David in the eye while I detail the horrors of our marriage. It's the very last thing I want to do.

'Yes,' I say.

Because it's time. It's more than time.

\* \* \*

Dee comes in after lunch. She looks at me like she's going to cry.

'Fuck,' she says. 'That fucking bastard. I knew this would happen one day.'

'Are you looking after the pub?'

Dee rolls her eyes. 'Trust you to worry about the pub when you're in ICU. Yes, I'm looking after it.'

'But is David there? In the flat?'

'No. I think he's gone to his mum's. He dropped his key off.'

I nod. I'm not close to David's mum, but things have always been pleasant between us. How does she feel about this? Do you just let your child in, at any age, no questions asked, if they need somewhere to go? Or do you put your foot down, if they've done something you find abhorrent? David has probably spun her a story, though. He probably said I slipped. For a moment, I panic. What if everyone believes that? What if the police do?

'How are you doing it all?' I ask. 'My job and yours?'

'I roped my sister in. I hope you don't mind. She's been driving me mad since she got back from uni, moping around waiting for the perfect job to fall in her lap. I said she might as well earn a bit of money and help me while she waits. She's turned out to be surprisingly good at it. Derek likes her, so that's half the battle, right?'

'Thanks,' I say. 'Maybe we'll keep her on. We never did replace Mary, we just all took on her shifts between us. Will you thank her for me?'

'Mary?'

'No, your sister, you idiot.'

'There she is. There's the Shell I know and love.'

There's a levity to the pair of us, but then worry takes over. 'I'll have to go to court. I'll have to look at him, and tell everyone what he did. I'm so ashamed.'

'You're ashamed? Christ, Shell, you've got nothing to be ashamed of. He's the one who should be hanging his head.'

'But I let it happen. I didn't leave.'

'But he did it, Shell. Don't ever forget that. Not leaving is one thing, but he was the one who was a violent prick.'

I nod. I know, on a practical level, that Dee is right. But believing it is going to take some time.

When Dee gets up to leave, saying she needs to get to the pub, I wish so fervently that I could go with her. All the boring jobs, like putting in an order with the brewery or doing a stocktake or sorting out the staff's wages. I'd take any of them over this. This lying around and waiting. I tell myself to be patient, that I'll be back there before I know it, no doubt moaning about those jobs again, this longing entirely forgotten. And besides, going home will mean facing it all. The fact that I now live alone, that I have to go through a court case and a divorce while still managing to keep my pub running. I need my mum, I think. It isn't something I think very often.

So after Dee's kissed me on the cheek, leaving behind her scent of mint shampoo and cotton fabric conditioner, I find my mobile in the bag of things she brought in with her, and I call my mum before I can change my mind.

'Shell?'

'Hi, Mum.'

There's a pause that feels awkward, and I think of the times I've overheard Dee and her mum on the phone, both of them battling to get their words in. No pauses, no gaps, or at least they fill any there are with love and compassion.

'What do you want, love?'

That's our relationship in a phrase. Mum knows I must want or need something to have called, but she still adds an affectionate tag on to the question, because there's still hope.

'I'm in hospital. In Intensive Care. It's David, Mum. He pushed me down the stairs.'

'The General? I'll be there in an hour.'

I sob after I've ended the call. At the fact that Mum and I haven't spoken for several years, but she will still put everything to one side to come to me when I need her. And I do need her. If I've ever needed her, it's now.

When Mum arrives, I am moving the remains of a jacket potato around my plate. I push it away, take a big drink of water. Mum looks different, older, though I would never say that. She doesn't have any visible bruises. I have enough for both of us. She stands there, at the end of the bed, as if afraid to come any closer, and I see tears in her eyes.

'I never wanted this life for you,' she says.

'Did you want it for yourself?' I ask.

She doesn't answer that. She comes over to the chair, sits down. 'I didn't bring anything. I left in such a hurry. I should have stopped for flowers or grapes or something.'

'No, I don't need anything like that. I just needed to see you.'

'Is this how it's been? Your marriage?'

I don't want to admit it. Still feel shame about it, even now it's over. 'Not always,' I say. 'He's not all bad.'

And I hate myself for defending him. If this was an ordinary hospital visit, an ordinary mother and daughter relationship, I would maybe ask how Mick is, but I don't care how he is and so I don't. But as if she knows I'm thinking about him, Mum brings him up.

'You know Mick still works here.'

I go a bit cold. Of course. He's a porter. He wheels people to and from the operating theatre or appointment rooms or scans. I've always thought the people in hospital deserve better than him. Chances are they need a friendly face, a bit of kindness. Not Mick's gruff, unsmiling face. Will I see him, while I'm here? It's unlikely, I decide. The hospital is big.

'I don't want him to know I'm here,' I say.

'What? I can't keep something like that from him, Shell.'

'Why not?'

'Because he's my partner. We talk about our days. I can't just ignore the fact that I've been to see my daughter in Intensive Care in the very place where he works. What would he think if he found out?'

'I don't care what he'd think.'

Mum bites at her short nails, gives me a look as if to say 'I knew you'd be like this.'

'Mum,' I say, wishing we could start again. 'Thank you for

coming. I'm a bit lost, if I'm honest. I'm not going back to David, and I don't know where I'm going to live or anything.'

'I can ask Mick if he minds you using the spare room for a while. He's put some of his things in there but there's still a bed.'

The spare room, as she calls it, is my old bedroom. I'd always thought the deal was that you could go back, to your home, if you needed to. But I don't want to so there's no point arguing about it.

'No, I didn't mean that. I'll sort it. I just feel a bit… untethered.'

Mum looks a bit blank. I can't help but wonder whether she's ever got to this point, of being determined to leave. I suspect not. Is it because the violence has never escalated to this level for her? Would I have got here without ending up in hospital? I'm not sure.

'Shall I get you a sandwich?' Mum asks. 'I passed a WH Smith on the way in. That potato doesn't look too appealing.'

'Yes please,' I say. 'Maybe something with salad? Ham, or chicken?'

When Mum is gone, I bite my lip to hold in the tears. How has it come to this, where all my own mother can offer me, when I've come pretty close to dying, is a sandwich? There's no support, practical or emotional. I resolve to ask the question I've always wanted to ask the second Mum gets back. It's not as if there's anything left of our relationship to protect.

'Why do you stay, Mum?'

She looks about her wildly, as if she thinks I might be talking to someone else. 'I got you tuna and cucumber, and a packet of cheese and onion. Here. Now, what are you saying? Why do I stay where?'

'With him. Mick. Why have you let him get away with it for all these years?'

A cloud passes over her features, and I think she's going to shut down completely. So I'm surprised when she answers.

'You don't just throw away a relationship, love, because everything isn't perfect.'

'It wouldn't be because everything isn't "perfect". It would be because he hurts you. Physically hurts you. And because he hurt me, too, for years.'

Mum puts her hands in the air as if warding off an attack. 'Now listen, Shell, I didn't come here to talk about that. And from the looks of things, you're not really in a position to preach about happy marriages, are you?'

She looks at her watch, and I know she's going to make an excuse to go and it doesn't really matter what time it is.

'You can go,' I say. A pre-emptive strike.

Mum opens her mouth and closes it again. 'Shell, I drove for half an hour in traffic to get here. I cancelled my nail appointment. And now you're asking me to leave?'

'I'm not asking you to leave. I'm giving you permission to leave, because it looks like you want it. I'm sorry I called you. It was a mistake. I thought we could come together, because we're both victims of the same thing, but it seems like I got that wrong.'

'I'm not a victim of anything,' Mum says, standing up and putting her coat on. 'You know, Granny Rose would hate to see us like this.'

And then she's gone, and I am left with those final words, and I know they are true. Granny Rose would hate the fact that her daughter is still with a man who is abusive to her, and the fact that her granddaughter has married an abusive man. And most of all, Granny Rose would hate to know that I am in hospital, that I came close to losing my life to the man who was supposed to love me. But Granny Rose isn't here. And there's nothing that anyone can do about that.

## 29

NOW

Physio Fern is so pleased with my progress that she gives a little clap when she sees me walking. I've been practising over the weekend, when she wasn't working, going a bit further each time. I can comfortably get around the hospital now. Not that there's really anywhere to go, other than the various coffee shops. Then it hits me – I could go to visit Matt for once, rather than him visiting me. I store the idea away for later.

'You're doing brilliantly,' Fern says.

And despite myself, I smile. I've always been something of a teacher's pet. Always wanting to please.

'Well enough to go home?' I'm joking, but not entirely.

'From my perspective, yes. I'm sure you're capable of getting around your home, getting in and out of the bath, up and down stairs, all of that.'

I think of the flat above the Pheasant that I shared with Dee and then David. Do I still live there? I'll ask Dee. 'It sounds like there's a but,' I say.

'There is, I'm afraid. I think the medical team want to keep an eye on you for a bit longer. Because of the bleed.'

I nod. 'Fern?'

She tilts her head to the side, checks her neat bun with one hand. 'Yes?'

'Thank you for what you told me, about your husband.'

'Ex-husband,' she says.

'Of course. Ex-husband. Can I ask something? Did he go to prison?'

She shifts a little, puts her small feet together and clasps her hands. I can see she's uncomfortable, and it's possible I could put a stop to it by taking the question back, but I really want to know.

'No, he... I mean, I never reported him. I just found the strength to leave.'

This hits me hard. I don't know why I assumed that her situation was like mine, that it had all come to a head, somehow.

'So he's just out there? Potentially doing the same thing to someone else?'

She drops her head, then lifts it and looks me dead in the eye. 'I shouldn't really have got into this with you, Shelley. I just wanted to help, but this is my personal life and it's not really appropriate for you to judge...'

'I wasn't judging,' I say. 'I'm sorry, I see how it sounded like that. It's just... The reason I was asking is that I know my ex-husband will be out one day, and I don't know how to feel about that. I don't know whether he'll come looking for me, because I testified against him. Because I effectively put him in prison.'

'He put himself in prison,' Fern says, and I just nod, because she's absolutely right.

For about half a minute, we look at each other. Two women of the same generation but on entirely different tracks, with this one awful thing in common.

'I moved away, after I left him,' she says. 'I don't think he knows where I am.'

I take a moment to let this sink in. She uprooted her life, moved away from her family and friends, presumably, to live in hiding. It isn't something I want to do. I've got no family to speak of, but I've always lived around here. It's home. And there's Dee, and her family who I'm keen to get to know again. And the pub. Or is there the pub? I can't know for sure. It's something else to ask Dee about.

'I don't think I could do that.'

She raises her eyebrows a tiny bit, and I think she's saying that sometimes you have to do things you don't want to do. Things you think you can't do.

'He might come out changed,' she says.

'He might.' I don't think either of us believe he will.

'And he might just want to start afresh. He might move somewhere new, or at least avoid settling somewhere too close to you.'

I think about finding out he's been released – would someone notify me? – and starting to sleep with a kitchen knife under my pillow, just in case. I don't want to live like that.

'I suppose all I can do is wait and see,' I say.

She nods in agreement. 'I'm sorry all of this has to be a consideration for you,' she says.

'I'm sorry it is for you too.'

She reaches out and gives my hand a quick squeeze, and then she disappears towards the doors. I watch her until she's gone. How many women are there out there, like Fern and me and my mother? How many of us are living in fear, weighing up our options, starting again? It's astonishing, really. It's outrageous. I still haven't seen my mum, and I feel a sudden pang for her. It's built up in early childhood, that bond, and it doesn't always matter what's happened since. Where is she?

\* \* \*

In the afternoon, I decide I'll go to see Matt. The restaurant's on the ground floor, and I'm on the third, but I can use the lift. Still, it feels like a big deal, like a mission. I go to the toilet first, take a good look at myself in the mirror. I've got used to seeing myself without makeup on, and now that the bruises are fading, I just look like myself. Just a few years older than I'm used to, a few more lines here and there. There's still fear in my eyes, but it's lessened. It isn't the most prominent thing. I wait until Jamie's done my obs, because I don't want him to come round when I'm gone and wonder where I am. And then I slide out of bed and out of the ward and I think, for a fleeting moment, about what would happen if I just walked straight out of the hospital and back into the world like this, in my pyjamas and with my dressing gown flapping in the wind.

On the way to the lift, people pass me and I half expect someone to stop me and send me back to my bed, but of course no one does. Everyone in a hospital has somewhere to be. No one is paying me any attention. I get in the lift and press the button for the ground floor, look down to avoid eye contact with my fellow passengers. It's busy on the ground floor, and cold, with various doors sliding open and closed, the wind rushing in. There are lots of people in coats, coming in for visits or appointments, and everyone seems like they're in a rush. I pause for a moment, think about turning back, but then I see a sign for the restaurant, Fresh, and I decide I've come this far and I can go a bit further.

The noise and smells when I push open the heavy door to Fresh are overwhelming. Coffee and some kind of spice. And what sounds like a thousand people talking. I locate the counter and walk over. I can't see him, but he could be out the back, in the kitchen. An older woman in a crisp white apron and a hairnet beams at me.

'What can I get you, dear? Soup of the day is parsnip. We're not selling much of it, if I'm honest.' She laughs, puts her hands on her hips.

'Is Matt here?' I ask.

'Matt Thornton?'

I stammer, realising I don't know his last name. 'The manager?'

'No, love, he's not.'

'Oh.' I don't know what to do. Why would he not be in? 'Do you know where he is?'

'Yes, he's at the refuge where he helps out. Do you need to get hold of him? I could take a name and number...'

The refuge. 'No, thanks.' I back away. Matt helps out at a refuge. Is that a coincidence, or is that the reason he's been helping me, because he knows about my situation with David? But no, that isn't why I'm here. Not now.

'Sure I can't get you anything? Soup? Coffee?'

I think about how nice it would be to join the buzz and sit drinking a cup of tea as if I'm a normal person living a normal life for a few minutes, not a hospital patient with memory loss.

'Thanks, I'm okay,' I say.

And all the way back to the Brain Injury Unit, I keep my head down. I don't know why, but I feel foolish, like I've been tricked. If he's not working at the hospital today, I can probably safely assume he won't visit, and the disappointment I feel over that is wrenching. It's an alarm bell. I'm letting this man become more important to me than I should. He's little more than a stranger, and there's a woman in his life already.

I spend the rest of the afternoon dozing, in between Jamie's checks. The trip to the restaurant took it out of me, and it's a reminder that I need to be careful about what I do. My progress has been good but there's a long way to go before I'm back to normal. I'm thinking about this, drifting in and out of sleep, when I hear a familiar voice.

'I can come back later, if she's sleeping.' It's Matt. He sounds weary.

I force my eyes open, ready to tell him I'm awake. I don't want to miss a visit, especially on a day when I wasn't expecting to see him. But he has his back to me, talking to Jamie. Their heads are bent in close, and I can't make out the whole conversation, but I hear Matt saying something about it being hard and us all having to wait and then Jamie says something about being thankful, about how things could be worse.

'Shelley,' Matt says when he turns for another look at me.

'Hi,' I say, and I can't help it, my face breaks out in a big grin.

'Do you want me to go and come back? If you're tired?'

'No,' I say. 'I'm fine. Stay.'

He puts a polystyrene container on my tray table. 'Coffee cake. From the restaurant.'

It's a strange thing, when you know someone's lying to you and you don't have any idea what their motive might be. 'How was your day?' I ask. 'In the restaurant.'

'Oh, you know, the usual. Busy busy, an average amount of complaining. Although I did have a new one today. A woman said she didn't like coriander and could we take it out of the carrot and coriander soup.'

'The soup was parsnip,' I say.

'What?'

'Today. I went to the restaurant, to say hello, and you weren't there, and the soup wasn't carrot and coriander. It was parsnip.'

He goes white. 'Ah. Okay. The thing is...'

But I never get to hear what the thing is because I feel like someone has reached into my chest and taken hold of my heart and squeezed it. I don't know why he's lying and I don't particularly care, but I don't want to have anything to do with it.

'I think you should go,' I say.

'Shelley, I can explain.'

'I don't want you to explain. I want you to go.'

He doesn't argue, just stands up and brushes his hands down the front of his jeans. He's wearing glasses and he has a few days' worth of stubble and I want to be able to point him out to Dee, to say I like him and what does she think. I know what she'd think. She'd say he's cute but not my type. But David was my type, and look where that got me.

'Do you want a tea, before I go?'

Despite myself, I do. The machine tea is pretty terrible but it's a change from water. He disappears and comes back with a tea and a KitKat, puts them on my tray alongside the coffee cake without a word. Slips out. And the second he's gone I wish I could call him back. Because maybe there is a reasonable explanation. And anyway, he doesn't have to explain himself to me, does he? We're not in a relationship. He's a hospital volunteer, someone who's made my time here so much more pleasant. I overreacted. And I can't even apologise. He probably won't come back. I wouldn't, in his shoes. I eat the cake and the KitKat one after the other, and it's only when I pick the KitKat up that I see there's a slip of paper under it. I unfold it, my heart in my mouth.

*Shelley – I'm sorry. The last thing I want to do is upset you. Call or text me if you want me to come in again. Otherwise, I'll leave you be. Matt x*

And at the bottom, he's scrawled his number.

## 30

THEN

Leaving hospital after David's attack is an anti-climax, because I have to wait around for hours for my medication. I've got the discharge letter by ten in the morning but the medication doesn't come until gone three. Because I didn't know what time I'd be able to leave, I haven't asked Dee to pick me up. Besides, Dee's running the pub. She's got enough on. So when I step outside and take a big breath of fresh air, I have no plan, no lift home. I look around for a taxi queue.

Just as I'm about to get in a car, a woman touches my shoulder, and it takes me a moment to realise that it's Angela, one of the nurses who's been caring for me these past few days. She must be on her break, and it's strange to see her in her coat, out in the world.

'You finally got it?' Angela asks.

I hold up the paper bag in my hand to show that I did.

'Well, good luck. In the nicest possible way, I hope I never see you again, Shelley Woodhouse.'

I tip my head back and laugh. 'I hope that too.'

And then I'm in the car, leaning forward to tell the driver to take me to the Pheasant, pulling on my seatbelt.

Dee's face is a picture. She's pulling a pint when I walk in the front door, having failed to rouse anyone at the back, and she just keeps the tap running as the lager starts spilling all over her hands and the floor.

'Shell, what the hell are you doing here? Why didn't you call me? I would have come to pick you up!'

'Dee, turn the tap off,' I say.

And it's only then that Dee looks down and presumably sees the lager pooling at her feet. 'Shit!'

I cross the pub, aware that all eyes are on me. Go through the hatch and behind the bar, reach into the cupboard at the back for a mop.

'Don't you dare, Shelley!' Dee is giving the man his lager, holding out the card machine for him.

But I feel fine, and I've never been one for sitting around reading a book or watching Netflix. Plus, Dee looks like she's got her hands a bit too full. She's the only one in and there's quite a crowd, with it being a Friday afternoon. I have been working in pubs long enough to know that this is just the start of it. Some of these people are settling in for a long night.

'I'll take my bag upstairs, get changed, and then I'll come and give you a hand.'

'Er, no,' Dee says. 'I'll take your bag upstairs, you can get in some pyjamas and lie on the sofa. I'll bring you some food.'

'How are you supposed to do all that?' I say, laughing. 'I know you're very capable but you're only one person, Dee. Let me help. Besides, it's my pub.'

Dee shakes her head, knowing I will do what I want to do regardless of what she says. I go up the stairs, trying not to think about the last time I was here, the last time I was on these very stairs, the fear I felt at that moment. The fact that I thought I might die. The flat is cold and feels slightly different, like a home always does after a period of time away. I can smell David. The stuff he puts in his hair. His deodorant. That strong cheese he always insists on buying, which has probably been sitting in the fridge getting more and more ripe. But David is not here. Dee has told me that he's moved back in with his mum for a while. And she's had the locks changed, just in case. So why do I feel like my heart is about to explode as I make my way through the rooms?

As I'm getting changed into some jeans and a navy and white striped top, I realise that Dee must have been in here and tidied things up. Everywhere's pristine. And before she did that, did the police come? Suddenly, my home doesn't feel like my own, and it hits me that, for the first time in my life, I now live alone. I sit on the edge of the bed for a minute or two, take some deep breaths. And then I go downstairs to the pub, give Dee a smile that I hope will look genuine.

'Have you been looking after Whiskers?' I ask, standing next to my friend as we both pour glasses of wine.

'Yes. Let me know when you want me to bring her back. She's been pining for you.'

It'll feel better when Whiskers is there. More like it used to be.

For the next couple of hours, I let myself get lost in the work. The dull repetitiveness of it. Making the drinks, taking the money, judging who's up for a bit of small talk and who wants to be left in peace. Collecting glasses, loading and unloading the dishwasher, wiping tables. I've always loved this about the job – I can close off the thinking part of my brain and just do it. I'm jolted out of it at about half-eight by Dee, who puts a warm hand on my arm and whispers in my ear.

'Can you serve Liam?'

I look up and see Liam across the bar from me, looking hopefully in Dee's direction, then at me.

'Shelley, you're back. I didn't even know you were out of hospital, let alone working.'

'Well, here I am. Usual?'

I wonder whether Dee and Liam have gone on another disastrous date. At the end of the night, when we've closed the door on the last drinker and Dee's taken off her shoes and put on the slippers she keeps in the back room, I ask her about it.

'It's just awkward as hell,' Dee says. 'He's been in twice, while you've been in hospital, and the first time he was asking about you and the second time he asked me out again and I panicked and said I had to change a barrel.'

'I don't get it,' I say. 'He really likes you. And I think maybe you like him too.'

Dee does her most scathing eye roll. 'If he liked me, he would make some kind of grand gesture or something. Coming into the bar where I work isn't really good enough, you know?'

I laugh. Dee's always had high expectations, and the men she's met have always failed to meet them. I think about how I can help Liam out, point him in the right direction.

Dee asks if I fancy a drink, and when I nod gratefully, she makes us both a vodka and tonic while I do the last of the tidying, and we take them upstairs. We do this occasionally, and I am grateful that Dee sensed I didn't want to be alone in my flat.

'I don't think I can carry on living here,' I say once we're upstairs and I've found some crisps to tip into a bowl.

'Really? I wondered about that. Is it about him knowing where you are?'

I take a slug of my drink. 'No, not really. It's just... ruined, I suppose. I can't go up and down those stairs a hundred times a day and keep thinking about what he did, and how it could have gone. People die falling down stairs, don't they?' I shudder.

'So where will you go?'

I shake my head. 'I don't know. There's so much I don't know. I need to get a divorce, sort everything out. But this place sort of comes with the pub, and I don't want to give the pub up. I don't want him to take that from me.'

'What if I moved back in?'

Dee's been living alone for a few years and always says she'll never share with anyone other than me. I consider it, the two of us living together again, watching films under one of our duvets on winter days, taking it in turns to cook. Would that be enough, to stop me feeling scared and sad in this place?

'Maybe,' I say. 'Let me think about it for a while. I'm not going to do anything immediately.'

Dee looks away, and I see that she is hurt.

'It isn't about living with you again,' I say. 'I'd do that in a heartbeat. It's whether or not it can be here.'

Dee nods but I'm not sure she believes me. We don't say much while we finish our drinks. I'm working up to asking about David, and when Dee looks like she's getting ready to leave, I blurt it out.

'Have you seen him? David? Since that night, I mean?'

'Only when he came to drop off his key. I was behind the bar, and he came in the front door and everyone glared at him. They all knew what he'd done. He looked at me and he said, "It was an accident, Dee. It's not what you think." Of course, I knew it wasn't true. I knew he'd been getting worse and worse and I should have known that it would lead to this.'

'You couldn't have known. I didn't know. Or if I did, I shut it out. Pretended I didn't.'

'I just don't get it, Shell. Why do men claim to love us and do things like this? It doesn't make any sense.'

I have thought a lot about that. Over the past few days, in hospital, but also in the days and weeks and months and years since David first hit me. Since Mick did.

'It's about power, I think. And control. It's small men who don't like women having a voice, being strong. And it's everywhere. Hidden away behind people's front doors, but it's there.'

We are silent, and there's a kind of hum of anger in the room. I feel like, if I stuck out my tongue, I would be able to taste it.

'I should go,' Dee says after a long moment. 'Shall I bring Whiskers in with me in the morning?'

I smile. 'Yes please.'

'Tomorrow,' Dee says, walking down the hall to let herself out.

'Tomorrow.'

I go to bed in the spare room. I don't want to be in our room, with his things. And I don't sleep, anyway. Not until the early hours of the morning. There's too much fighting for space in my head, and I'm jumpy, too. I get up to check every time I hear a creak or a tap. This is what he's done to me. It isn't only about the physical injuries, which will heal. It's about this, the loss of my peace of mind. And I'm furious. I'm incandescent with rage.

# 31

NOW

Dee bustles into the ward in the early evening with a little boy holding her hand. 'This is Callum,' she says.

He laughs. 'Aunty Shelley knows who I am!'

'Well, remember we talked about how Aunty Shelley's had an accident and some of her memories have gone?'

Callum looks at me, his expression serious. 'Did they fall out of your head, the memories? What about the one from when we went to the farm and that goat tried to eat your dress?'

Dee smiles. 'That was pretty funny.'

The goat story rings a distant bell, and I close my eyes, try to let more of it come. 'Was it pink? The dress, that the goat tried to eat?'

Callum shakes his head. 'I don't remember. Have some of my memories fallen out too, Mummy?'

'No,' she says, playing with his hair affectionately. 'We all forget some things. I don't think there'd be room in anyone's brain for everything.'

Callum seems to accept this. He sits on the bottom of my bed and I give him the remote control to move it up and down, lift my head and then my legs. He thinks it's wonderful, and I take a moment to appreciate the simple joy of children. I watch Dee, too, the way she watches him, alert to his movements. Ready to catch him, I suppose. That's a big part of what motherhood is.

'Why don't you show Aunty Shelley the things you chose for her?' Dee asks, handing him a rustling white plastic bag.

Callum looks a bit shy, tucks his chin into his chest. 'You do it.'

'I will if you want, but you chose them. I thought you'd want to do the honours.'

Callum looks from her to me and then back to the bag. 'Okay.'

The first thing he pulls out is a plastic dinosaur about the size of a tennis ball. 'Stegosaurus,' he says. 'You always choose him when we play dinosaurs.'

I hold it in my hand, look at it intently. It's green, a little battered. Clearly well-loved. And there's something a bit familiar in the weight and feel of it. I do a sort of roaring noise and make as if to attack Callum with it, and he shrieks and giggles.

'That's what you always do!'

I think about muscle memory. About how the body remembers things the mind has hidden. But not for long, because Callum reaches into the bag again and pulls out a packet of Skittles. I wonder whether these are significant, or whether he just chose them because they are bright and they are sweets, and he likes them. Perhaps he's hoping we'll share. I ask if he wants one, and he nods very solemnly.

'Greens and yellows,' he says.

'What?'

'I like the greens and yellows, and you like the oranges, purples and reds.'

'Perfect,' I say.

The last thing he's brought is a colouring book and some pencils, and we pass twenty minutes or so colouring a picture of a robot together. He's the project manager, telling me which bits to do

and in which colour. He shakes his head if I go outside the lines.
Dee sits back and watches us, and I know it must have made her
happy, this relationship I've clearly built with her child. I am deter-
mined to keep it going, to not let it slip.

And then something comes to me, as I'm looking down at his
crown, at his dark hair spiralling out from this centre. I hold my
breath, trying not to let it disappear, the way dreams are sometimes
snatched away on waking. I am colouring with Callum. There are
dinosaurs scattered on the floor, and Dee comes into the room with
a tea and a ham sandwich for me, tells Callum there's one for him
on the table, and he runs off to get it.

'I remembered,' I say, and Dee flicks her eyes over to meet mine.
'What?'

'Just a flash, playing with Callum, you bringing us sandwiches.'
'Where were we?'

'Your place, I guess? There were dinosaurs on the floor.'

'There are always dinosaurs on the floor,' she says. 'That's bril-
liant, Shelley. Hopefully that will start to happen more and more.'

Callum is watching this exchange, his head swivelling back and
forth. 'Was it me? Was it me bringing the dinosaur and the
colouring that made the memory come back?'

I beam at him. 'I think it was. Will you come again?'

He nods his head, over and over. Soon after that, it's time for
them to go. I say that I'll walk them to the door, but in the time it
takes me to get up and out of bed, Callum's gone back and forth to
the door at least seven times.

'Thank you for bringing him,' I say to Dee, before they leave. 'It
means a lot, to see you both.'

She pulls me in for a hug, and I breathe in the scent of her. She
smells more like home to me than any place.

Ten minutes after she leaves, Jamie appears, wheeling his blood
pressure monitor, humming. 'Did you know the Queen died?'

I flick my eyes towards him. 'No.'

'Last year. We've got King Charles now. Big Coronation party, all that.'

I know the Queen was getting on, so I'm not sure why this news shakes me as much as it does. 'It's disorienting,' I say. 'To know I must have known that, and I've forgotten it.'

Jamie stops what he's doing and looks at me. 'I can't imagine.'

'But you must see people like me all the time, working on this unit?'

'All the time. But every case is different. Some people wake up with a different personality, or not recognising their own parents, or constantly shouting and swearing. It's devastating, but it's fascinating, too. I love working here. I love finding out more about how the brain works.'

I am silent, because I don't know what to say. And Jamie seems to sense that it's time for a change of subject.

'Is your friend coming in today?'

'Dee?'

'No, the cute, scruffy guy who comes to see you.'

I think about Matt, about how he is cute, about whether he is really my friend, and whether I'll see him again. When Jamie leaves my bedside, I reach for the phone Dee brought. I'd forgotten how clunky these things were, and it takes me ages to add him as a contact. Then I spend several minutes composing a text, and send it before I can change my mind.

Hi, it's Shelley, from the hospital. I'm sorry for the way I was earlier. Please call in next time you're here.

I turn the phone over to stop myself watching it for a reply. It might be a while before I see him, and days feel like weeks in here. I go for a walk around the corridors, trying to get my strength up, and when I get back to my bed, I can't resist turning the phone back over, and there's a message from him. I try not to pay too much attention to the way my heart lifts when I see his name.

It's fine. I shouldn't have lied. I'll come tomorrow and explain. Matt.

Tomorrow.

* * *

Next time I see Jamie, I ask if there's any good news from the past few years. He thinks, tapping his pen against his lips. 'The news is all pretty shocking, I have to say. But how about the fact that in 2017 you were married to a man who was hurting you, and now you're free of him, and he's in prison? That seems pretty good.'

I don't realise I'm crying until his expression changes. 'What did I say? I'm sorry, Shelley. It's just... Well, I haven't told you this, but I remember you from last time.'

My head jolts up. 'Last time?'

'From 2017, when David pushed you down the stairs. I was here, looking after you, when you were recovering from that. And I see all sorts of things here, but I found your story really tough. You were obviously such a sweet soul and he'd taken so much away from you, and I was rooting for you to take it to court, for him to be properly punished for what he did. Now, this time, you've been seriously injured but it was just an accident. It wasn't anyone's fault. In this job, we often get to see people for a few days at a certain point in their lives, and we never get to find out what happens afterwards. When I heard you were back, that you were in a coma again, I thought he was out and you'd gone back to him, or that you'd met someone else who was just as bad, and it was such a relief to hear that you'd been in a car accident – strange as that might sound.'

'I would never go back to him,' I say.

'Well, good. Because you're a good person, Shelley. You deserve good things. And it feels like you have good people in your life now. I hope it stays that way.'

He takes his monitor and wheels it to the next bed, and I sit very still and quiet, trying to keep hold of what he said so that I can process it. And while I'm doing that, something comes into my mind, as clear and bright as a photograph. It's the trial. David's trial.

## 32

### THEN

I grip the sides of my chair so hard that my knuckles go white. It's all been building up to this, to today. I look at David across the courtroom, and he looks so small, so pathetic. He won't meet my eye, hasn't looked at me once, this whole time. When I close my eyes, I can see him on our wedding day, on the day we met, on the day he pushed me. And I cannot quite believe I let it go on the way I did. If it hadn't come to a head like that, if I hadn't nearly died, would I still be living with him, still at the mercy of his whims and moods? Possibly.

He's just a man, I tell myself. Just an average, insecure man. But he's a monster, too. I hate him for pleading not guilty, for dragging me to court to live through it all again. For several days, we've battled it out, him saying I slipped, me saying he pushed me. The lawyers are clever and they don't miss a thing. At times, I have doubted my own story. But now the jury have a verdict and the courtroom is in silence, waiting for it to be read.

The foreperson is a woman, maybe ten years older than me. She has thin, mousy-brown hair in a chin-length bob, glasses that are too big for her face. Has she ever known violence from a man?

There's no way to tell. I can picture her being pushed against a wall, a meaty hand around her throat, but I can also picture her sitting at a table opposite a man with kind eyes who pours her a glass of wine and asks about her day; about her jury service. I'm back in the room, focused on the matter in hand. If they have found him not guilty, I fear for my future. And if they have found him guilty, I fear for his. Because you don't stop loving someone overnight. You don't stop caring about how their life turns out.

This woman who is holding mine and David's future in the palm of her hand steps forward, clears her throat. The judge asks if the jury have reached a unanimous verdict, and she says they have. A couple of people on the jury look down at that point, and I wonder if they were the ones who didn't agree at first, the ones who were talked around. When the judge asks the foreperson what the verdict is, I take a deep breath in. Time slows, and I look at David again. There's no fear on his face, just exasperation. His mum is sitting in the public gallery, and I question the steps that led from us all eating roast beef around her dining room table to being here, in this courtroom. Remind myself that David took the steps that brought us here. I did not.

'Guilty,' the foreperson says, and I exhale.

David's shoulders slump and I keep looking at him, can't look away. Because I was sure that he would acknowledge me at some point, flash me the smallest of apologetic smiles. But there is nothing. Has his lawyer advised him to look away from me? And what could it possibly matter now, when it is all over?

He is given ten years. GBH. A term I've only heard before on TV. After he says it, the judge glances at me and I try to interpret the meaning of the look, but there is nothing. I want to thank him, for taking my life seriously. But I don't, and then it's all over. Dee drives me home.

'Ten years is longer than I've known him,' I say.

I'm not sure what my point is. I'm just trying to grasp what a decade actually is.

'He might not do the full ten,' Dee says.

'Still, he'll do at least five. Five years is a long time. Five Christmases, five birthdays.'

'I would have given him twenty.'

I watch Dee, whose eyes are on the road. I want to say thank you but I can't find the words. I hope Dee knows. When you get married, you're essentially tying your life to a person and putting everyone else second. But when the person you married isn't the person you thought they were, sometimes you need those secondary people to step up, to get you out.

Back at the flat, Dee asks whether I want her to open up the pub.

'No, let's stay closed for today.'

'We never stay closed.'

'Well, it's not really a normal day, is it?'

I have changed out of my stiff court clothes and into jeans and a hoodie. It's cold and clear outside, and we go for a walk, get a coffee on the way to warm our hands.

'I can't stop wondering what he's doing. Do you think that will stop, eventually?'

Dee tilts her head. 'I think so. It's just all so fresh. And he's somewhere you know nothing about, so you can't even really imagine it.'

'Most of my prison knowledge is from *Coronation Street*,' I say. 'Or crime novels.'

Dee links my arm and we walk on, through the park where some toddlers are taking turns to go down the slide, past the church. And when we circle back round to the pub, there's a woman hammering on the locked front doors, and it's David's mother.

'We're not open today,' I say, trying to keep my voice even and level. 'Are you looking for me?'

David's mother, Janet, looks like she's been crying for days. She looks at me with pure hatred in her eyes. 'He wouldn't do this,' she says.

'But he did,' I say. 'I'm telling you, and a jury has told you.'

'He's my boy. I didn't raise him that way.'

I think about what I have heard of David's childhood. His father left before he finished primary school, and his mother was strict and worried. Where did it come from, his tendency to violence? I believe that it didn't come from this diminished woman standing in front of me.

'I know you didn't. But he's an adult, Janet. And for whatever reason, this is what he's become.'

'You could have given him another chance.'

Dee steps forward, then. Not so close to Janet that it's intimidating, but enough to shield me from her words. 'That's enough,' she says. 'This wasn't a one-off, or an accident. Your son has been hurting her for a long time, and now he's being punished for it.'

Janet slumps, and I am reminded of the way David's body took the blow of the sentence. I know that David is all she has, that she probably hoped for grandchildren in the nearish future. Not prison visits. I find myself about to say sorry, but I stop myself. 'I'm going inside now,' I say. 'I think you should go home.'

Janet turns to go. There's no fight left in her. I watch her turn the corner before I take out my key and let myself in. Dee stays for another couple of hours. I try to get her to talk more about Liam, but she won't, and it's the first time I've known her to be reticent like that. Maybe this is really something. After lunch, she looks like she's got something to say.

'If we're not opening, I could do with going out for an hour or two. But...'

'But what? You don't have to babysit me.' It comes out harsher than I meant it to.

'I know that, Shell. I'm just trying to be a good friend.'

'I'm fine. Go. Really, go.'

Dee gathers her things together and leaves the flat, and I sit on the sofa thinking that I will cook something nice for the two of us, to thank Dee for everything, and then there's a noise from downstairs and I jump. I am not okay. Haven't been since the attack. Physically, I've recovered, but there's a part of me that is always scared. That's what David's done, and it's worse than black eyes and bruises. Worse, even, than a coma. I pull my knees in to my chest and wrap my arms around them, so I'm as small as I can be.

For the first time in a long time, I don't know what my future looks like. I thought I'd met the man I was going to spend the rest of my life with, but that's over. And I'm starting to think that the Pheasant isn't my future either, after years of feeling certain that it is. I go downstairs, into the bar area. I rarely see the place like this, still and empty. Before and after we're open, I'm always rushing. Now, I just stand here, taking it all in. I've done a good job with the place. Toned down the garish décor, replaced the awful patterned carpet with wood-effect flooring. A year or so ago, I hired a local artist to paint on the walls. I am so proud of this pub, but somehow it no longer feels like mine. I have to determine whether that's something David has done, or whether it's something my own heart is telling me.

The next morning, I search online for local women's refuges. I find three in Loughborough and call the first one listed, before I can change my mind. The woman who answers the call has a lilting Welsh accent. She asks how she can help.

'Do you take volunteers?' I ask.

'To help out here at the shelter? We certainly do.'

'Can I fill in an application, or have an interview, or whatever I need to do? I run a pub, so I'm busy most evenings but I have mornings free.'

There's a pause, and I think she's going to tell me that's no good, but it must just be a brief fault on the line.

'Why don't you come in tomorrow morning at ten and we'll have a chat?' she says. 'My name's Rose, by the way.'

After I've hung up, I feel like I've made something good out of a difficult day. I think about what I might wear to meet Rose, what I might say when she asks why I chose a domestic violence charity. For a moment, I feel slightly panicked. I'm not ready to tell a stranger about my own experiences. But I don't have to, I remind myself. I can take this one step at a time. And if I get someone out of the kind of situation I was living in, it will all have been worthwhile.

## 33

---

NOW

Hamza steeples his fingers and asks how I'm feeling today.

'Lost,' I say.

'Lost. How so?'

'I'm worried that my brain is blocking out something really awful. It can do that, right? I've read about it. When someone's been through a terrible trauma and their brain just shields them from it.'

Hamza uncrosses his legs and recrosses them the other way. 'There have been cases of that, yes.'

'So what I want to know is, if my brain is taking me back to seven years ago when my husband had just tried to kill me, what the hell happened in the intervening years that is worse than that?'

'I don't think you should think along those lines, Shelley. I don't think that's what's happening in this case.'

'But how do you know?'

'Because I know a bit about what your current life is like.'

'I'm glad one of us does.'

'Shelley, I understand this is hard. But your loved ones are just trying to do as you've asked. To let you piece it all together yourself.'

Which loved ones? Dee? Who else? How terribly sad that I can only think of one person who loves me. And then I think of my mum, remember that I asked someone to call her for me and it all came to nothing. But I have a phone now. I can do it myself, if I still want to.

'Shelley, we can move forward in a couple of different ways. We can continue waiting for your memories to come back or we can show you photos and tell you things and go on your social media and basically try to fill in the gaps.'

'I'm worried that if people just tell me, I'll never know for sure whether I remember those things or just know them because I've been told.'

He nods and pushes his black-framed glasses up his nose. 'I understand that.'

There is a temptation to ask for it all. To have it laid out in front of me and see what feels familiar. But I know, deep down, that I want to get there on my own. I want to fight my way back, not have it all handed to me.

'I am remembering things,' I say. 'I remembered waking up from my first coma, and David's trial.'

Hamza smiles a small smile, and I know he's pleased. 'That's great. Anything else?'

I start to shake my head, but then I realise it's not true. 'I remember my friend Dee being pregnant. I remember playing with her son, Callum. I get flashes, like photographs. A red car. A kitten. I can't piece them all together yet, and I don't know what's from my life and what's from something I've seen on TV, but I feel like it's happening, even if it's very slow.'

'That's good,' he says. 'You know, it can be very disorienting to lose your memory. You're coping admirably. I hope you'll let me know if you need any extra support.'

When I get back to my bed, I send a message to Dee.

Am I in touch with my mum?

I stare at it for a while, thinking about the absurdity of it. Of not knowing the answer myself, and also of potentially not being in touch with my own mother. She replies quickly.

Can I call?

When I answer the phone, she doesn't say anything for a minute.

'What is it?' I ask. 'It's bad, isn't it?'

'It's bad,' she says. 'Are you sure you want to talk about it on the phone? I can come in later.'

But now I know there's something, I need to know what. There's a question lurking in the back of my mind, and I have to know the answer or I'll go mad.

'Is she dead?'

'God, no! I'm sorry you thought that. It's not that bad.'

I feel like something's been pressing down on my chest, and it's just been lifted off. I feel like I can breathe again.

'She disappeared,' Dee says. 'A couple of years ago now. Didn't tell anyone where she was going. I think it was the only way she felt able to leave Mick.'

The joy I feel at the thought of her finally leaving Mick is like a wave. I bask in it for a moment, but then I catch hold of something else Dee said. That she didn't tell anyone where she was going. 'Me,' I say. 'She told me.' I don't know where this came from but I'm sure it's true. I try to concentrate, try to think of a place, but nothing feels right.

'If she told you, you kept it from pretty much everyone,' Dee says. 'Even me. Which is possible, of course. Look, Shell, this is a lot. Try to just let it sink in for a bit, okay?'

When we end the call, I sit still for a few long minutes, getting more and more angry. And when I feel like I'll explode with it, I throw back the covers and get out of bed, and I go in search of Mick. At the main entrance to the hospital, there's a reception desk with a bored-looking woman sitting behind it.

'Where could I find a porter?' I ask her.

She eyes me, in my gown. 'The nurses will call one if you need to be taken somewhere.'

'I don't need to be taken somewhere,' I say. 'I'm just looking for the porters' room. Lodge, is it called? Where they wait in between moving people around.'

She can see the rage in me, and I wonder whether she's going to do something about it. Call security, ask for me to be taken back to where I belong. But maybe she knows Mick, or maybe she just doesn't care, because she points down a long corridor and tells me it's a room near the end on the left. And I thank her, and go.

When I knock, it's him who comes to the door, and he looks so shocked to see me that I get one big push in before he can react. I put my hands out against his barrel chest, and I shove him as hard as I can. He doesn't fall, but he stumbles. Someone else in the room jeers, then gets up to see if he needs to intervene.

'You fucking bastard,' I say.

Mick smirks, and it makes me want to kill him. All the anger I feel about David is mixed in with the anger I feel about him, and there's so much of it spilling over. I think about Fern, running away from the man who hurt her. About Mum, going into hiding. About me, unable to let go of the memories of being pushed and hit and broken.

His friend is a wiry, tall man with a shaved head. 'Come on now,' he says. 'I don't know what's going on here but let's not resort to getting physical with each other.'

I laugh then, and it sounds bitter and cold. 'This man,' I say, gesturing with my head towards Mick, 'this shitty excuse for a man ruined my mum's life.'

The wiry man opens and closes his mouth, clearly unsure what to say.

'Domestic,' Mick tells him. 'I'll deal with it.' He steps out of the room and pulls the door closed behind him, and I see what he's doing. He's making sure there are witnesses. Something Mum and I were never able to do.

'I haven't seen your mother for about two years,' he says, keeping his voice low.

'Because she's uprooted her life to hide from you!'

He folds his arms across his chest, smirks again. 'Is that what she's told you?'

'She hasn't told me anything, because I don't know where she is. And that's down to you, and I despise you, Mick. I was scared of you when I was growing up, because you were big and powerful. But I'm not scared of you now. Are you beating up someone else and their kid? How do you live like that? How do you sleep?'

'That's enough,' he says.

It isn't. It isn't enough, but he goes back into the room and leaves me standing on my own in the corridor, my fists clenched so tight there are little crescent moon shapes on my palms.

\* \* \*

Matt comes in at lunchtime, and I'm so relieved to see him that I almost burst into tears. He puts a plastic cup of tea and a KitKat down on my tray, gives me a smile that's so genuine and simple.

'I've had a shitty day,' I say.

He looks at his watch. 'Already?'

'Yep.'

'Do you want to talk about it?'

I shake my head. But even as I do it, I'm thinking that part of me does. It's all too raw and recent at the moment, but at some point I do want to talk about this with him, because I feel like I can trust him.

'I want to know why you lied to me,' I say. 'I'm not angry any more. I just want to understand.'

Matt sighs and sits down, sipping his own drink. 'Sometimes I help out at a women's refuge,' he says. 'And I hadn't mentioned it, so I just pretended I'd been at the restaurant. It was stupid. I guess I was trying to simplify things.'

'A women's refuge? For, like, women who are victims of domestic abuse?'

'Yes,' he says.

He looks at me, his eyes steady and level, and I think about when I said to him, the first time we met, that my husband tried to kill me. He knows about this world. I feel suddenly as if I'm naked, completely exposed.

'Is that a volunteer job too? Are you some kind of saint?'

He chuckles, and I'm glad I've managed to lighten the mood, because the air was thick with it.

'I just help out a bit, with the food. It's really not a big deal.'

I nod. 'You must see some awful things.'

'I do.'

I leave a gap for him to go on, but he doesn't. Of course he doesn't. He's not about to tell me these women's stories as if they're gossip. I hear him swallow. It strikes me as ironic that I married a man who hurt me and only now I'm meeting a man who works in a job that helps other women in that position. What might life have been like if Matt had walked into the Horse and Wagon the night David did?

'I know you went through that, and I'm sorry,' he says.

I shrug. 'It's one of those things.'

'No,' he says, shaking his head vehemently. 'It's not "one of those things". "One of those things" is getting caught in the rain just after you've had your hair done, or missing lunch with friends because you were stuck in traffic. What you went through, what the women at the shelter have been through, it's someone's fault.'

He's right, and I'm stunned into silence for a minute.

'I'm sorry,' he says, 'I didn't mean to raise my voice. It's just... something I feel so strongly about.'

Does he have personal experience of this? 'It's all right,' I say. 'You're right. It's all someone's fault. I'm not saying it's okay.'

In the quiet that follows, he reaches out a hand and puts it over mine where it's lying on the white sheets. It's deliberate, not a mistake or a careless brush. It has meaning. I can't look at him, so I look down at our hands, his large one covering mine, and I have another flash of something like memory. My hand, and a man's, held just like this. And I'm in a wedding dress. And it isn't the one I wore to marry David.

Suddenly I know something. I know that I have met Matt before, outside of this hospital, back in my real life. But I'm not ready to say that to him yet, so I wait until he goes before I open the door to the past.

# 34

---

## THEN

It's a slow night and Dee's dragged two barstools round to our side of the bar, and she and I are chatting to Liam. Besides the three of us, there's only Derek, sitting at his usual barstool, and a man and woman sitting at one of the corner tables. I know I should be wiping tables or doing an impromptu stocktake, but my feet are rubbing from new shoes and I can't resist the opportunity to take the weight off them for half an hour.

'Shelley needs to get back out there, don't you think?' Dee asks.

Liam grins. 'I know better than to tell Shelley what she needs.'

Dee flashes me a look. One that says that she's going to continue to tell me exactly what she thinks, but that I should remember she only has my best interests at heart. I marvel at the fact that we can speak without words like this. It's born of long nights in pubs with sleazy men and, before the Pheasant, shitty bosses.

'David's gone, thank god, and it's been a while, and you're fully recovered from the attack, and I don't like to see you lonely.'

*Physically recovered*, I think. Fully recovered physically. I don't know whether I'm ready to meet someone, don't know, in truth, whether I ever will be. How can I trust someone again, after falling into the trap of a man like David? Wouldn't I always be waiting for things to turn nasty, always wincing when I made a mistake or said something sharp, expecting to pay for it with blood and broken bones?

'What does Shelley think?' Liam asks, blowing Dee a kiss to apologise for challenging her.

They both turn to look at me, to see how I'll answer.

'Don't you want some romance?' Dee asks. 'Some passion? That feeling you get when you meet someone and know there's something between you?'

I look from Dee to Liam and back again. They are properly together now. Have been for months. And they have a silent communication thing going on, too. I feel a pang of something. Jealousy? I am happy for them, but I am waiting for Dee to tell me she's moving out, and I can't help but think that the last time she moved out it was because I was moving in with David, and now it will be because she is moving in with Liam, and I feel like I've gone backwards while Dee has moved forwards. It's stupid, because I don't want to be in the marriage I was trapped in. But still.

'Sometimes,' I say. 'Sometimes I think about going on a date. About getting dressed up and doing my hair and makeup and having someone pick me up and going for dinner and drinks and wondering whether he's going to kiss me on the walk home.'

It's true, I do think about all of that. It's hard not to, sometimes. Love and sex are everywhere. In books, on TV, in conversations. There's no avoiding it.

'And?' Dee prompts.

'And then I remember that I spend most mornings at the shelter and most afternoons and evenings standing here, and I'm not sure when I'd fit in a love life. And I also remember what happened to me last time I fell in love,' I say.

Dee makes an angry face. 'Not all men are like David.'

'We're not,' Liam agrees.

'But how do I know?' I ask. 'Nobody thought David was like David until he was.'

Neither Liam nor Dee has an answer for this, and the man from the corner table is standing at the bar with two empty glasses, so I slide off my stool and go to serve him.

When I sit down again, Dee gives me a tentative smile.

'Liam's got this friend...' she says.

'I can vouch for him, Shelley. He's one of the good ones,' Liam adds.

I want to be cross with them for this intervention in my love life, but I find I can't be, really, because I know they both want the best for me. They want there to be double dates, and all of that.

'What's his name?' I ask.

'Pete,' Liam says. 'Pete Parker.'

'Peter Parker? Like Spiderman?'

'Yes! He's a gem, Shelley, honestly.'

'Why is he single?'

Liam shrugs. 'Why is anyone? He hasn't met the right woman yet. Can I give him your number?'

I'm mulling this over when the door is pushed open with force and a frantic-looking woman bursts in.

'We need help! My boyfriend, he's been attacked, outside. Please help us!'

Then, action. Liam, Dee and I rush to the door, followed by the man from the corner table. He steps forward.

'I'm first aid trained. Can I help?'

I watch him, relieved. I, too, have done first aid training, and I was going to tell them, of course I was, but it's been a long time since I sat in that church hall learning about bandages and bleeding, heart attacks and the recovery position. The man who's volunteered is confident, and he kneels on the cold, wet ground before the man who's been attacked. The man whose face is a mess of blood and pain.

'Has anyone called an ambulance?' I ask, and then I go inside to do it in the quiet and calm of the pub.

Derek is still sitting at the bar, unperturbed. I glance over to the corner table and the woman has gone. I'm not sure when that happened.

Once the ambulance is there and everything is being dealt with, I invite the first aider back inside for a drink on the house.

'Oh, I should go,' he says.

I find myself thinking that I don't want him to disappear. I take him in. He's messy and dishevelled, his hair looking like it needs a cut and his clothes rumpled and damp from the rain and the kneeling. But when he looks at me, I sense a kindness in him, and I am warmed by it.

'Stay,' Dee says. 'We absolutely insist.'

I wonder whether I'm giving off some kind of vibe of being interested in this man, or whether Dee's just being friendly.

'Well, okay,' he says, coming back inside.

Derek finishes his third pint and leaves. If he's even noticed any of the kerfuffle, he doesn't show it. So now it's just the four of us. Me and Dee on one side of the bar, Liam and the helpful stranger on the other. As I get us all a drink, I think again about double dates, and laugh to myself.

'I don't think I've seen you before,' Dee says. 'Are you local?'

I have my back to them all, dispensing shots of vodka into two glasses for me and Dee, but I am listening.

'Sort of. Well, yes. But only recently. I'm from around here, and then I moved away for ten years or so, and now I'm back. My sister – she's the one I was here with tonight – she's taken me under her wing and is trying to make sure I have a social life of some sort.'

I am surprised by how relieved I am to learn that the woman was his sister.

'Well,' I say, turning and passing Dee her drink. 'I'm Shelley and this is Dee, and Liam.'

The man holds out his hand for me to shake. 'Matt,' he says. 'It's nice to meet you.'

## 35

---

NOW

I remember being in Paris, climbing the dimly lit, narrow steps of the Eiffel Tower, my sandals rubbing at my heel. I remember painting a kitchen in a minty shade of green, splotches of paint on my clothes and in my hair. I remember stepping off a plane in Greece. The air, hairdryer warm, and the sky, the kind of blue that looks fake in photos. I remember walking around a supermarket, choosing between types of melon and trying to decide how many eggs I – we – needed. I remember saying 'I do' on a beach, the sand warm under my bare feet. I remember.

Matt. In all of those memories, Matt is beside me. There's a feeling of panic as they wash over me, because my brain has insisted this man is a stranger. A kind, attentive stranger, when this man is my husband. I get out of bed, because I can't stay still with this new knowledge. I go to the restaurant. I need to tell him that I know. And I'm scared to, as well. But the decision is taken out of my hands because he isn't there. A cheerful woman tells me he's at the refuge and I know, the second she says the word, that she is talking about my refuge. I am not a pub landlady. Not any more. I run a women's refuge. How could I have forgotten that?

I've brought some money so I order a pot of tea and a slice of Victoria sponge. I sit at a table right in the middle of the buzzy restaurant, and I think. Before, I was trying to do a jigsaw when I only had half of the pieces. Now, I have most or perhaps all of the pieces, but they still need to be slotted into place.

When I get back to my bed, there's someone sitting in the chair next to it waiting for me. My heart jumps. Could it be Matt? But no, he's already been in once today, and anyway, the hair's too short. Too neat. As I approach the bed, he turns and smiles, and it's Liam.

'Shelley,' he says, his voice thick. 'I'm sorry I haven't been in before now. It's hard, you know, with Callum and work and everything. I hope Dee's been sending my love.'

I have to do some mental adjustments, because seven years ago Liam was a regular at the pub and sort of a friend. But now he's Dee's husband, of course, and I know we've spent a fair bit of time together over the years. I want to tell him that I know about Matt, about all of it. But I feel like I have to tell Matt first.

'Hi,' I say, getting back into bed and pulling the stiff sheets over my legs.

'You're looking great,' he says.

I laugh because it's so far from the truth, but it's kind of him to say it, so when he looks hurt, I cover my mouth and tell him I know what he means.

'I'm not the best company,' I say. 'I get so tired and I'm still pretty confused. You know I thought it was 2017? That I thought David had just attacked me?'

'Yes, Dee said. But you don't have to be good company for me, Shelley. I'm just here to try to pass a bit of the time with you, maybe cheer you up. Dee's working but my mum came over and offered to have Callum, so I thought I'd come and find you, see how you're doing with my own eyes.'

There's a brief silence and I can't think of a way to fill it. It's ridiculous, because I've always been a master at small talk. It's part of the job description when you work behind a bar. You're constantly feigning interest in something boring a customer's telling you or filling silences like this one to keep things smooth with a customer who has nothing to say. But here, now, it's different. I can't talk about the weather, or where I'm going on holiday, or what I've been up to lately. And what else is there?

'Shall I do the talking?' Liam asks.

And I'm so grateful I could kiss him. I nod. 'Please. Tell me stories. Tell me anything. I feel like my brain is deteriorating. I've forgotten how to have a conversation.'

So I lay back and he tells me things. About his work as an IT consultant, and a day out he went on with Callum at the weekend, and a story about his friend Pete having a run-in with Tesco over some defective pyjamas and ending up with practically a whole new wardrobe out of it. I know he's exaggerating and I don't care. He's right, it passes the time.

'Do I know this Pete?' I ask, because I don't know whether there are still gaps, so I'm trying to identify and fill them.

'You might have met at the wedding. And I tried to set you up with him once.'

I fish around for a memory. 'What happened?'

'Well, you went and met someone else before I could organise something,' he says, his voice soft.

Ah, yes. The night I met Matt. Liam was talking about setting me up with a friend earlier in the evening.

Jamie comes over to do my obs and he has something to say. 'Good news, Shelley. The doctor says you can go home tomorrow.'

I've been waiting for this, of course, but I'm a bit stunned. I expected it all to be very gradual, but this feels like a leap.

Jamie must see the confusion on my face. 'They need the bed,' he says. 'Don't they always? The doctors will fill you in when they do their rounds in the morning.'

When he's gone, Liam turns to me. 'That's great news, isn't it?'

It is, and yet... I've started to feel protected here, in this world away from the real world, where I don't have to think about anything beyond what I want for my next meal. I'm not sure I'm ready for whatever is waiting for me in the real world beyond the hospital doors. But I don't say that to Liam. I just smile and nod. 'Brilliant news.'

A few minutes later, Liam says he has to go, and he leans over and kisses my cheek and says how nice it's been to see me, and it isn't until five minutes after he leaves that I think again about going home. About where home is. I know it's with Matt, and if I close my eyes I can picture the house. I think I could direct someone there in a car. But am I ready to move back in? I know Matt isn't a stranger now, but he still feels a little like one.

I send Dee a message.

I'm being sent home tomorrow and I don't know where I live.

Half truth, half lie. I know where I live, but if I tell her that, I'll have to tell her I remember everything, and I'm determined to talk to Matt first.

She replies almost immediately.

I knew you'd be stressed about this. You're welcome to stay in our spare room, of course.

I think about this. How will Matt feel if I tell him I remember our past but I'm not quite ready to move home? My brain supplies the answer almost immediately. He'll be fine with it. He's a good man. He isn't David.

Spare room sounds good.

* * *

I don't sleep much. I keep dreaming that it's morning and it's time to go home and I'm still in my pyjamas, wandering around with a little bag packed and no one to pick me up. I wake up, again and again, fearful and anxious. And eventually it's morning and Jamie opens the blinds and asks me how I slept and I lie and say I slept fine.

'Usual for breakfast?' he asks.

I nod. My breakfasts in here are a small bowl of bran flakes, buttered toast and orange juice. The toast is always cold but it tastes great, somehow. What do I usually eat for breakfast, at home? I close my eyes, see myself biting into toast smeared with Marmite. See Matt turning his nose up at the smell, me purposely breathing all over him after I've eaten it. It makes me smile.

Dr Jenkins appears shortly after nine o'clock. 'Did Jamie tell you we're sending you home?'

'Yes.'

'I've discussed your case with a number of colleagues and we're all happy that we've monitored you for long enough. There's no sign of the bleed starting up again.' She stops talking, looks at me. 'I thought you'd be happy about that. Most people can't wait to get out of here.'

I look away, feel the sting of tears.

'Shelley? Are you worried about going home?'

'I'm going to stay with a friend for a bit.'

She nods, and it seems like she's about to speak again, but she doesn't. 'I know you're still recovering your memories, Shelley, but you've come a long way. I think you'll get there. Your physical recovery has been very quick.'

When she's gone, I get dressed and brush my teeth. I stare at myself in the mirror for a long time. I am no longer thirty. I am no longer the landlady of the Pheasant. But I am still Shelley Woodhouse.

Jamie comes over to say goodbye, and Angela is with him. She's come down from Intensive Care with another patient, possibly the one who's moving into my bed.

'In the nicest possible way...' she begins.

'You hope you never see me again,' I finish.

She widens her eyes in surprise.

'You said that last time,' I say.

She laughs. 'I say it to everyone when they go home. But it's great that you remembered that.'

'Take good care,' Jamie says, and he puts a hand on my arm, and it is warm and reassuring.

I tell him I will. And then I go. Outside, Dee is waiting. On the drive to her home, I think about the night I told Matt about my past.

## 36

THEN

'Will you close up?' I ask.

'What's it worth?' Dee wraps a few strands of hair around her finger, then lets it spring free.

'My eternal gratitude.'

'Nah.'

I smile and go back to serving. It's nine o'clock and Matt is coming in at ten to take me out for a drink at a different pub before closing. It's something we've been doing for a couple of months. In the early days, Matt would come to the Pheasant and I would snatch time to chat to him when I could, and then one day he asked whether I missed being on the customer side of the bar, and I realised I did, a bit.

When he comes in, I'm serving a group of women who are all drinking different wines. I know he's there before I turn my head and see him. I'm not sure how this is possible, but it's like he changes something in the atmosphere, so I can sense him. When I turn and we make eye contact, he flashes me a smile and I am reminded of that first night, when he helped the guy who'd been attacked out the front. If that hadn't happened, if that scared girl-friend hadn't run in, I might never have met him. He'd told me, later, that his sister was taking him to every pub in town. He might have walked in and out of mine without me noticing him. And what a loss that would have been.

I finish pouring all the different wines and give the woman who's buying the round the card machine. Then I go over to where Matt is leaning on the bar, and he leans further and gives me a kiss. Someone makes a jeering sound. Someone always does.

'How was the hospital?' I ask him.

Matt shrugs. 'You know, the same. Lots of sad people waiting for news.'

I think that the people at the hospital are lucky to have him there, a friendly face at their worst moments. Almost say it, but it's early days in our relationship, so I stop myself. At ten, I run upstairs to the flat and reapply my mascara.

'Ready to go?' Matt asks on my return.

I look at Dee.

'Go,' she says. She gestures around the pub, which has emptied out a fair bit. There's Derek, of course, and the wine women, and a couple of other stragglers. 'I have this all under control.'

'I owe you one,' I say.

'You owe me several.'

Outside, the cold March air hits me and wakes me up. Matt takes hold of my hand and asks about my day, and I tell him a story about Derek getting locked in the toilets earlier, and we both laugh. It is easy with Matt. It feels right. But he is pushing for more, for commitment, and I'm not sure I'm ready.

'I have to tell you something,' I say once we're seated in a corner at the White Hart.

'Sounds serious.'

'It is.'

Where to begin? With David, or with Mick? I take a sip of my vodka and tonic. I am playing for time. Now that I've begun this, I'm not sure I want to go on. Because won't it affect the way he sees me, when I let him know how damaged I am? 'This is hard. You know I volunteer at a women's shelter?'

He nods.

'And you know I was married?'

Matt nods. He looks afraid of what I might say. I put a hand on his arm to reassure him, and he takes my other hand in his.

'My ex-husband, David. He's in prison.'

This was unexpected, I can see. He reaches for his pint and takes a long gulp. 'What for?'

'GBH.'

He raises one eyebrow, silently urging me to go on.

'He... well, he tried to kill me. Pushed me down the stairs. I was in a coma.'

'Fuck, Shelley.' He shakes his head as if trying to dislodge the words.

'This was a couple of years ago now. But, it wasn't only that. He'd been... abusing me... for a long time.'

He stares at me, waiting for me to go on. So after a deep breath, I do.

'He didn't do it at first. I knew he had a temper, but he kept it under control until things were serious between us. And then the first time he was so apologetic and said it would never happen again and begged me to give him another chance. He used to mess around with my mind, too, make me think I didn't remember things correctly. I'm such a cliché, aren't I?'

Matt squeezes my fingers. 'Shelley, this is your story. It doesn't matter how many other people have been through something similar.'

'I put up with it. I stayed. And then I nearly died, and I swore I'd never go back to him, and now he's in prison.'

'Where he belongs.' His voice is a bit choked. 'I'm so sorry, Shelley, that you've been through that.'

I shrug, bite my lip hard to stop tears from coming. 'It's a pattern,' I say, determined to get it all out now. 'My mum was married to a man who abused her too.' I pause to gather myself, take another sip of my drink. 'Mick. He was violent with both of us. It's why I hardly have a relationship with my mum. I couldn't forgive her for not getting us out of that situation. But now that I've lived with it myself, I understand a bit more how hard getting out actually is. And the reason I'm telling you all of this is because I'm scared. I'm scared of it happening again. And that's why I hold back sometimes, why I want to take things slowly. I don't want to ever be in a situation like that again.'

The end of this speech comes out in a rush and I exhale, exhausted, and look to Matt for his reaction.

'Is she still with him?' he asks.

'Yes.'

'My mum...' he says, and I'm confused, because this isn't what I'd expected him to say. I silently urge him to go on.

'My parents, they had this explosive marriage. Lots of shouting and throwing things. Sometimes my dad hit her. We left when I was six, so I don't remember too much. Mum says she knew that if she didn't get me and my brother and sister out, I would grow up thinking that was normal.'

We look at one another, both in pain.

'Thank you for telling me,' Matt says. 'For trusting me with it. I'll be patient. And if you ever need me to be more patient, just let me know. It's been my biggest fear, that I would hurt someone else in that way. But I wouldn't, Shelley. I couldn't.'

I believe him, and I hope he knows that. It doesn't mean I can

forget about my past, my experiences, and leap into a serious rela-
tionship head first. I'll always have this fear, this trepidation. It's
something he'll have to adjust to, if we carry on with this.

'What about your mum now?' I ask.

'She's remarried. She met my stepdad a few years after we left. I
don't see my dad. She's really happy, Shelley. This is going to sound
like such a cliché, but there's a life beyond it. I'd love you to meet
her one day, to see that.'

This feels big. A suggestion of meeting parents. My mouth feels
dry and I go to sip my drink but find it is empty.

'One more?' I ask.

While I wait at the bar, I list good men I know. It's a thing I do, to
remind myself that they exist. That what happened to me won't
necessarily always happen. I think of Liam, of Derek, of Matt. I am
sure that Matt belongs on my list.

We have another drink and talk about less heavy stuff. Some-
thing he's reading, something I've seen on TV. I like hearing what
he thinks about things, especially things I've read or seen or heard
about myself, because his take is always slightly different and
usually fascinating. It's like getting a glimpse of the world from a
different angle. When we walk back to the Pheasant, we are hand in
hand, our coat hoods up because there's a hint of rain in the air.

'Do you want to stay?' I ask.

'I'd better not. Early start.'

I am disappointed, and when he pushes me gently against the
side door and kisses me, I'm ready to plead with him to come
inside. But then he pulls away, looks at me seriously with his eyes
like pools. 'I didn't know, about your husband. I feel like now I do,
I'll understand you better. Thank you for telling me. I know it can't
have been easy.'

I put my head down and Matt lifts it again with one finger

under my chin. 'I love you,' I say. I hadn't planned to say it, and I cover my mouth as if I can cram the words back in. But Matt is smiling, his whole expression full of joy, and I am glad I said it, because it's true.

# 37

NOW

Dee's chatting away on the drive back from the hospital, and I'm looking out of the window because it's the first time I've been out of the hospital in days and I'm working out how much is familiar. We go through the town centre, past the church, and then I see a road on the left and I expect her to indicate but she doesn't.

'Can we go left here?' I ask, a note of panic audible in my voice.

Dee shrugs and flicks her indicator on, swings into the turn at the last minute. 'Where now? We're going the wrong way for my place.'

My instinct is telling me where to go and I don't want to lose sight of it. 'Left again, just here.'

She looks across at me and I know that she knows where I'm leading her. We take a right and then a final left, and then I tell her to slow down.

'Here,' I say, pointing at a small, ordinary-looking house.

Dee pulls over, and we both look out of the window at the house. It has a green front door and shutters on the downstairs windows. The recycling bin is out, ready to be collected. In many ways, it's like every other house on this street. But it's also not.

'This is where I live,' I say.

I look at Dee and she has tears in her eyes. 'Yes.'

But I didn't really need her to confirm it, because I know. I stare at the front door, as if waiting for someone to come out of it.

'Do you want to go in?' Dee asks.

I shake my head quickly. 'No, not yet.'

I don't know how to tell her that it's scary, feeling so out of control in your own life. Feeling like it's a game you've been playing and you're trying to remember what the rules were.

'Back to mine, then?'

'Can we make one more stop?'

'Anywhere you like.'

When she pulls into the car park of the Pheasant, the familiarity of the place really hits. I know exactly what angle she needs to turn at to get into the corner space, and so does she, because she reverses in expertly.

'Are we going inside? Or did you just want to see it?'

I take a deep breath. 'We're going inside. Just for a minute.'

We unclip our seatbelts and get out of the car. For a moment, I just stand there, not quite ready to go in, and Dee takes the lead from me. Just waits. I notice that the outdoor tables and chairs are new, and the car park that used to be gravel has been tarmacked. Slowly, we make our way to the door which is looking a bit neglected, the black paint a bit chipped here and there. I push it open and go inside, and the warmth and noise of the place is like a wall and it's like going back in time. Derek's sitting at the bar and he turns the way he always does when someone comes in. Like a cat keeping watch of his territory.

'Shelley,' he says. 'It's good to see you up and about again.'

And then, when he spots Dee behind me, he speaks to her. 'The Stella's off, you know. I'm on Carling. If I have to have another pint of it, I'll be going to the Three Kings.'

'You'll never go to the Three Kings,' Dee says. 'Not after last time, when they let someone else sit on your stool.'

So Dee still works here. I'm piecing things together, bit by bit. There's a young guy behind the bar who looks like he could break hearts as a hobby. He's got this dark hair that falls in his eyes, and when he brushes it away, his eyes are a glorious green.

'Hey boss,' he says, holding up one hand in a wave. 'I thought we weren't going to be seeing you today.'

'Change of plan,' Dee says. 'But I'm not staying, so don't expect me to start serving. Why's the Stella off?'

The man rolls his eyes and nods towards Derek. 'It's only five minutes since he told me. I'm waiting for a quiet moment to go down and change it.'

I am standing next to Dee on the wrong side of the bar we've spent so many nights behind.

'This is your place now.' I feel like things are slotting into place, like I almost have the full picture.

She nods in confirmation. 'When you left, I moaned so much about having to get used to a new manager that you and Liam talked me into it. Turns out I'd picked up pretty much everything I needed to know from you over the years.'

It makes sense, Dee being the landlady. And it's a relief, too, to know that I didn't totally let go of this place that I love. That there's still someone familiar here.

'Do you live upstairs?' I ask.

Dee laughs. 'No. We did for a while but we moved out when I was pregnant with Callum. It didn't seem like the right place to raise a family. It's rented out now. So, what do you think? Are we sticking around for a drink or going home? I don't want to get in trouble with your doctors for taking you straight from hospital to the pub.'

I laugh. 'Home, then,' I say.

'Good, because I find it impossible to be in this place and not get to work. I don't know how you do it.'

'Do I come in a lot?' I ask.

But I know the answer. I do. This is where we all spend our time. My friend Dee, her husband Liam, Matt and me.

'Can't get rid of you,' she says.

Back at Dee's house, which I also managed to pick out of the houses on the street, Liam and Callum are watching an animated programme about numbers. They turn their heads in unison when we enter the room and I see how alike they look, while still seeing bits of Dee in Callum's face too.

'What's brown and sticky?' Callum asks.

And I know the answer, but before I can say it, Dee and Liam both shout it out.

'A stick!'

'His favourite joke,' Dee says to me.

'I knew it,' I tell her. 'I knew the answer.'

'Well, aren't you coming on leaps and bounds today? Liam, Shell took me to her house.'

'Oh yes? That's great. Did you go in?'

'No. I wasn't ready.'

Liam takes this in his stride. 'There's a cottage pie in the oven.'

And Dee goes over and kisses him, and I feel a stab of envy for this sweet life she has. I feel like mine, by comparison, is in pieces, and I have to put them back together before I even know whether it's what I want.

We eat dinner, Callum chatting non-stop about someone at school who had a nosebleed in the playground and a dinner lady who just gives you more if you say you don't like it, and then stands over you making sure you eat it all up. I'm quiet, trying to take it all in. I notice Dee and Liam checking on me every few minutes, exchanging looks with unspoken words behind them. I feel like an intruder here, though they've done nothing to make me feel that way.

'I won't stay too long,' I say when Callum pauses for breath.

Dee fixes me with a look. 'You can stay as long as you like.'

'Nanny is coming in a couple of weeks,' Callum says. 'And Mummy said if you're still here then her and Daddy will have to give her their bed and sleep on the sofabed.'

Dee goes red. Says his name a little sharply.

'It's fine,' I say. 'Really. This is your home. Your family.'

'You're my family too.'

It's the kindest thing she could say, and it's almost too much to bear. I think of my mother, how she could be anywhere, or nowhere at all. How she could have died and I wouldn't even have known.

'I'm trying hard, to remember. And once I have, I'll go back home.'

We're all quiet then. Even Callum. But afterwards, when Liam is washing up and I search out a tea towel to dry, when Dee has taken Callum up to run a bath, he reassures me.

'Shelley, we really don't mind how long you stay. What Callum said, we were just talking logistics. We don't want you to do anything before you're ready.'

I thank him. And I wonder if he knows that the thanks are for his kindness towards me but also the way he has helped Dee transform from a sceptical single woman to a calm, contented wife and mother. It's like he's steered her away from danger, into calmer waters. He smiles at me, and I feel like we're going to hug but his hands are wet and soapy, so we don't.

I go to bed early. Dee's been to my place and brought my toiletries and clothes, pyjamas and underwear and a few books. Everything I might need. I imagine her there, talking to Matt, him leaning against the kitchen counter, and her, talking with her hands and trying to reassure him. I pick up a paperback and the beginning is familiar. It's about a woman who's having a baby and finds out that her husband is leading a double life. Have I read this before? Was I halfway through it when the accident happened? I flick ahead fifty pages or so, try to see whether I recognise it, but I don't. Frustrated, I throw it across the bed and it lands with a thunk on the floor. A few seconds later, there's a knock at my door, and I get out of bed in my pyjamas to open it, expecting Dee.

Callum's on the landing, dancing about. 'I need a wee, and I heard a noise.'

'It was me, throwing a book,' I say. 'Let's get you to the toilet.'

I follow him to the bathroom and he sits down on the toilet.

'You know, you shouldn't throw things.'

'I know that. I'm sorry.'

'It's okay. You probably did it because you've forgotten that rule.' He washes his hands carefully, pumping the soap and splashing his pyjama top.

'When will you remember things?' he asks, looking at me with wide eyes.

'I remember some things.'

'Is it scary?'

I consider this. It is, a bit. 'It's more like feeling out of control. Like if you're on a swing or a roundabout and it's going too high or too fast and you can't do anything to stop it?'

'Want to see my room?' he asks.

I'm not used to kids, to how quickly the subject can be changed. 'I do.'

He pushes open the door. A little light comes from a bee-shaped nightlight next to his bed, and there are books and toys and pictures on the walls and soft toys lining the wall at the edge of his bed. He points to a poster which a map of the UK with a big arrow showing where we live.

'It's wonderful,' I say.

'You can come and stay in here with me, if you ever get frightened,' he says.

And then he gets into bed, turns on his side to face the wall, and is asleep almost instantly. I stand there for a few more seconds, just watching him. There's a swell of love that can't just be the result of knowing him for a couple of days. I remember him. I remember that I love him.

Back in my room, I reach for my phone and send a message to Matt.

> I'm not at the hospital any more. I guess you probably know that.
> Can we talk?

His reply comes quickly.

> I'm not at work until midday tomorrow. Want to meet somewhere in the morning?

We go back and forth, finally settling on the park at ten. Unlike Callum, I take a long time to get to sleep. It isn't until I tell myself the story of proposing to Matt that I finally fall.

## 38

THEN

'I'm talking big dreams,' Matt says.

'Big dreams,' I repeat. We are in bed, lying on our sides facing one another, propped up on our elbows. I close my eyes, try to visualise what I want. And for the first time, it isn't the Pheasant that I see. It's him and me, side by side. Travelling, seeing things, making each other laugh. But I know that isn't what he means. So I think again, about different ways I could spend my days and evenings, different ways my life could be arranged. This pub life is all I've known, but it doesn't mean it's all there is. Mum showed me how to work behind a bar and how to fall for someone bad for me, and now I'm learning how to do other things.

'I'd like to open my own shelter,' I say.

'Wow, really?'

'Yes. Rose at Female Aid is so great, but she can only do so much. We're always having to turn people away, send them back to situations that aren't safe. I hate it. There's just all this need, and a huge void where the help should be.'

Matt furrows his brow. 'Don't you think you'd find it hard, like living through it all day in day out?'

I love that his reservations are around the toll this might take, rather than my ability to do it. I consider his question. It would be a bit like that, but I am confident that the satisfaction I'd get from doing something useful would outweigh it. Matt knows, though, that the scars run deep. A couple of times, he's jumped up or moved quickly and I've flinched as if expecting to be hit. And he's seen me after tough sessions at Female Aid, when I've been on my knees with the fear and frustration of it all.

'There are so many women out there like me, living that awful life. And you just don't know. I want to help them.'

'Then we should do it,' he says.

'We?'

'I mean you, but I could help out.'

I'm not expecting this. But it means something to me, that he doesn't only want to hear about my big dreams, but wants to help me make them a reality.

'I don't know enough about it,' I say.

'We'll find out. Rose would help, I'm sure. And we can do research.'

I resolve to start looking into it the next day. Matt makes life seem easy. It's a way he has. Whenever I go to him with a problem or a worry, he talks it over with me until I can see a path through the darkness. And it makes me believe in myself. Perhaps we could open a shelter, between us. I feel a bead of excitement travelling around my insides, and then it bursts, fizzing all through me.

When I was with David, it was all fear and trepidation. Hoping I wasn't saying the wrong thing, that nothing would set him off. I didn't know, until I met Matt, that it could all be lightness and support. We argue, of course we do, but it's not frequent and I am never, ever, made to feel frightened. And that's worth everything to me.

When I try to explain it to Dee, the following day as we're

preparing to open up, I say I feel like I am wrapped up in a blanket. Warm and protected.

Dee pulls a face. 'Not very sexy, though, is it? A blanket?'

I flick a tea towel at her. 'It's sexy enough for me.'

And it is. Sometimes, Dee tells me about arguments she's had with Liam, about how they've made up. Ten minutes from shouting at each other to having sex. It works for them. But I don't want or need that. I need this, what I have, with Matt. I feel settled.

'I'm going to ask him to marry me,' I say.

Dee is sweeping the floor but she snaps around to look at me.

'Are you?'

'Yes.' I didn't know it for sure until I said it, but now it seems obvious and like the only course of action. 'And I'm going to give up this place. Not immediately, but I don't think we'll live here, after we're married. I'd like to buy a house.'

'Woah, that is a lot, Shelley Woodhouse. And you seem pretty sure that he's going to say yes.'

I am sure. I can picture myself proposing in a hundred different ways, and I can picture a multitude of reactions from him, but I cannot picture him saying no. He's made it clear that he loves me. He makes it clear every day.

'I'm not going to steal your wedding thunder,' I say. 'I can wait until after yours to propose, if you want.'

Dee shrugs. 'Up to you.'

Dee and Liam are getting married in a month's time, and Dee swings between being relaxed, like this, and being a total nightmare. I feel like I've been living the wedding for months, hearing on a daily basis about the caterer and the flowers and the cake. I am Dee's Maid of Honour, and I'm giving a speech. I've been dress shopping, seen the rings, and it's been amazing, but it's also made me realise something. I don't want any of that again. I did it with David, and if Matt wants it, I'll do it again. But I suspect he won't. I want to go somewhere, just the two of us. Or maybe with Dee and Liam along for the ride. Somewhere hot. Write down all the things I love about him and tell him on a white-sand beach. I will ask him tonight.

But before that, there's a long shift to do. Dee opens the doors and it isn't long before Derek appears, and after him, a group of older women who sometimes come in for coffee after their weekly walk. And then they keep coming, couples and families and groups of men. Sometime in the early evening, my phone pings with a message but I don't have time to look at it, and it goes out of my mind. By the time I open it, it is almost midnight and my feet are aching and Dee has waved and gone.

It's from my mum.

I'm going to leave him, Shell. Will you help me?

I feel as if all the air has been pushed out of my chest in an instant. I have been waiting for this day for years. Immediately, I type a reply.

Anything. I'll do anything. I'm so happy.

Upstairs, Matt senses the lightness in me. 'Has something happened today?'

'Two things,' I say. 'Mum is leaving Mick.' Just saying it, I feel my legs start to shake and I have to sit down. Matt is quiet, thoughtful. He brings me a cup of sweet tea, and it is exactly what I need.

'That's great,' he says. 'Does she have somewhere to go?'

I tell him I don't know, that I will call her in the morning and talk it through with her. Once Mick is at work.

'I don't know whether I can fully forgive her,' I say.

'For letting him into your life?'

'Not that, so much, but for standing by when he was hurting me as well as letting him hurt her. It's just, it's your number one job as a parent, isn't it? To protect your child. I feel so let down. It's so complicated, the way I feel about her. I'm desperate for her to get out, couldn't have been happier when I saw her message just now, but there's a part of me that's still angry with her and I think maybe I always will be.'

Matt is silent for a moment. He doesn't rush in with words. He is considered, careful. 'I think that's okay,' he says. 'I think it's fine to feel both of those things at once.'

'But she's my mum. I want to just love her, the way you love yours. I want it to be simple.'

He takes my hands in his when I put the empty mug down on the floor. 'I don't think you can choose that, at this stage.'

He is probably right. 'I wish Granny Rose had seen this.'

'I wonder what's made her decide, after all these years.'

Perhaps something's happened, like it did with David, I think. Perhaps Mum sent that message from a hospital bed. I send her another message but there's no reply. Eventually, tired of waiting, I stand and say I'm going to bed, relieved that this decades-long ordeal is going to be over.

We go through our night-time routine. Brushing our teeth side by side at the sink, playfully pushing each other out of the way to spit. Matt strips to boxers and I pull on pyjama shorts and a vest top, and we climb into bed. I am quiet, my mind still racing, going over escape plans and possibilities, when Matt speaks into the silence of the room.

'What was the second thing?'

'Oh, yes. The second thing is that I wanted to ask you something.'

'Ask away.'

I turn over so I'm facing him. He is on his back, but I put a hand on his arm and pull him onto his side. We lock eyes. This isn't how I had thought it would happen, but so what? With David, I had a romantic proposal story and a body full of bruises. You don't always get what you think you want.

'Will you marry me?' I ask.

He bolts up into a sitting position. 'Are you serious?'

Something about his reaction makes me laugh, and then he is laughing, too.

'Shelley, really, do you mean it? I can't tell whether you mean it.'

I gather myself, stop laughing. Suddenly, it's not funny. It's deadly serious. 'I really want to marry you,' I say, and there are tears in my eyes threatening to spill, and I'm not sure whether they're left over from the laughter or newly there because this is the most important thing I've ever asked anyone in my entire life.

'I really want to marry you, too,' Matt says. 'I didn't know whether you would, after David.'

He kisses me, and I fall into it. And before I stop thinking, I remember what Dee said about it not being sexy, the way I feel about Matt. Dee knows me so well, but she is wrong about this. For me, right now, feeling safe and loved is the sexiest thing of all.

# 39

---

## NOW

Dee offered to take a day off, but she was off yesterday and I know what it's like when you run a pub. She has orders to do, wages to sort. I tell her to go, and she kisses me on the forehead with her lips scratchy from toast crumbs. Liam walks Callum to school, and the bustle of their family life is replaced with a deep silence. Dee asked what I was planning to do today, and I said I was going to take it easy. Read a book. Maybe go for a short walk. She told me to come to the pub for lunch if I fancied it.

I didn't tell her what I'm really planning to do. I feel like this meeting with Matt should just be between the two of us until afterwards. But I'm as nervous as if I was going on a first date. I blow-dry my hair, put on a bit of makeup. I go through the clothes Dee has brought me, wishing I had something better while trying to remind myself that this man has seen me at my best and my worst, that for the past week he has seen me in nothing but pyjamas. That he has stood by me, even when I didn't know who he was.

Our agreed meeting point is a café, and I get there early and go inside to buy us both drinks to take away. I'm hoping we will walk. It's easier to talk, sometimes, when you're walking alongside a person rather than sitting or standing opposite them, with the full force of their gaze on you. When Matt appears in the distance, I watch him approach. How did I ever not know this man? Everything about him is familiar, from the way he moves to the way his hair falls in his eyes, and he blows it away.

'Hi,' he says.

'Hi.' I hold out his coffee and he smiles, but the sadness in his eyes doesn't lessen. 'Can we walk?'

We set out walking. It's a cold, bright late winter day, and I'm astonished by how much beauty there is everywhere. The clear skies, the bare trees.

'I know,' I say, after a minute or two of silence.

'What do you know?'

'Everything, I think. That we're married. That you're not a hospital volunteer.'

He stops walking and I turn to him and we both grin. 'I didn't want to lie to you...'

'No, I get it. I understand. Dee has told me how hard I found it when people were trying to fill in the blanks for me.'

'You wanted to do it yourself,' he says.

'And I have.'

'Can I give you a hug?'

We move towards each other and our bodies fit, his arms around my lower back and mine around his shoulders. It feels right and uncomfortable at the same time. I pull away. 'I'm sorry, I'm not sure I'm ready. I need to take this slowly.'

'Of course,' he says, and he sounds a bit dejected.

'I'll get there,' I say. 'I'm just still working on it all. You know I'm staying at Dee's, I suppose?'

'She called me. And listen, I can't wait to have you home but it takes as long as it takes, all right? I hate the fact that you had to go back to all that stuff with David. You're bound to be shaken. But I'm here, for chats and support and, eventually, marriage.'

'And KitKats?'

'Always KitKats.'

'Thank you,' I say. 'I can't believe I got it so wrong with one husband and so right with the other.'

We walk on in silence, and I drink my tea, feeling it warm my insides. When we reach a bin, we both put our cups in the recycling, and he asks whether I'm getting tired, whether I want to head back. I realise that I am tired, and I know I'll probably spend the afternoon napping on the sofa, but I'm not quite ready for this to end.

'Just a few more minutes, just back to where we started.'

I mean the walk, but that is what we're doing here, isn't it? Getting back to where we started. Whenever we pass someone with a dog, he quietly gives it a cuteness rating out of ten, with most of them scoring twelve, and I make up some commentary for the ducks who are swimming across the lake but getting nowhere because of the breeze. And when I can see the café, and I know it won't be long until we go our separate ways, I reach for his hand and hold it in mine, and out of the corner of my eye I see him smile. And it's so easy and right.

'How did you come up with the volunteer thing?'

He laughs. 'Well, you'd been coming round on and off for a few days. And every time you saw me you'd ask who I was. It was like a knife to the heart every time. I told you I was your husband over and over, and you'd get really upset and say your husband was David and I'd try to explain that David was in prison and you'd moved on but it was just so scary for you. I had a long chat with the doctor and your Intensive Care nurse, Angela. Also Dee. I said I wanted to come in to see you but didn't want to upset you, and I think Dee suggested it. She said she'd been in hospital once as a teenager, to have her tonsils removed, and there had been this lovely volunteer who came round to chat and bring drinks and so on. It just seemed like the best way to still get to be around.'

I think about how it must have felt, him knowing that we shared a life together and me not knowing who he was.

'Thank you,' I say.

'For what?'

'For finding a way. I felt pretty low in there at times. I felt like Dee was the only person I really had in my life who cared about me. But you made everything better, you really did.'

'Well, that's what I'm here for.' He looks at his watch and pulls a face. 'But unfortunately I have to make a move. That restaurant's not going to run itself.'

It's odd to think of him still going to the hospital now I'm not there.

'Will you come to Dee's for dinner later? I'm making toad in the hole. It's Callum's favourite, apparently.'

'And one of mine. But I'll be working late. I'll tell you what. Could I take you out on a date, tomorrow night?'

I feel the smile spreading over my face, working its way up to my eyes. 'I would like that.'

'It's a deal, then. I'll pick you up at seven.'

He blows me a kiss and walks away, and I stand there for minute or so, just watching him go. Knowing that he'll come back. I feel the absence of his hand in mine, and stuff it in my pocket for warmth, and then I head back to Dee's house, stopping off at the super-market for sausages and wine. It feels like such a normal thing to do, to walk in the park and then pick things up for dinner.

It's not until I'm back at Dee's, washing up the breakfast dishes with the radio on, that I think about my mum. Did Matt get in touch with her, to tell her about my accident? And if he did, why didn't she come?

## 40

---

### THEN

'Are you ready?' Matt asks.

'I think so.'

We get out of the car and knock on my mum's front door. I haven't been here since Granny Rose died, but when Mum opens the door, it still smells familiar. Like her washing detergent and potpourri, with undertones of Mick. He's not there, but he's everywhere. His boots by the front door, his coat slung over the banister. I can tell he chose the picture hanging in the hallway, which is bold and bright and nothing that Mum would pick.

For a minute, we look at each other. She's lost weight, and her nails are bitten down. There are no obvious bruises, but I know that doesn't mean anything. She pulls me in for a hug, and I can't let myself relax into it, but I want to.

'Are you packed?' I ask.

She nods. Over the past few weeks, since she asked for my help, Matt and I have searched for places she could go. Not too far, but not close enough that she might run into him. We settled on Nottingham, found a room for her to rent in a shared house with three other women. We set her up with a new bank account and gave her some money to tide her over until she found a job, helped her with the paperwork to set up a restraining order. And all the time, she went back and forth, not sure she was really going to go through with it. It's her house, this, and she owns it outright, having paid the mortgage for more than two decades. It should be him who's going, but we both know there's no way that will happen. He won't let her go, either. That's why we're here while he's at work, why she's packed her bags in a hurry in the two hours since he left.

Not for the first time, I question whether I should have offered for her to stay in our spare room. I haven't offered and she hasn't asked. We're not close now, haven't been for years, and living together again would put our relationship under immense strain. Still, I mention it, tentatively.

'It's the first place he'd look,' she says.

We both know it's true.

'You know, you can't tell him where I am, no matter what,' she says.

Until now, it's been us telling her this. 'I know, Mum.'

'You too, Matt,' she says, looking at him.

I know that she doesn't trust any man, and I understand why.

'I wouldn't,' Matt says. 'Really, I can't think of anything I'd be less likely to do.'

I can see that she is torn, wanting to believe him but not quite able to. Still, she doesn't have a choice. Matt's been in on this with me. He's had to be. The organisation was more than I could manage alone.

While she looks around the house, trying to decide whether she wants to take anything else, Matt makes us all hot drinks. The tea tastes weird, has probably been in the cupboard for years, but he's dug out a packet of Hobnobs and we dunk them, none of us saying much.

'I'm ready,' Mum says, draining her mug.

I notice that it says 'World's Best Mum' on the front. A Mother's Day present from years ago. I notice that she is not taking it with her.

'Let's do it,' Matt says, and when he puts a gentle hand on her shoulder, I see her flinch, and he pulls it away as quickly as he placed it there.

I drive and Mum sits beside me in the passenger seat. Matt is quiet in the back. The silence is too thick, so I reach over and put the radio on, and there's a ballad from the eighties on and Matt starts singing along, his voice deep and out of tune. I smile, can't help it. I join in. It's one of those songs I haven't heard for years but which I remember all the words to. I glance across at Mum as the final chorus approaches and there's a hint of a smile on her face, and I see that she's mouthing the words, not quite singing along, but almost. He's taken everything from her, but it will come back. Her voice, her strength. It will come back.

When we pull up outside the red-brick terraced house, Mum looks at it for a long time before taking her seatbelt off.

'You know, I've lived in that house for thirty years. I wonder how long I'll live in this one.'

I point out everything positive I see. The flowers in the front window, the way the paving stones at the front are swept clean, the way the sun is shining, hitting the front of the house. I want her to see these things, to know that she isn't only losing parts of herself, but gaining something too.

We press on the doorbell while Matt gets a couple of boxes out of the car boot. The woman who opens the door is a similar age to Mum. She's short and slight, and her wavy hair is the colour of caramel.

'You must be Tina,' she says. For a moment, I don't think she's going to step aside to invite us in, but then she does. 'Rosemary,' she says, by way of introducing herself, wrapping her thick cardigan around her.

I wonder how she's ended up here, in this strange houseshare for middle-aged women. Perhaps she and Mum will become friends. Or perhaps they'll both keep to their rooms, occasionally crossing paths in the kitchen or the hallway. I wonder whether we should warn her about Mick, about the possibility of him turning up here. It's possible she has a Mick of her own, of course. I decide I'll leave it for Mum to navigate.

Rosemary gives us a very quick tour. The kitchen's old-fashioned but clean, with peeling sticky labels on the cupboards – one for each resident. There are padlocks on the cupboard doors, and the sight of them makes me feel wretched. We go upstairs to Mum's room, and it looks a bit shabbier than it did in the photos on the internet, but it's liveable, and that's enough for now.

'Well,' Mum says, once we've put her folded clothes away in a chest of drawers that's slightly uneven and missing a handle. 'You probably want to be on your way.'

I look at Matt but I can't read his expression. 'We can stay as long as you want, Mum. We could go out for something to eat, see what the city's like?'

'No, I can eat here. Better get used to it.'

She brought some food with her, but not a lot. Teabags, a few tins of soup, some crisps and biscuits.

'How about I go out for some fresh stuff? Milk, bread, cheese, that sort of thing. You can make me a list if you want.' Matt is being so helpful, but I feel a flash of worry about him leaving me alone with her for the hour or so it would take him to complete this task. It's been so long since we spent any real time together, and there's something about this room that makes me feel claustrophobic.

'I can do that,' she says. 'Honestly, you go.'

Matt gives me a shrug and we grab our jackets and head for the stairs.

'Will you be all right?' I ask in the hallway. There's a piece of wallpaper that's starting to come away in the corner, and I want somewhere better for her. Somewhere that is her own, with no Rosemary and no locks on the kitchen cupboards.

'Yes,' she says, but her eyes look frightened.

It's hard to walk away, to not bundle her back into the car and take her home. But it's for her safety, I remind myself. It's for her.

We're subdued on the drive home. Matt's at the wheel; I'm in the passenger seat.

'She'll be okay,' he says after a lull in conversation.

'I just hate that she's ended up there, after setting herself up with a life. I hate how much he's taken from her.'

'I know. Me too. But she's better off in a slightly dingy house-share than at home and in danger.'

'I wonder whether he knows yet, that she's gone.'

He shrugs. 'I expect we'll get a visit later. Or maybe tomorrow.'

I think about seeing him, about how much I hate him, and I decide that if he comes in the pub, I'll bar him for life. I almost hope he does, just so I can get some of this rage out. I feel full with it, itchy and bloated.

When we get home, he is there already. Standing at the bar with a pint in his hand. Dee flashes me an apologetic look and I know that she didn't know what to do for the best.

'Where is she?' he asks, and I can tell from his voice that he's already had three or four drinks.

'Who?' Matt asks.

Mick goes for him then. Lunges forward with his fist swinging, but he trips and Matt dodges out of the way, and Mick ends up on the floor.

'Am I supposed to believe it's a coincidence that you've been off out somewhere and Tina's disappeared?' He scrambles to his feet.

I look at him. 'Disappeared?'

'Oh, fuck you both.' He sweeps an arm around the pub. Everyone has stopped talking and turned to look. 'Fuck the lot of you.'

He storms out and I watch him leave. Gradually, the hum of conversation starts up again, gets back to its usual level. Matt puts his arms around me and I let myself be held, there on the wrong side of the bar.

'Good day? Other than him?' Dee asks, and I know she's really asking if it's true. If I was lying when I said Matt and I fancied a trip to the seaside. If I was really getting my mum away from danger.

'Good day,' I say.

It's safer for her if she doesn't know. That's what I need to remember.

'Did you bring me back a stick of rock?'

'No rock,' I say.

She keeps her eyes fixed on me, doesn't look away. 'Another time,' she says. And then, 'Are you going to call her?'

'Call who?'

'Your mum. If she's missing.'

'Oh, yes. I'll go upstairs and do that. She won't have gone far, though. You know my mum.'

I hate lying to her. Hate keeping secrets. But sometimes there's no other way.

# 41

_____

NOW

I wake up breathing hard, and there is sweat gathered around my hairline. Mum. There was a call, a frantic phone call, and I was about to leave for the shelter when I took it. She didn't phone often. When she did, it was always something important. I put the phone to my ear, said hello. And then those words.

'He's found me. Shelley, please come. He's found me.'

I didn't think, didn't answer, didn't call the police or Matt or anyone else. I just got in the car and started driving towards her. Because she was my mum, after all, and she needed me. I'd only been driving for a few minutes when it happened. I misjudged the roundabout, thought I had time to get around ahead of that huge people carrier, but I didn't. I saw the panicked look on the driver's face, saw that she was doing what she could to stop, as was I. But it was already happening by then. Our cars were colliding, the steel and glass bending and shattering.

I feel sick at the memory. I reach for my phone and call Matt. 'Are you at the hospital?'

'Yes. Do you need something? I can come, or phone Dee...'

'I need to go to my mum. Can you come?' I hear Mum's voice in my mind again. *Please come.*

'Give me half an hour,' he says.

I know I can't ask him to be faster but half an hour seems like an endless amount of time to have to fill. I search for Mum's number, call her. But there's no answer. What if he's killed her? What if, when I was in that hospital and Mick was in the same building, going about his daily life, he knew that my mum was lying lifeless somewhere because of him? I feel cold, go upstairs to pull on a jumper. And then I pace the living room, waiting for Matt.

When there's a knock at the door, I feel overcome with relief for this man. This man who stands by me and shows up, no questions asked.

'Can you take me to her?' I ask. 'I need to find out if she's okay.'

'Do you remember where she is?'

I speak without thinking. 'She's in Nottingham.'

'I'll drive,' he says.

It takes the best part of an hour to get there and I am anxious, so I don't say much. Matt fills some of the silences with questions, but he keeps things light. Doesn't ask anything that relates to my memory. I want to go into all that, want to peer into the corners and pull out the memories that are lurking there, but that's for another day. Right now, all I can focus on is this. She called me, asked me to come. And I tried, I went racing off to her, but I had an accident and lost my memory and now almost two weeks have passed and it might be too late.

I remember the question I needed to ask Matt. 'Have you been in touch with her? While I've been in hospital? Does she know what happened to me?'

He takes his eyes off the road for the briefest moment, and I see that he's weighing something up. I remember him carrying boxes.

Helping to move her in. First to that shared house, and then later to the small terraced house she lives in now, alone.

'Matt, the road!'

He looks away from me, straight ahead, and we weren't in any danger but I'm nervous about being in a car and I don't need to tell him why.

'I haven't been able to get hold of her,' he says. 'I've tried, lots of times.'

There's a stone in my stomach, smooth and heavy, and it's sinking. 'And my number won't have been working, if she's tried to call me.'

Yesterday, I finally sorted out a proper phone, and I've carried my number across. But there's no way of knowing what calls or messages I received in the intervening days.

When we pull up outside her house, I'm reluctant to get out of the car. There is something to be said for being trapped in this unknowing. If we find out today that she is dead, there's no undoing that. And yet. There's the flipside, too. She might answer the door and have a reason for being unavailable and another one for calling me, terrified, saying that Mick had found her. Matt turns to me, unclips his seatbelt.

'Ready?'

I am not. But I nod anyway, and we get out of the car, meet by the front door. The paint is peeling. I reach and scrape some flakes off with my thumbnail. And then I knock. The seconds feel like hours, but I wait a reasonable amount of time before knocking again. Matt takes a step backwards, looks up at the windows, searching for signs of life. What's the next step? Calling the police? How do you explain that you were called out on a mercy mission and it's taken you two weeks to get here?

'I have a key,' Matt says, reaching into his pocket. 'If you want me to...'

He has a key. I'm so grateful that we have a way to get inside, to check. He passes the key to me and I slide it into the lock and turn.

'Will you go in first?' I ask.

He knows what I am asking. If my mother is dead inside this house, will he please be the one to discover her? I've watched enough crime dramas to know that if she's been lying in here for all this time, we'll know almost immediately from the smell. But still, I want him to go in first. To act like a shield. And he agrees, without question. I think about what a good man he is, and then I push the door open and he takes a step inside.

There is no smell. No body on the living room floor or lying on the bed. If my mother is dead, she's also elsewhere. But something awful has happened here. Matt and I move through the rooms, silent. All the curtains are closed, and the front room has a chair with rope tied to the legs, an upended coffee table. In the bedroom, the bed is unmade, and there's a bottle of whisky on the bedside table, a dirty glass. Mick has been here.

When the search is over, we come together in the living room and Matt looks at me, his eyebrows raised as if asking what comes next.

'I don't know what to do,' I say. 'Do we call the police?'

Matt looks pained at this suggestion that she might still be in danger. 'We should report her missing,' he says.

He's right. So we go back to the car, locking the door carefully behind us. Matt searches for the nearest police station on his phone, and then uses the GPS to drive us there. When he's parked and is reaching for his seatbelt clip, I put a hand on his arm.

'Will you come in with me?' I ask.

'Of course.'

I see that, as far as he's concerned, we're in this together. This rescue mission. This life. I want to thank him, for coming to my rescue and my mum's. For going ahead of me when I can't face going into the house where she might be decomposing and for coming with me now, when I have to explain something almost inexplicable to the police. I give him a smile that I hope conveys all of it, suspect it doesn't. And then I get out of the car and we walk into the police station. I'm not going to be fobbed off, or told they don't look for adults who might just have taken themselves off for an extended holiday.

Over the next hour, we explain it all more than once. The historic abuse, the recent run-in with Mick, the house my mother escaped to, that only we know about. A police officer named Denny listens, takes notes, asks me to repeat certain things. I explain the car accident, the coma, the memory loss. How it's coming back to me, how it started like a trickle but now it's like a flood. I have an image of me standing on a beach with a piece of wood or metal in front of me like a shield, trying to hold back the tide. Denny is patient and he seems reasonable.

'He's a dangerous man,' I say at the end. 'Please take this seriously.'

'Thanks for coming in,' he says. 'We'll do what we can and keep you posted.'

I want to ask exactly what they'll do, but I know I can't push it. I told him what we'd found, at the house. The state of things. It's clear she hasn't just gone away somewhere without telling me. We stand up and he shakes my hand and then Matt's, and I notice the flash of a gold band on his wedding finger. What sort of a man is he? The kind like David or the kind like Matt? He seems ordinary, pleasant, but you can't know. If life has taught me anything, it's that.

Back in the car, I take a few deep breaths.

'You did good,' Matt says.

'It's just such a convoluted story. I think he just thought I was a bit unhinged. It isn't normal, any of this.'

'It isn't normal,' Matt agrees, 'but it's true. I'm sure he's used to sorting lies from truth. Try to have faith. Now, do you want to do anything else before I drive you home?'

'Is there anything you can think of?' I ask.

'Well, we could go into the town centre, ask around in shops and pubs...'

'The pub!' It's so obvious, I can't believe I didn't think of it before. 'The pub where she works.'

'Do you know what it's called?'

I'm about to shake my head but I speak instead. 'The Bull's Head.'

He puts the name into Google Maps and we go there. It's a bit dingy, a real drinker's pub. No food menus on the tables, no women to be seen other than the one behind the bar. For a second I think it could be her, but then she turns and I see she's just a similar age and build. She comes to us, her arms folded across her chest, and asks us what we're drinking.

'We're looking for someone,' I say. 'She works here, or she did. Tina Woodhouse.'

I keep a close eye on her face, but she gives nothing away. 'Who's asking?'

'I'm her daughter.'

She tilts her head a little as if trying to see the resemblance, and she must be happy with what she sees. 'She's gone. Just didn't turn up for her shift one day and no one could reach her.'

'But didn't anyone think maybe that was something to worry about?'

The woman shrugs. 'Not my business.'

'Look,' I start, but Matt puts a hand on my arm, and it's gentle but firm.

'Let's just go,' he says. 'We're not going to get anywhere here.'

I give the woman one last look, try to put a bit of pleading into it, but she is unmoved. When we get back in the car, Matt starts driving without asking me what I want to do, and it's clear that we're going back. That this phase of the mission is over. For the first twenty minutes of the journey, my mind is racing with possibilities, but then I calm down, reach some kind of equilibrium.

'Want to play a game?' Matt asks.

'I think I just want quiet, if that's okay?'

'Sure.'

I close my eyes and think about our wedding.

## 42

---

### THEN

'How hot is it?' Dee asks.

'My makeup is literally sliding off my face,' I say.

'Oh man, I wish I was there.'

'Me too.'

There is a brief silence, which is rare between us, and I imagine we're both thinking about how she and Liam would have been here with us if they didn't have a newborn to take care of.

'Did you find witnesses?' Dee asks.

'A couple of hotel staff are going to do it.' Matt and I met them yesterday. They were sweet and seemed excited for us, but it isn't the same as having someone you love. I'm sitting in my hotel suite, looking at myself in the gold-edged circular mirror. I'll have to do my makeup again, but my hair looks good. Soon, I'll put my dress on and it will really feel like a wedding.

'How's Callum?' I ask.

'I'm pretty fond of him. But god, if he would just sleep a little bit. Anyway, I don't want to put you off. I hope you and Matt are busy trying to make him a playmate.'

I laugh, because I know that is what's required of me, but I'm not sure children are on the cards for me and Matt. We've talked about it, and it's something we both want, but I'm not pinning my hopes on it. I'm in my mid-thirties, and I've seen all those articles about what happens to your fertility after thirty. If it's just me and Matt, that's enough for me.

'I'd better go,' I say.

'T minus one hour, right?'

'Right.'

'I'll be thinking about you. Please make sure there are photos.'

I feel suddenly close to tears. It's like it's just hit me, the enormity of what's happening. After David, I thought I would never trust anyone enough to get married again. It took forever to sort out the divorce, with David in prison, and I felt sure I would never risk putting myself through it again. I even told Matt that, in the early days. But now I'm here, on a beautiful island in the Caribbean, and I don't have a single doubt about saying yes to this man. As second chances go, it's a good one.

Matt comes to the door twenty minutes later. He's been having a drink at the bar, giving me some space. He claps a hand over his mouth when he sees me. I'm in my dress, which is long and simple, with no sleeves and some beading on the bodice.

'I can't believe I get to marry you,' he says, pulling me into his body.

We're both ready with half an hour to spare, and we only have to walk out of the hotel's front door and onto the white-sand beach. So we sit on the edge of the bed, holding hands.

'Are you nervous?' he asks.

'No.' I'm not. I was, the first time. 'Are you?'

'Only about getting my vows wrong.'

'You won't.'

He looks at me, his eyes intense, and part of me wants to look away, but I force myself not to.

'I will never hurt you,' he says.

And I swallow, keep looking. 'I know.'

The setting is perfect and there's a bit of a breeze. Enough to cool things down a little but not so much that the sand is being blown around. The hotel staff have set up a little archway with flowers for us to stand under. As I walk towards it, my hand tightly in Matt's, I look at the place where the chairs would be, if we had guests. Is it selfish that I don't really want to share this with anyone? I know I would be happy if Dee and Liam were here, but I'm all right with the fact that they're not, too. Matt gives my hand a squeeze and then lets go, because we are there, under the archway, and the celebrant is smiling at us, and it's time.

Afterwards, the celebrant and the witnesses disappear and Matt and I dance on the sand to a song he hums. I'm the happiest I've ever been. I run through different iterations of myself – the one who let Annabelle push me around, the one who Mick used to let out his frustration on, the one who became David's victim. Who am I now? The one who is loved, perhaps. Matt's love is something I am sure about, something that feels almost too big to be true.

On a folding table nearby, there are glasses of champagne, bubbles fizzing to the top. We take them and sit down, and I take off my shoes, bury my toes a bit in the sand. The tide is out and the water seems so far away, but I know that it will reach this place in an hour or two, that it will wash away our footprints, as if we've never been here.

'I want to give up the pub.'

He looks at me, astonished.

'What?' I ask.

'I just... I didn't know you were there yet.'

'What do you mean, there?'

'Big dream time.'

I remember the conversation we had, about me wanting to help people. Think about the shelter where I spend a few hours a week. Is that what I mean? I think it is. In one sense, it's terrifying to think about walking away from the Pheasant, from everything I've worked towards and built up. But I've done that, and now I want to do this.

'There's this place, an old office building,' Matt says. 'I'll show you when we get back. It's on the outskirts of town, near that restaurant with the good fish. It belongs to the council but it hasn't been used for years. I was thinking about whether they might do a deal with you – let you use it rent-free to do something good for the community.'

I don't say anything. I am thinking that this is what it's like to have a real partner. Someone who remembers what you told them and bears it in mind, thinks of you when you're not together, when he sees a place that might just fulfil a dream you once mentioned. A smile spreads across my face, and I lean over and kiss him, and then he's kissing me back and I feel a bit dizzy, but in a good way. When we stand up and he takes my shoes from me, I notice that the sea is already creeping in, already making its move. Nothing stays the same.

* * *

A week later and we're home, our skin a shade darker than usual and our heads full of memories. Dee invites us for dinner, and when we get there, she says she had this whole Moroccan thing planned but then Callum wouldn't let her put him down the whole day so do we mind if it's Dominos?

'We've got some news,' I say. 'It's kind of big.'

Dee stops with a slice of pepperoni pizza halfway to her mouth.

'I'm giving up the Pheasant.' It's only as I say it that I realise I've never talked with Dee about this possibility. This is going to come out of absolutely nowhere for her.

'You are not,' Dee says, biting into the doughy pizza.

'I am. I'm starting a new venture.'

The day we got back from holiday, Matt took me to see the building he'd mentioned. We stood in front of it, hand in hand. It needed some work, but not a huge amount. I thought about how we might turn the small office units into bedrooms, a couple at a time. Build as we went. And the next day, I made an appointment to see someone at the council about it. I have all these ideas, about filling the place with flowers and books and having space for kids to do their homework and for Matt to do some batch cooking when he has time to help out. Whenever I think about what I'm going to do, I feel this fizz inside me, and I know it's right.

'What kind of new venture?' Liam asks.

I clear my throat. I'm not used to saying it yet, feel a bit like people will think I'm silly, or a do-gooder. 'I'm going to open a shelter for victims of domestic abuse.'

There is silence for a beat.

'Are you serious?' Dee looks like she might cry.

'Yes, but it doesn't have to be a bad thing. Maybe you could take over.'

We have worked together for years, and I knew it would be a wrench.

'I think it's brilliant,' Dee says. 'I think you're brilliant.'

She comes over to the armchair where I'm sitting and pulls me up and into a hug, and I wonder what I'll do without this woman at my side every day. I tell myself that in the evenings, which I will no longer work, I will sometimes sit on the other side of Dee's bar and it will be just like always. I'll probably end up collecting glasses.

'To new ventures,' Liam says, holding up his beer bottle.

We raise our glasses, and I look across at Matt and I feel so damn happy.

'Was it hard not being able to have your mum at the wedding?' Dee asks.

And just like that, my contentment falls away. Dee doesn't know that I'm in contact with my mum. Like everyone else other than Matt, she believes my mum has disappeared. I've had 'phone mum' on my to-do list for days, ever since we got back, and every day I've prioritised other things. Last time I visited her, she seemed like she was settling into her new home. She'd found work in a local pub and was volunteering at the library. There was a greenhouse in her garden and she was experimenting with growing vegetables. When I told her that I was getting married again, she'd made a noise that sounded a lot like a grunt. She still thinks there are no good men. I know that. Mick has been hounding me, trying to find out where she is, and though I've told him nothing, I'm terrified that he'll find out anyway.

'She was at my first wedding,' I say. I'm trying to make a joke but it falls flat, and I wonder whether I've offended Matt until he flashes me a look of solidarity across the room.

'We bought you something,' Dee says, and it's like she's trying to backtrack, after killing the atmosphere.

'I told you not to,' I say.

'I know you did. But since when do I listen to you?' She gets up and leaves the room, and when she comes back she's holding a large picture frame.

She turns it, so we can see, and I gasp. It's us, me and Matt, sitting on the beach just after our wedding, my shoes on the sand, but it's been changed from a photograph into something more like an abstract painting, all bold colours and thick lines.

'How did you do that?' I ask.

'I found this guy who does it.'

'But how did you get the photo?'

'Oh, that. I contacted the hotel. Asked if someone would take a photo of you after. I knew that's when you'd look most yourselves, when all the formalities were done.'

I think myself back there, can feel the sand between my toes and the sound of distant waves crashing. Salt in my hair, and Matt beside me.

'It's perfect,' I say. 'Thank you.'

I am quiet on the walk home. Matt doesn't push me, and I'm grateful for that. He knows that sometimes I have to process things, and he gives me the time to do it. It isn't until we're back in our own kitchen, above the pub, that I speak.

'If we never have a baby, will it be enough?'

Matt doesn't look surprised. He hesitates just long enough so that I know he's considered the question, isn't just answering automatically.

'You and me, holidays and sunshine? Afternoon cinema trips and beer gardens and working together. Helping people. Yes, Shelley, that's enough for me.'

And just like when he said, on our wedding day, that he'd never hurt me, I believe him.

# 43

---

NOW

Matt drops me back at Dee's door and I ask if he wants to come inside. It's started to rain, so we hold our jackets over our heads as we go to the door, and once we're inside, it feels deathly quiet. We're still standing in the hallway, taking our shoes off, when my phone rings, and we both jump. And when I see the name on the display, it's sort of like seeing a ghost.

'Mum?'

'Shelley.' Her voice is a croak but unmistakably hers. It sounds like childhood.

'Oh, Mum. Where are you?'

'Hospital,' she says. 'Shelley, I've been calling and calling.'

At first, I can't compute it. I imagine her lying in that same building I was in, the same one where Mick is, and feel a jolt of panic. But then I realise that she won't be there; she'll be in the closest hospital to her new home.

'Oh, Mum. I went to the house. I knew he'd been there.'

'I thought he was going to kill me, Shelley. He had me tied to a chair. Gagged.' Her voice is full of tears, and I think about seeing

Mick, about him saying he hadn't seen her for more than two years, and I want him to be dead.

'How did you get away?' I ask.

'I managed to get some of the knots untied, but it took days. One morning he came in and I was behind the door, and I just ran. Knocked on someone's door, and they called me an ambulance.'

'Jesus. Are you all right?'

'I don't know. They're saying I can go home but I'm so frightened.' Her voice breaks.

'I'm coming,' I say. I look at Matt for the first time and he nods, and I know he's saying he'll take me back there.

'Please.' She tells me which hospital. Which ward, which bed.

It's only after I've ended the call that I realise she doesn't know I've been in hospital too. It doesn't matter. Not now. Matt holds up the car keys and, when I nod, he turns back towards the door and reaches for his shoes. He looks weary, I think.

'Are you sure you're okay to do the drive again?' I ask.

'Absolutely. I wish we'd thought to check the hospital when we were there, though. How did she sound?'

I fill him in while we drive. There isn't much to say, since I don't know the details of her injuries, but when I talk about Mick keeping her prisoner there, in her own home, he tightens his grip on the wheel until his knuckles are white. When we arrive and are walking through those squeaky hospital corridors, I try to prepare myself for what she might look like. But when we find the ward and step inside, she waves from her bed and she doesn't look too bad.

'I'll get some drinks,' Matt says, and I appreciate him letting me see her alone.

She's propped up with pillows and has lipstick on. There's no visible damage to her face, but her left arm is in plaster.

'Mum,' I say, reaching for her hands. 'How are you?'

'Much better than I was. They say I can go home later.'

'Is your arm...?'

'Broken,' she says. 'Other than that it's just a few bruises.'

I look at her other wrist, which is the yellow of mustard. 'Have the police been involved?'

She looks a bit uncomfortable.

'Mum, we have to report this. You need to be safe.'

She gives a tentative nod but doesn't say anything.

'What is it? What's making you hold back?'

She looks me dead in the eye. 'I'm not strong like you, Shelley. I can't stand in a courtroom and go over the things he's done to me.'

Strong. It isn't a word I associate with myself, but I try it on for size. 'Do you know what made me strong?'

She doesn't look away from me, and she nods to encourage me to go on.

'Thinking about the cyclical nature of it. I saw it happening to you and it ended up happening to me. I don't know whether I'll have a child, but I wanted to put an end to it. A full stop. And now David is in prison. And we could get Mick sent there too, between us.'

Her eyes flash with something I can't quite name. 'Why did it take you so long to come?'

'I tried to come, and I had a car accident. I've been in hospital, in a coma.'

She looks stunned. 'And are you—'

'I'm okay. Matt's been looking after me.' I don't tell her about the memory loss. I can go into that another time. 'And he's been trying to get hold of you, too.'

Matt is back and he's holding a tea in each hand and there's a plastic bag swinging on his wrist that I know will contain KitKats. I think about the first time I saw him, in the hospital, how kind he was.

'You're really okay?' she asks again.

And there's something about it that breaks me. Perhaps it's because she never asked that when Mick was hurting me. Perhaps it's because she is asking it now, when she's the one in hospital.

'I'm alright,' I say.

* * *

It's a long day. When she's discharged, mid-afternoon, we drive her home. I want to offer to take her back with me but I know it isn't possible, and besides, where would I put her? I'm still staying in Dee's spare room. Matt and I clear up the mess as best we can. And then Matt makes a trip to Tesco and buys her a stack of ready meals and pre-prepared sandwiches, because she only has use of one hand. He brings flowers, too, and a couple of magazines. While he's gone, I put a load of washing on and make sure things like teabags and biscuits are somewhere she can reach them. I'm standing at the sink, looking out of the window, when she says my name. When I turn, she's in the kitchen doorway, and there's something about the way the light hits her that makes her look old. I think of Granny Rose, of how simple my love for her was compared to this.

'I will go,' she says. 'To the police. I told them at the hospital that it was an accident, but you're right. If you come with me, I'll go.'

I'm so relieved. They have to take this seriously, with her living in hiding and him tracking her down and her arm now in plaster.

'He's a monster, Mum,' I say. 'And...'

I need to say this next thing, but it's hard, because I spent so many years believing the opposite.

'And?' she asks.

'And it isn't your fault. None of it.'

It's like the words unpin her because she falls to the ground, sits with her back against the wall, sobs rushing through her. I sit down beside her, not quite touching. Just there. By the time Matt returns, we've wiped our eyes and blown our noses, and we're sitting with mugs of tea in the living room, the sun shining bright through the windows. He empties the bags into the fridge and cupboards. I can see from the way he keeps checking his watch that he's eager to get on the road again. We go into the kitchen and speak in hushed voices.

'I need to stay,' I tell him. 'Just tonight. We're going to the police in the morning, to report Mick.'

'That's great,' he says.

'You go back. I'll let Dee know.'

'I'll come and collect you,' he says. 'Tomorrow?'

'I think so. I'll call.'

He nods and there's a moment when I think we're going to hug, but neither of us is quite able to initiate it. After he leaves, Mum waits a few minutes before speaking.

'Thank you for staying.'

'It's fine.'

'You know, I felt safe here. Before he found me. It was the first time I'd felt safe for years.'

'You'll feel safe again,' I tell her. 'Because he'll get what he deserves.'

'I hope so.'

I have to believe that, because what else is there? Mum living in fear for the rest of her life? I have to believe she can start again, the way I have.

We eat a pizza and salad and we go to bed early. Mum lends me a pair of pyjamas and a toothbrush, and I sleep in her spare room, trying not to think about how unfamiliar it is. Trying not to think about Matt. In the early hours, I have vivid, repetitive dreams about Mick. That we're both in hospital, that he's found us, that we're running away, but we're not fast enough. And I wake up furious, because I shouldn't have to live my life like this, and neither should she. A locksmith's coming later to change the locks, but she'll probably have to move again to feel safe now he knows where she lives.

It doesn't occur to me until the morning to ask what she thought when she called me asking for help and I didn't come.

'I thought you were done with me,' she says. 'I didn't know you'd been in an accident, of course. I thought you'd reached your limit.'

I nod. 'Matt said he was trying to get hold of you, to tell you about me.'

'I thought...'

I gaze at her, and see a world of fear in her eyes.

'I don't trust him. I can't.'

I have something she doesn't have, and it's worth everything. The ability to start again, to trust. I hope she'll have it someday. When we set out to walk to the police station, I notice there are trees with blossom on them and I don't mind as much about the wet pavements and the chilly breeze. Spring is coming. It's a new start. It makes me consider another new start I made.

## 44

### THEN

With a new pub, I think, you open with a bang. A party to launch you. With a women's shelter, you open quietly, without fuss. No party, but still a day when you open your doors for the first time. And this is that day. Matt is at the hospital, and I'm walking from room to room, trying to imagine what this place might feel like for someone coming to it from a dangerous home situation. I hope it is welcoming.

When we first got the keys, I thought I'd taken on more than I could handle. The empty rooms, which had seemed to be in pretty good shape when I'd had a look around, suddenly revealed themselves to be littered with cracks in the plaster and stained carpets. I went to the Pheasant that night and told Dee all about it, said I was worried I couldn't manage it.

'Can I take a look?' Derek asked.

I looked at him. Dee and I were used to speaking freely about anything and everything in his earshot and he rarely joined in.

'Why?' I asked.

'I've done a bit of all sorts in my time. Painting and decorating, laying carpets. I was even a carpenter for a while. I could help.'

I looked at Dee and she raised her eyebrows, as if to say 'who knew?' And then I thanked him, and he said he'd be there bright and early the next day. He stuck to his word. Over the next few weeks, while I made the transition from pub landlady to shelter manager, Derek was there every day. When there was something he didn't know how to do, he'd make a call to an old contact and a plumber or an electrician would be there within an hour or so, always offering mates' rates.

When it was done, and I was looking around the place, hardly able to believe the transformation, he stood back and watched me.

'I didn't say much,' he said at last, 'when you went through all that business with your ex-husband. I didn't think it was my place. But you've been good to me, you and Dee. I'm glad I could help make this happen.'

'What you've done is unbelievable. I'll never be able to thank you enough.'

He reddened. 'A pint will do me fine as a thank you.'

We were silent for a minute, and I didn't think he was going to say anything else, but then he did.

'My wife, Theresa. She left me for another man and it broke my heart, but I decided that if that's what she wanted, if she was happy, I'd let her go. But two years later, she was dead.'

I widened my eyes.

'He killed her, Shelley. What I've done here, I've done it for you and I've done it for her.'

There was a tear in his eye, and I watched him brush it away.

'For Theresa,' I said, lifting the can of Diet Coke I was holding as if in a toast. 'Thank you.'

\* \* \*

For weeks, we've been letting the other shelters in the area know that we're going to be opening, and the people who run them have all said that there is a need for more space, more beds. But even so, I am sort of surprised when my phone rings at around eleven and someone from Women's Aid asks if I can house a young mum and her two sons. I say yes and when I hang up the phone, I don't know what to do first, so I go upstairs and make up a room with three beds.

The woman arrives within the hour. She has a black eye and a cut on her cheek that could have been made by a ring. She is flanked by two similar-looking boys with dark hair and dark eyes. They look about two and four, and I wonder what they've seen and heard. Whether they clung to one another beneath the covers the way I used to cling to Granny Rose.

'Ella,' she says. 'I was told you'd be expecting me.'

'Come in,' I say. 'Please. Make yourself at home.'

During the months of preparation, I have thought about whether I'll reveal myself as a fellow victim of domestic abuse to the women I'm trying to help. The only conclusion I've come to is that it will depend on the circumstances. And here I am with my first guest, and I ache to tell her she is not alone. That it is not her fault. But there's no opportunity to do it, while I'm giving the tour. When we get to the living area and the boys see the buckets of toys, their eyes flash brighter. I have gathered these toys and books and games carefully from charity shops and car boot sales, constantly checking that every age group is covered. The boys go over and pull out little cars and soon they are racing them across the carpet and I ask Ella if she wants to go into the kitchen for a cup of tea.

'I'll be through here,' Ella says to them, but they are lost to their game. She leaves the door propped open.

'How do you take it?' I ask, putting the kettle on to boil.

'Just milk.'

The silence grows around us, so when Ella speaks again, it's a jolt.

'This isn't how I thought my life would go,' she says.

'I'm sure,' I say. 'I wanted to be a pop star.'

Ella smiles and I feel something breaking down between us, some familiarity creeping in.

'What are your sons called?'

'Jack and Harry. Jack's almost four, Harry's two. I didn't...'

She stops, and when I look over, I see that Ella is frantically swiping at tears, as if she thinks she can hide them, or force them back in. I wait, in case she wants to finish her sentence.

'I didn't think I'd be a single mum.'

I run through a couple of different things I could say to this, but they all sound glib. I am not a mother and I can't presume to know what it's like to be one, to have all that responsibility piled at your feet, to know that it's going to last for decades. What I really want to say is that there are worse things than being a single mum, and that living with a violent man is one of them.

'Do you want to talk about him?' I ask.

'No.' The answer is abrupt, sharp. Sure.

I think about the pain one person can inflict. The physical side of it, and the mental. Why would anyone choose to do that to someone they claim to love? It's a question I'll never stop asking.

'What made you get into this line of work?' Ella asks.

I'm not sure how to respond, but then Ella looks straight at me for perhaps the first time since she arrived, and the information passes between us with no need for words.

'Oh,' Ella says. 'Oh. You too.'

I nod. I'm distant enough from my experience with David to talk about it, and if Ella wants me to, I will. But not today. Today is about making her feel safe, making her sons feel protected and secure.

'I'll get some lunch on the go,' I say, opening the fridge. 'And then I'll walk you through the legal and practical support we can offer.'

\* \* \*

Later, Matt is cooking dinner and asking me how it all went, and I tell him about Ella and her sons. The haunted look she has. He doesn't turn away from the hob, where he has a stir-fry sizzling, but I know that he is listening.

'So many women,' he says. 'I'll never understand it.'

'About one in three, I think.'

I have read a lot, in the past few months, about domestic abuse. I know from my own experience how it works, how it builds and erupts, and how people are often persuaded to stay. What I don't know, and suspect I will never know, is why some men like to hurt women.

'So how do you feel, about your first day?'

'Hopeful,' I say. It's true.

Matt pushes the wok off the heat and comes over to me, wraps his arms around me.

We stand like that, in the middle of the kitchen, for a minute or two, and then I pull away and get bowls out for our food.

When I gave up the pub, I had to give up the flat above it, too. It was strange, after so many years, to be looking for somewhere new. But Matt told me that he'd scraped a deposit together in the time he hadn't had to pay rent while we lived above the Pheasant, and now we have this little place that we own. When we came to look at it, we both knew it was the one for us. It's not ostentatious or flash, but it has everything on our checklist, from two bedrooms to a small garden. It's close enough to town that we can both walk to work, and it's only a short walk from Dee and Liam's. We've been here for three months, and we're making a list of things we need to do to it, but none of them are urgent, and besides, I am looking forward to doing them. The flat never felt like a proper home, I realise. It was an extension of the pub. And the pub had become a sort of identity for me. Who am I now?

When the phone rings, I know it will be Mum because she's the only one who uses the landline.

'Shelley, it's me, it's Mum.'

'I know. How are you?'

There's a slight pause, and I fill it with worry. Is she about to say something has gone wrong? That she has decided to go back to him?

'I wanted to let you know that I feel settled. Like I can relax for the first time in years.'

I let out a breath. 'That's good to hear.'

Mum's voice is different, but it's familiar, too. This is how she used to sound, before Mick. I didn't notice at the time, and it probably happened gradually, but the fun and light went out of her. And now it's back.

'How's the pub?'

'I've been promoted,' she says, and I can clearly hear the pride in her voice. 'Assistant manager. I mean, there are only five of us so it's not as fancy as it sounds, but the last one left and Clive said I was the best one to step into the breach. So here we are. What about you?'

'I opened the shelter today,' I say.

I've told her about it, and despite thinking I'm foolish to leave the safety of my own pub, she has been supportive, in her way.

'I hope it's what you need,' Mum says.

'What do you mean?'

'Well, I've always felt like you're looking for something. You've always had this way about you, like you can't bear to settle and you've got your eye out for the next opportunity. I hope this is it.'

I don't say anything, but to myself, I say that it's Matt I was looking for, not this new venture. Or perhaps it was both. Still, Mum isn't the person to talk to about how good my marriage is, how safe and protected I feel.

'Do you ever see him?' Mum asks. 'Mick?'

I curl my free hand into a fist and imagine throwing a punch towards Mick. I see his nose gush with blood.

'Never,' I say. 'And I hope I never do.'

## 45

NOW

In the early hours of the morning, while Mum rests upstairs, I think about telling Matt I'm ready to come home. But every time I imagine the conversation, it doesn't seem quite right. Maybe another day or two. It feels like there's something missing, one piece of the jigsaw still lost. But perhaps it's just the strangeness of it all. The unfamiliarity of what was once my cosy life. The last time I look at the clock, it's gone four, and I sleep in until nine. I send Matt a message.

Can you pick me up today? Any time.

He arrives when Mum and I are eating toast spread thickly with honey. I've told her I'm going, and I know she's scared, but what can either of us do? We have to go on living despite these men who have tried to ruin us, or what else is there? At the door, she holds me close for a fraction too long, and when she pulls away, she can't quite look at me.

'I'll come more,' I say. I will find a way to make it true.

In the car, I feel like a weight has lifted. I feel as light as air.

'Did it go okay, with the police?' Matt asks.

'Yes. Because Mum still has visible injuries, it felt like they were taking it seriously. I wish I could be there when they turn up at the hospital to arrest him.'

'You and me both.'

I look out of the window at the houses racing by. Inside each of them, a family, or a couple, or friends, or a person on their own. And so many of those people living in fear, with violence as present as if it were another being in the household. But not me, now. And not Mum, either. I have to focus on that, and on what I can do with the shelter, because otherwise it just feels too big and too impossible.

'I was thinking,' Matt says, breaking into my thoughts, 'we never got to go on that date.'

I'd forgotten all about it. Him, in the park, asking me if we could go back to basics, go out for a drink. I was looking forward to it, and then everything got complicated again.

'We could still do it,' I say.

'We could. Tonight?'

I don't need to check my diary. I have no plans whatsoever. 'Tonight.'

And then I close my eyes and I must have fallen asleep because the next thing I know, we're pulling up outside Dee's house. I stretch and yawn, shake my head to try to wake myself up. Everything feels just a little foggy.

'I'll pick you up at eight,' Matt says, and I lean across the space between us in the car and kiss his cheek.

I can tell he wasn't expecting it, and he holds his hand to the place where I kissed him, as if he wants to preserve it somehow. It makes me feel like the sun has broken through the clouds.

\* \* \*

I spend as long getting ready as I used to when I was going on a first date. Because that's what it is, in a way. Matt and I are married, but this feels very much like a fresh start. I choose a jumpsuit with a floral print, white trainers. I put gold hoop earrings in my ears and a delicate chain with a gold 'S' on it around my neck. I put my hair up, take it down again. I do my makeup, concentrating on making my eyes stand out. And after all of it, when I look in the mirror at the full effect, I get a bit of a shock. Because here I am. Shelley Woodhouse. No longer lost, or confused. Nobody's patient or victim. Ready to go for a drink with the best man I know.

We don't go to the Pheasant, and I'm glad. I don't want to be watched or talked about. I want to be in a pub where no one knows me, where I am just another customer, where I have never stood on the other side of the bar. Matt chooses a quiet bar with a long list of colourful cocktails and asks whether I'm drinking.

'They didn't say I shouldn't, but I might not. Just to be on the safe side.'

He orders non-alcoholic cocktails for both of us, and then we take them and slide into a booth, side by side. Not a soul in earshot. 'I've missed you,' I say.

He cocks his head in a way that asks me to explain what I mean. Because he's been here, hasn't he, all this time? Even when he had to conjure up a different persona to do so.

'I got so lucky with you, and I know I forgot all about that, but I think I knew that something was missing.'

'I missed you too,' he says. 'It was so weird acting like we didn't know each other, like I didn't love you.'

'There's one thing I was sad about, when I realised it wasn't 2017.'

He looks serious, a little pale. 'What's that?'

'That I don't have a cat any more.'

I watch him relax. 'We can get a cat.'

'You're allergic,' I say.

And that is what it takes for him to know I'm fully here, fully back. That I remember it all, from the foods he doesn't like to the places he wants to go.

'I *am* allergic.'

I wave a hand. 'It's fine. I'd rather have you than a cat.'

'Well, good. Another?' He gestures at my empty glass.

'I'll get them,' I say.

When I return to the booth, it's with a question I can't believe I haven't thought about until now. I suppose my brain has had enough work to do.

'What's happened to the shelter? Did it have to close while I've been away?'

'No,' Matt says. 'Annabelle's looking after it.'

Annabelle. At first, her name in his mouth doesn't make sense. Annabelle was my childhood friend, and we drifted apart after she went to university and I stayed here. But then it comes back, like a shift from blurriness to sharp focus. Of course. Three months after we opened the doors, a familiar face came walking through them, with a six-month-old baby in her arms. And once we'd got her back on her feet and talked about the relationships we'd fallen into and how they had broken us, once we'd caught each other up on the years we'd been apart, it was like old times. But better, because we were on a level footing, and there were none of the games she liked to play when we were younger. She stayed on, first as a volunteer and then, when she was able to, as my second in command. Sometimes Dee jokes about me choosing to work with my old best friend over her, my newer one. But I know she isn't threatened. Annabelle and I will never be as close as we once were, and Dee and I are rock solid. But it's good to have Annabelle back. She understands the parts of my past I find it hard to look directly at.

'Is she okay on her own?' I ask.

'Well, I've been helping, and we haven't taken in anyone new. She's been fine. That said, I know she's looking forward to you coming back. I asked her not to visit because of how confused you were about everything, but she's dying to see you.'

'I'll go there tomorrow.'

'Just for a visit, though, right? Don't go in there and start working.'

I smile, because he knows this is exactly the kind of thing I would do. 'Not tomorrow, but I'm nearly ready to go back.'

'Well, that's great. There are so many people who've missed you.'

I think about the low times in the hospital, when I thought I didn't have anyone other than Dee. There is Matt, and Mum, and Annabelle. I have a whole life, with purpose and love. I have been so lucky.

He walks me back to Dee's. We hold hands, and the air is cold and I haven't brought a thick enough coat so the warmth of his skin is welcome. I feel the smooth metal of his wedding ring.

'You weren't wearing your ring,' I say. 'When you were visiting me. When you were being Hospital Matt.'

'Yeah, I thought it might confuse things.'

I look down at our hands. 'And where's mine?'

'It's at home. They asked us to remove any jewellery while you were in Intensive Care. Do you want me to drop it round for you?'

'I'll pick it up,' I say. I picture walking up to the front door of the house that was my home, that will be again. I don't know where my key is, but I know how that place smells when you open the front door, where I'll see a small pile of recent post and Matt's discarded shoes.

And then I go back to what he said about taking his ring off because it might confuse things. I think of him and Dee in the aftermath of the accident, frantic and having to make all these decisions about what was best for me. How, for Dee, it wasn't the first time she'd almost lost me. We reach Dee's front door, and I ask if Matt wants to come inside, and I'm torn over how I want him to reply. It isn't my home, isn't really my place to be inviting people in, though I know Dee wouldn't mind. But at the same time, I don't want this evening to end.

'I'd better get home. I've got an early start in the morning. Is that okay?'

I look him in the eye and nod. And then I reach up and put one hand on the back of his neck, and I lean in and kiss him. I mean for it to be a chaste kiss, a commitment to finding my way back to him. But I'm back. I'm all in. And it turns into something else, into something passionate and full of all the longing we've both been feeling. It turns into a promise of what's to come.

'I'll be home soon,' I whisper into his ear.

He grins, and it's so reassuring to know that he's there, ready and waiting for me to step back into the life I was living. The life I forgot.

'Goodnight, Shelley Woodhouse,' he says, walking backwards down Dee's front path.

'Goodnight, Matt Thornton.'

I let myself in, and the house is quiet. Callum and Liam must be in bed, and Dee will still be working. I make myself a cup of tea and sit in the kitchen, going back over things Matt said tonight. I feel like a teenager with a crush.

I've been doing what Angela suggested, all this time. Letting in a bit of my past at a time, until I was totally up to date. There isn't much left. Just the accident itself. And I'm ready for it. I'm not scared. I've spent too long being scared. So I look back over it with something like compassion. For my mum. And for me.

## 46

---

### THEN

I take a deep breath and try not to think about how many people are beyond the curtain. I step through, and just like I've been told, the lights mean I can't see the audience. I know they are there, but it's just an abstract idea. I clutch the notes I've written on little cards. I have my talk memorised but I need them as something to hold, to keep my hands from going to my pockets. Into the silence, I speak.

'Whether you're aware of it or not, you all know women whose lives have been affected by domestic violence.'

At the end, when they burst into applause, it's a shock. I've tricked myself into believing it's just a rehearsal. But it empowers me, too, makes me feel like I can conquer the world. Shelley from seven years ago couldn't have done this. But this Shelley can. I take a few questions from the audience and leave a stack of cards with the details of my shelter. I know there will be women here who are living through this, and I want them to come to me, when they're ready.

As I'm heading for the door, a woman approaches me. She is tall and strong-looking, with an expression that is half worry and half anger.

'My sister,' she says. 'I think her husband is abusing her. But every time I try to bring it up, she won't talk.'

I hear this a lot. It's a hard one, because the right answer means waiting it out, knowing someone you love is in pain. 'She might not be ready,' I say. 'The best thing you can do is make it clear that you'll be there when she is.'

The woman looks frustrated.

'I know,' I say. 'It's really hard. But the women who come to our shelter have nowhere else to go. Your sister is lucky that she has someone looking out for her.'

'I love her,' the woman says simply.

We say goodbye and I make my exit. I do this a couple of times a month now. Go to talk to a group of people about what I've been through, and what I've learned. Women's Institute meetings, youth groups, workplaces. I will go anywhere that will have me. But now, I'm ready to go home, after a long day at the shelter and my evening spent here. I know Matt will have cooked for us, and after dinner we'll curl up on the sofa and watch an episode of something light and cheerful. No crime. I see enough of that.

When I get in, Matt comes to the door to greet me. He always does this, and I love it.

'How was your day?' he asks, kissing my lips.

'Long,' I say, 'but good. How was yours?'

'Same old. We ran out of soup and you would have thought the world was coming to an end. I sent someone out for some tins of Heinz tomato in the end.'

He takes my coat and puts it away in the cupboard while I remove my shoes. 'Dinner will be ready in ten.'

'Okay. I need to nip upstairs for five minutes, freshen up.'

In the bathroom, I take out one of the tests I keep in the drawer. It's a formality, really. I already know. My body doesn't feel quite like mine. I'm off tea, and my breasts are sore. I watch the test for the two minutes. How many of these have I taken? And how has my life come down to this – taking tests over which I don't really have any influence of the outcome? There have been so many periods, so many tears. Not a single positive. But this time, I am so sure that a second line will appear. Still, when it does, I make a small gasp of excitement. I wrap it up in toilet roll and sneak it back into the drawer where Matt never goes. It is our anniversary at the weekend, and I want to give it to him as a present. I imagine the look in his eyes, how we will talk about names and plans. It is perfect. It is a new starting point. It is our future.

'Is it taking too much out of you, the shelter?' Matt asks, grinding pepper over his mushroom tagliatelle and then mine.

'No, it's like, it's the opposite. Yes, I never get away from the topic of domestic abuse, but the fact that I'm doing some good, helping some people, it's like it feeds me.'

'Good. Because I think it's an amazing thing, but if it ever gets too much, you need to focus on yourself, you know.'

I feel so lucky to have someone who cares about how I'm doing. Who monitors me, checking for signs of burnout.

'I'm fine. Now, what do you want to do at the weekend? Dinner out? Or cinema? Or I could see whether the Royal are still doing those spa days?'

Matt reaches across the table and holds my hand. 'I don't care,' he says.

And I know he doesn't mean it in a rude way. I know he just means that he wants us to be together, and the details don't matter much.

'I'll sort something,' I say. 'Keep it as a surprise.'

I think about the test, upstairs, what it means for us. Next time we're celebrating our anniversary, there will be three of us. The joy of it fizzes in my stomach. I don't like keeping secrets from him. It isn't normal, for us. But this will be worth it. Two days, and I'll tell him, and he will be overjoyed.

'How is tomorrow looking?' he asks.

This is something we do, each evening. Talk about the day we've just had and the one ahead. Discuss who needs to be where and at what time.

I shrug. 'Just a normal day at the shelter,' I say. 'You?'

'Hospital. But I'm finishing at three, so if you need me at the shelter after that, I'm all yours.'

We have an early night. Our days start at six, and we both like our sleep. Matt is gone almost immediately, as he always is, but I read for half an hour or so, trying to switch off, to stop my mind racing. When I do fall asleep, I dream of babies. I dream that I'm in the hospital after the birth, that there are rows and rows of babies and I have to identify my own. They all look the same, in their white sleepsuits and little matching hats.

In the morning, he leaves first. I don't feel rested. I feel stressed. What did that dream mean? And will I dream like that for the next nine months? I can't wait until I can share the secret with Matt, until something like this will be a funny story we'll tell friends rather than something I have to keep to myself.

I'm just about to go, have one earring in and the other in my hand, when my phone rings and Mum's name flashes up on the screen. It's like an alarm bell, because she rarely calls to chat. She typically only calls when she is in need.

'Mum?'

'He's found me. Shelley, please come. He's found me.'

The line goes dead and I grab my bag and go to the car. My head is spinning and I know I should call Matt, let him know, but I just want to get there first. It's impossible to know whether Mick's already been or if he's on his way. If I can get there quickly, I might stop something awful from happening. I try to focus on the fact that Mum sounded all right. Frightened, but not hurt. She was able to make the call.

I haven't even got out of town when it happens. The round-about, the people carrier, the impact. The blackness.

# 47

---

NOW

Dee and I stand on either side of her kitchen island with mugs of tea.

'Do you think you had your kitchen done like this so you basically had a bar in it?' I ask.

She laughs. 'Tell me everything. How's your mum?'

So I tell her everything, or almost. How I was on my way to Mum's rescue when I had the accident. How no one else knew that she needed help. How Mick had kept her prisoner but she'd managed to escape with a broken arm and cuts and bruises. Dee is one of the most expressive people I know and her face changes as the story goes on – worry, horror, fear. But it has a happy ending, or I hope it will. I leave it where I left Mum, after the trip to the police station.

'Shit,' she says. 'Both of you, in hospital at the same time, and not knowing anything about each other. And I can't believe you've known where she is all this time.'

'I couldn't tell anyone,' I say.

'Oh, I know, I get it. It's just a lot to take in, that's all.'

We are silent for a beat.

'What's going on with you? I feel like I hardly know.'

'I'm really tired,' she says. 'I keep feeling like I'm going to actually fall asleep on the bar.'

'Do you need to see a doctor about that?' I ask.

'No. I know what it is.' She flashes me a grin. 'It's exactly like last time.'

Last time. Does she mean...? 'Pregnant?' I ask, barely a whisper.

'Yep. Knocked up. Who'd have thought it?'

I take her hands and clasp them in mine and I want to tell her that I'm pregnant too so badly, but there's someone else I have to tell first. It's nice, too, to anticipate telling her. I know exactly how she will jump up and shriek and take me in her arms.

After we've talked it all through, imagined Callum with a baby brother or sister and she's told me all about how Liam's terrified because he says the last labour was pretty traumatic for him, I tell her there's something I need to say too.

'I'm going home,' I say.

'Really? You're ready?'

I nod.

'Do you think you remember everything?'

'I think so. I still can't believe you and Matt made up the volunteer thing.'

Dee laughs. 'Seriously, if you could remember how angry you got when we tried to tell you he was your husband, you would get it. He didn't want to stop seeing you altogether, so he had to make up something.'

'God, I love him.'

'And he loves you. What a happy coincidence.'

'Do you know where my key is? I want to surprise him.'

Dee goes over to the kitchen drawer where they keep takeaway menus and elastic bands and stamps and Callum's drawings. She pulls out a key attached to an Eiffel Tower keyring and throws it across to me.

'Paris,' I say. 'I thought I'd never been anywhere.'

'You guys are always going somewhere.'

Not for a while, I think. It's going to be nappies and naptimes for the foreseeable future. Dee gives me a tight hug on the doorstep.

'Tomorrow?' she asks.

'Tomorrow.'

And I walk home, my feet taking me there, my brain not having to do any of the work. Once I've let myself in, stood in the hallway letting the familiarity wash over me, the first thing I do is go up to the bathroom and retrieve the test I wrapped in toilet paper. It's still there, still wrapped. Still positive. I take another one, just to be sure, but I know it will be positive, and it is. I put a hand on my belly, try to determine whether it's more curved than it was before. Probably not. But it will be. I wanted to give this test to Matt on our anniversary, but I've missed that and we've probably been through the biggest test we'll ever face. So now there are no big plans. I'm just going to hand it to him, and when he looks at me like he can't quite believe it, I'll nod a confirmation.

I'm in the living room when I hear his key. Was it a mistake, wanting to surprise him? Will I give him a heart attack? I stand up and go out to the hallway, so he can see me straight away. He jumps a bit but doesn't seem too alarmed.

'Hello, you,' he says.

'Hello, you.'

'Is this just a visit or...?'

'I'm home,' I say.

He steps forward and takes me in his arms and I breathe in the familiar smell of him. Our washing liquid, and whatever he's been cooking, and his apple shower gel.

'Thank you for waiting for me,' I say.

I pull back from him and we both have tears in our eyes. We move through to the kitchen and I put the kettle on, because he likes a coffee when he gets back from work. I know where everything is, the mugs and the coffee and the spoons, and the familiarity of it is such a comfort after all this time of feeling displaced and not knowing quite who I was.

We talk about this and that, and then he takes hold of my hand and there's a serious look in his eyes.

'When you didn't know me, after you woke up, that was the most scared I've ever been. That's permanent, for some people, and there was no way of knowing. You must have felt so weird, so adrift.'

I try to put it into words. 'It was awful thinking I was back there in that time with David, but you know, you made all of it easier. I didn't know who you were but I knew you were kind, and that I loved you being there.'

'I have to tell you something,' he says, his expression darkening. 'There was a letter from the prison service. I opened it – I hope you don't mind.'

I shake my head. I know what's coming. 'Is he being released?'

'It's a possibility. Later this year.'

How do I feel about that? I've always believed in redemption, thought that people deserve second chances. It wouldn't be right to wish he was locked away forever, and yet...

'I will never let him hurt you,' Matt says, covering my hand with his.

I appreciate him saying it, but he can't promise that. Promising me he'll never hurt me is one thing, but this is something he doesn't have control over.

'I think I can live in a world that has David roaming around in it. I don't believe he'd be stupid enough to come here.'

'No, I'm sure he wouldn't.'

I shrug. 'Then it's fine.'

'Do you worry about him doing it again, though? To someone else?'

I think about that. I know about patterns of behaviour, about how these people operate. I've heard enough women's stories.

'If he does, I just hope he gets caught again. But he might have changed. I have to believe that he might have.'

Matt nods, takes a big gulp of coffee. Into the silence, I clear my throat. Stand up, slide the test out from its hiding place beneath the letters on the kitchen side.

'There's something else,' I say.

I watch him look at it, see him realise.

'Someone else.'

He's up and out of his chair, his hands gripping my upper arms. 'Seriously?'

'Seriously.'

'I can't believe the hospital didn't pick that up, with all the tests you had.'

'I'm glad they didn't. I'm glad I got to remember, and be the one to tell you.'

And we cry, there in the kitchen, and it isn't perfect, but it's pretty close. Yes, Mick is still out there, although hopefully that's about to change, and yes, David might be free again soon, but I have everything I need in this small house with this incredible man, our future growing inside me, cell by cell.

# BOOK CLUB QUESTIONS

1. Did the novel mirror your perception of abusive relationships? If not, how was it different?
2. What do you think the future holds for Shelley's relationship with her mum?
3. Who was the most surprising character in the novel?
4. Do you believe Shelley has found her happy ever after with Matt at the end?
5. How would you compare Shelley's friendship with Dee to her friendship with Annabelle?
6. What are the overriding emotions that the book made you feel?
7. Who was your favourite character?
8. If you could say one thing to Shelley Woodhouse, what would it be?

# ACKNOWLEDGEMENTS

As always, I owe so much to a lot of people who supported me during the writing of this book. Thank you to my agent, Jo Williamson, and my editor, Isobel Akenhead, for listening to my scrappy idea and letting me run with it, and then helping me to shape it into a novel. Thank you to Boldwood – it takes a lot of work and creativity to consistently kill it the way you're doing.

Thank you to Louise Thomas and James Thomas, who talked to me about domestic violence and policing. And to Linda Everall, who talked to me about physiotherapy. On both fronts, any mistakes are my own.

Thank you to Nikki Smith, Lauren North and Zoe Lea, for being the most supportive writing buddies I could possibly wish for. You all listened to my ramblings when I was developing the idea for this book, and then read a draft and offered your usual wisdom and insight. I will never stop being grateful that we met.

Thank you to Jodie Matthews, Abi Rowson and Lydia Howland for keeping me company in my daily life through a WhatsApp chat. Thank you to my parents and my in-laws, for always reading my books and being generous with childcare so I can continue to write them. Thank you to my sister, Rachel, for her love.

Thank you to my husband Paul Herbert, who is probably checking my Amazon rankings as I type this. Thank you to my children, Joseph and Elodie, for asking great questions and being amazing cheerleaders.

# ABOUT THE AUTHOR

**Laura Pearson** is the author of issues-based women's fiction. She founded The Bookload on Facebook and has had several pieces published in *the Guardian* and *the Telegraph*. *The Last List of Mabel Beaumont* is her first title with Boldwood.

Sign up to Laura Pearson's mailing list for news, competitions and updates on future books.

Visit Laura's website: www.laurapearsonauthor.com

Follow Laura on social media here:

 facebook.com/laurapearson22

 x.com/laurapauthor

 instagram.com/laurapauthor

 bookbub.com/authors/laura-pearson

## ALSO BY LAURA PEARSON

# Boldwood

Boldwood Books is an award-winning fiction publishing company seeking out the best stories from around the world.

**Find out more at www.boldwoodbooks.com**

Join our reader community for brilliant books, competitions and offers!

Follow us
@BoldwoodBooks
@TheBoldBookClub

Sign up to our weekly
deals newsletter

https://bit.ly/BoldwoodBNewsletter

Printed in Great Britain
by Amazon